To Love Again

By

Anna Craig

Anna Craig

Copyright © 2025 Anna Craig

All rights reserved.

To Love Again

For my husband, who showed no interest at all.

Prologue

Kate

And there he stood, standing, staring. James. I hadn't seen him since he walked out my door nearly two years ago. "See you," he'd said, but I didn't.

One text, then nothing. Gone, disappeared as if he'd never existed. As if he'd never been part of my very being for five years. My soulmate. Except he wasn't. Now, on the eve of my twenty-fourth birthday, he appeared, just looking. His deep brown eyes pierced mine. He had changed.

James was always the one wearing chinos and a T-shirt, casual, understated, and cute. The James staring at me now was in a grey suit, tie, and yes, still cute. His hair was cut with precision; gone were the unruly waves that used to dip over his ears, the brown now flecked ever so slightly with grey. His face remained motionless. His body was a statue, upright and tall, so tall, still tall. And then he turned, and he was gone, again.

I breathed. I realised the groceries I was carrying were scattered along my steps. The ingredients for beef goulash now looked like raw, splintered beef covered in dirt and gravel. Ugh. Nearly two years later, and he was still able to fuck with my life.

I scrambled up the groceries and unlocked my front door. Sarah, my ever-suffering housemate, was bopping along in the kitchen with her earbuds in, oblivious, until she saw my face and stopped dead.

"You look like you've seen a ghost."

Sarah was dramatic at the best of times, but I had a feeling this was an accurate description.

"I saw James."

James was my first kiss, my first fumbled sex, my first carpet burns from my first fumbled sex. My first love. My first heartbreak. I loved James, totally and unconditionally. I gave him my heart, and he shattered it into tiny pieces. Sarah wrapped her arms around me.

Sarah and I had met at work about eighteen months ago. She was an accomplished surgeon of the general kind, appendixes and gallbladders, with the occasional bowel thrown in. I was a surgical and trauma nurse, ward-based, thriving on the throngs of wounds, blood, and vomit.

We'd met at a work Christmas party hosted by the surgical ward I was working in at the time. Sarah was wrestling with an overzealous junior doctor who was insisting on sitting far too close, one hand pawing her knee, while I was in battle with another junior doctor, drunkenly declaring his love about five minutes into our "relationship". I locked eyes with Sarah; we nodded towards the door and ran, quite literally, away. We collapsed in an alleyway in hysterics and relocated to the local pub.

To Love Again

Tall, slim, blonde and beautiful best described Sarah. Barbie adjectives often followed, chic, glamorous, stunning. Polished to my disarray. I was pleasant on the eye, as my grandfather had once described me; secretly, I hoped I was a little more than that. I had straight black hair with the occasional kink that the hair straightener made disappear. Shorter than Sarah, I was a little curvier but could still "rock" a two-piece.

Sarah, at the grand age of thirty-five, was at a crossroads where relationships were concerned. I was about to hit twenty-four, not so much at a crossroads as a stop sign. We both had many stories to tell, and many, many drinks later, I'd learnt that Sarah had been married to Michael John Abbot for nearly five years and divorced for one. Sarah had learnt that I'd surrendered my heart to James Simon Davy at the tender age of eighteen and that, for the following years, I'd lived in a utopia of love, until I didn't.

I described my life with James, teenage love evolving into grown-up love; dating evolving into cohabiting; girlfriend and boyfriend evolving into partners. The laughs, revelations of feelings, the squabbles and the make-up sex. The giving of each other to each other, and then the taking away. James taking away.

The last two years I defined as life phases, relatable to grieving the unexplainable death of a loved one, uncannily parallel and similarly sad. The seven stages of grief, except when I got past the shock, denial, and pain stages, I got stuck. Trapped in anger and misery. It had taken a long time to reach rebuilding and hope.

Sarah listened, with the occasional nod, but said nothing. No opinion, no advice, just listened.

Our friendship grew, Dr Sarah Turner and Registered Nurse Kate Dixon. We became inseparable, bonding over failed relationships, blood and gore and tequila shots. When Sarah and Michael's house was sold as part of the divorce settlement, I invited Sarah to live with me. It took Sarah a millisecond to agree. Neither Sarah nor I knew where our lives were going. Career-wise, we were pretty settled, but our personal lives continued to be one disaster after another. Our search for the "next one" took on the portrayal of a reality show. Starting with hope and intrigue but ending in despair and tears. Although Sarah seemed a little more settled with her current beau, Jack. Often, we would sit in pyjamas, mine a mismatch of T-shirt and shorts, Sarah in some silk or linen creation, dissecting the could bes and should bes whilst sipping a sauvignon blanc, before heading down the slippery path of tequila lip, sip, and suck.

Now, on my birthday eve, the sauvignon blanc was on ice, tequila and lemons poised.

1
The Beginning

James

I met Kate when we were both eighteen. She had just moved to London to start her nursing degree. I had also been drawn to the big city and the bright lights of London, leaving my family and Lancashire home to pursue fame and fortune at the London School of Economics, or LSE as it's coolly referred to, with an emphasis on fortune. I was proud to attend such a prestigious school. As my father observed, LSE's motto, *"to understand the causes of things,"* resonated with my curious mind. My father was always looking for connections behind life choices, inferring that fate had intervened.

I met Kate at a party, leaning against a wall, a pretty wallflower, seemingly knowing no one. The darkest blue eyes, a whisper of a smile, and black cascading hair descending over a tight floral dress. The neckline offered a glimpse of a breast, sending my eighteen-year-old hormones into a frenzy.

I watched from afar as my best friend, Miles, coolly swaggered over. Kate's face lit up as he worked his flirtatious charm. Miles was famous for his suave charisma; even at the tender age of eighteen, it was as if he'd been wooing girls since birth, natural and unrelenting. I had known Miles since primary school, bonding over Lego and water play. Miles had moved to the Big Smoke two years earlier when his family relocated, his father being some convoluted high-flying chartered accountant in the corporate world.

The music picked up a beat as Katy Perry belted out *"I Kissed a Girl."* I strode towards them, grabbed Kate's hand and asked her to dance. Miles gawped as I led her away.

"Subtle," noted Kate.

I grinned and was greeted by the most beautiful smile I'd ever seen.

We stayed together for the rest of the night, captured in a bubble of discovery. The conversation was tentative at first, exploring snippets of each other's lives, cautious not to divulge too much as we were both unsure where the evening was heading. Gradually, flirting and teasing crept in, occasional touches, legs and fingers brushing, punctuated by smiles as we both realised the feelings developing between us.

As night became dawn, I drove her home. I scooted around to open her car door and walked her to her front step. We stopped in that awkward moment of *"do I or don't I?"* I did.

I kissed her on her doorstep, gentle and tentative at first. Her mouth slowly parted as my tongue swept her lips. Our bodies pressed together as raw emotions deepened, tongues searching, exploring. Breathless, my hands cupped her face as we drew apart. I stood dazed. Kate smiled.

"Goodnight," she said, turning to leave.

I fell in love with Kate.

Kate was my everything. We grew together, sampling life, love and everything in between. Youth and naivety paved the way to worldly and experienced. We became inseparable, sharing the excitement of new beginnings. Kate was captivated by the joy of caring, thriving on the endless possibilities of making a difference. I became immersed in lectures, textbooks and numbers.

We both embraced university life, driven by the need to succeed. Kate was also driven by the need to outdo me. If I got a distinction, she'd strive for a high distinction. The fact that our studies were poles apart had no bearing. Her friends became my friends. We dated and double-dated. We laughed and we cried. We celebrated the successes and reflected on the failures.

Kate lived in her grandfather's house with Eva and Jesse. Eva had moved to London with Kate, like Miles and me; they had been friends forever, now both studying at Kingston University, located in the Royal Borough of Kingston upon Thames, which sounded very grand.

Jesse was a qualified registered nurse, working on an oncology ward at St Bartholomew's Hospital, or St Barts as it was commonly known. He'd answered an advertisement for a housemate and had no idea how living with these two females would affect his life. Jesse and I became cautious friends, as one does with a male who lives with your girlfriend. Miles was equally wary, though probably more so because Jesse was Australian and had that rugged outback appeal, although he was born and bred in Melbourne.

2

The Housemate

Kate

Eva and I had moved to London to start our nursing degree in the summer of 2009. My grandfather had passed away the previous year, and we'd moved into his Victorian terraced house, one in a row of many, with gabled trims and stained-glass windows repeated time and time again.

I was the apple of my grandfather's eye. He had only three grandchildren, me and my two brothers, Ben and Daniel. As the only female, I cherished our unique bond. Bob Dixon was a remarkable gentleman, kind but firm, in a no-nonsense sort of way. My father, William, or Will as he was known, resembled Bob in looks only. He was firm in a firm sort of way, the bad cop in my parents' relationship. My mother, Louise, was gentle and caring, always excusing my father's abrupt and dismissive manner.

I was excited to leave the clutches of my family, feeling humbled to have been left my grandfather's home in his will. It wasn't a big deal to the rest of my family; Bob Dixon had been a very successful businessman and had provided amply for my brothers and parents. His London house had always been *our place*, ever since I'd been allowed to visit him during school holidays. I'd keep him company, especially after my grandmother,

Rose, passed away just before I was born. *Kate Rose Dixon* became his pride and joy.

Eva often accompanied me on my visits to my grandfather's home. He welcomed her warmly, enduring our giggles and incessant chatter, indulging us in conversations he had no real interest in. Eva and I enjoyed exposing him to the devious ways of teenage girls. My grandfather would describe us as "angels sprinkled with wickedness."

Eva and I had been friends forever. We met in Year 1 of primary school in Leeds. Our classroom teacher, Mr Rathburn, had alphabetised his seating plan, I was Dixon, and Eva was Douglas, and that's how we remained seated throughout our junior school days. We became known as the "Double Ds". The label held no malice or innuendo; the innocence of youth had not yet been lost. The high school years, however, saw the loss of such innocence and the loss of the "Double D" tag, but saw our friendship grow

Eva and I travelled through our school days, mostly complying with the rules and expectations of others. We weren't members of the "cool girl gang," but we were well-liked. We attended a co-educational comprehensive school; our parents opposed private schooling, and we spent most of our days avoiding the entrapment of our male counterparts. As we entered our senior years, that distraction became impossible to avoid, testing both Eva's and my resilience to persuasive charm.

Eva didn't look dissimilar to me. We both had long dark hair, mine black, Eva's dark brown. Both slim, graced with breasts ample enough to be an asset but not too burdensome. We were tall enough to be noticed but short enough to be appealing to those who wanted to protect. We were pretty without being truly beautiful. Our clothes leaned towards the casual, a canvas of pale jeans, pastel sweats and tees, with an occasional pop of colour.

Moving into my grandfather's house was surreal. We were greeted once again by the pillar-box red door with the gold-plated knocker, my grandfather's one indulgence in showy opulence. Eva and I silently looked around, expecting to see Bob appear from every doorway, welcoming us in his inimitable way. Most of the furniture had been removed, leaving a blank canvas, though Bob's chair remained. We smiled as we both noticed it, threadbare on the arms and seat, assuring us of his presence.

We were pulled out of our morose mood and catapulted into a mania of excitement as we ran from room to room. The bay windows begged to be reading nooks, with a myriad of cushions and cosy throws. The wooden floors screamed out for tufted rugs, and the high ceilings and walls seemed desperate to be revived with the energy of youth.

Trailing through the famous London markets, Camden and Portobello Road being our favourites, the house soon began to feel like home. My grandfather's chair dominated the living space, a sort of shrine to the amazing man who embodied wisdom and kindness. We missed his presence, that male influence.

One night, as we were sitting indulging in crisps, chocolate and all things bad, watching *Pretty Woman* for the umpteenth time, we suddenly realised we needed a housemate, a *male* housemate. Someone to put the masculinity back into the house. We both grinned at the thought and immediately put our plan into action.

Jesse was one of hundreds who answered our advertisement. We soon learnt that having a spare room in a house in London was a rare commodity. My father insisted on being present for the screening process, as he called it, providing a rare glimpse of a caring human. Ben and Daniel, my protectors, also decided to hover; it was like interviewing a contestant for *Arrange a Marriage*.

Jesse took it all in his stride. The laid-back, seemingly unflappable Australian remained nonchalant as my father, Ben, and Daniel fired questions. Eva and I smirked as we watched on. Once it was determined that Jesse was not a serial killer, he was given the Dixons' approval to move in. Eva and I had already decided that, as soon as this handsome Australian native had appeared, he would be staying.

Jesse was a registered nurse who completed his studies at the University of Melbourne, then worked briefly at The Alfred before embarking on his adventure to London. His interest in oncology was driven by the passing of his mother, Julia, aged forty-six, from breast cancer. Jesse had witnessed exceptional care and cutting-edge technology at Melbourne's Peter MacCallum Cancer Centre, and gaining a registered nurse oncology position at St Bartholomew's Hospital assured him of continuing his mother's legacy of caring for others. Julia had been as dignified in death as she was in life. Jesse would never forget her courage in facing the relentless, evil barrage of cancer. Now, Jesse had joined that battle and took pride in continuing her fight.

Eva and I decided that we did not want our tampons sharing space with Jesse's condoms, a little presumptuous, maybe, or risk the confusion of his and her razors. So, Jesse got the attic room with an ensuite, and we continued to share the main bathroom. Like all London terraced houses, the attic was a little snug, especially for our tall, burly Australian, but it assured Jesse privacy away from his prying housemates.

Jesse's move into our abode went smoothly; a couple of his friends helped lug suitcases and various bags up the steep staircase to the top of the house. Eva and I closely supervised the three gentlemen as they flexed their very impressive muscles.

Two became three. Jesse fitted in seamlessly, being that bit older, at twenty-three, he brought a maturity we aspired to. In true Eva and Kate style, we decided to celebrate with a party. Jesse was very keen to join the celebrations, and planning began in earnest. House meetings were quickly organised, fuelled by multiple snacks and beverages. Eva and I took the opportunity during these gatherings to delve into the life and times of Jesse. Subtly, of course.

Jesse had not so much left Australia as fled from the clutches of Lily. He had met Lily during his registered nurse training. A few years older than Jesse, she was a qualified physiotherapist on a ward where Jesse had a placement in the early days of his degree. The friendship that followed developed rapidly into a relationship that soon spiralled in intensity, becoming suffocating and impossible.

He admitted to us that he had been snared by Lily's beauty and seduced by her charm. Jesse felt flattered to be "chosen" by Lily, older, wiser, and undeniably gorgeous. He enjoyed the flirtatious undertones; however, these soon became open interactions, blurring the lines of professionalism.

Jesse reached for his beer before continuing. Eva and I listened quietly, moving closer as his story unfolded. Jesse and Lily began seeing each other outside of work. Being a young nursing student, Jesse was content with a casual relationship, albeit boyfriend and girlfriend. Lily, however, was not, and her persistent expressions of devotion to Jesse became overbearing.

Jesse was reluctant to describe Lily as stalking him, but her constant calling, texting, and loitering around his ward began to have an adverse impact on his life. He paused. Eva and I didn't move, sitting steadfast, not speaking, silently encouraging him to continue. Jesse struggled to be released from Lily's grasp, and despite ending the relationship, she refused to let go. It became apparent that Lily was not going to leave, so Jesse did.

Jesse's colleagues and friends had acknowledged his bravery in leaving Australia to come to England alone. However, Jesse felt it was cowardice to run away from a relationship he could no longer control. Eva and I were novices when it came to relationship advice, and seeing Jesse clutching his beer in a shadow of sadness, we settled on a group hug. Jesse's initial confusion and surprise gave way to acceptance of this simple offering of friendship.

The bond was set, and in that moment, an unspoken pact was made to protect and defend; to take care of each other.

3
The Party

Kate

The day of the party started slowly. Jesse had insisted on practising party drinks the night before. Consequently, Eva and I crawled out of bed clutching our heads, squinting at the daylight. Jesse descended from the dizzy heights of the attic, skipping steps two at a time and grinning. As Eva and I rocked in a corner, Jesse bounded about the house, moving furniture and whistling as he went. He could be as irritating as he was endearing. Eva and I decided to access Panadol, water and bed, leaving our energised housemate to continue with the party prep.

Sometime later, we emerged to find Jesse gently snoring on the couch, cuddling an unopened can of beer. Looking around, packets of crisps sat ready, bottles of alcohol lined up, well, two, a bottle of tequila and a bottle of rum, the latter we'd found hidden in my grandfather's highest kitchen cupboard. We'd decided on a dual-nation theme. Jesse insisted on a barbecue, sausage-sizzle style, while the English contribution was red, white and blue balloons and streamers everywhere.

We crept around so as not to wake our sleeping friend and continued our inspection of the party setup. On opening the fridge door, we were greeted by cans upon cans of beer, sausages and chopped onions. Loaves of bread and the mandatory tomato ketchup occupied a small trestle table groaning under the weight of alcohol, crisps, plastic cups, serviettes, a bowl of lemons and the biggest container of cooking salt, not the Himalayan pink variety on Jesse's "to get" list. Eva and I smiled and high-fived. Done.

It was still a couple of hours before party time, ample time to transform hungover ducklings into beautiful swans. Eva's and my dress style was somewhere between streetwear and casual, streetwear without the statement of cultural expression, whatever that may be. Day to day, we wore a uniform of jeans, tees and hoodies; comfort was key. Party time, however, was step-up time, dress time. Pale yellow for me and pastel pink for Eva; legs on show, curves accentuated, necklines plunging, but not too low, flirtatious without being provocative. Makeup was simple: long lashes, soft blush and glossy pink lips.

Jesse scrubbed up well. Looking very dapper, as the British would say, in chinos and a white linen shirt, his wavy hair tamed with a touch of Eva's mousse, and he smelt divine. A smoky cedarwood scent lingered around him. On seeing us, his eyes gave a smile of approval.

Eva's and my friends were coming from Leeds, mostly girls. We hadn't ventured into the philandering world of dating. Eva had come close at a high school dance, but too many hands in too many places and a wet, slobbering attempt at a kiss had somewhat ruined the moment. Eva said it was like being fondled by an octopus. George, the octopus, had soon latched onto Emily. Poor Emily.

I hadn't had an encounter, close or otherwise. My parents' relationship wasn't exactly a shining example of happily-ever-after. I'd observed from afar, content until now to remain a spectator rather than a participant. Jesse was also on the sidelines. After his disastrous relationship with Lily, he was wary of any further female entrapments.

My brothers, Ben and Daniel, my so-called protectors, were making an appearance. Ben and Daniel were older than me by three and four years. Daniel worked in the entertainment industry, though details were always elusive in conversation. Ben, the eldest, was an accountant from the suit-and-briefcase brigade. Neither was married, although Ben had a long-suffering girlfriend, Lisa, who tolerated his many business trips and long working hours. Lisa was a paramedic; unpredictable shifts only added to their relationship's complexity. She was beautiful inside and out. Ben, roguish but with a heart of gold, worshipped her.

Daniel was the quieter of the two, three if you counted me, which seemed ironic for someone in entertainment. He was secretive, revealing only snippets of his life but nothing substantial about what he actually did. Daniel didn't have a girlfriend, at least not to my knowledge. My brothers were both good-looking: Daniel oozed handsomeness with quiet charm, and Ben was stylish and well-groomed. Both tall, some might say imposing, which added to their protective aura.

Jesse had invited new friends and workmates, a mix of male and female. He had one sibling, a brother named Luke, older by five years. Luke shared a close bond with their father, and after Julia passed, he'd resolved to stay nearby. A chef by trade, Luke had transitioned to owning a wine bar in the heart of Melbourne with a friend. He'd never travelled outside Australia and couldn't be persuaded to make the transatlantic voyage to London.

The party was a resounding success. Thirty or so revellers, full of beer and sausages, danced the night away. Music from Lady Gaga and Beyoncé boomed across the three levels of my grandfather's house. As new friends mingled with old, balloons popped, streamers adorned necks, and tequila was licked, sipped and supped. Jesse, Eva and I were impeccable hosts, ensuring everyone mingled, introducing ourselves to those we didn't know and encouraging others to do the same. As the night progressed, we all shared a commonality of alcohol-fuelled fun.

The night dwindled to a close. One of Jesse's friends, Dean, was chatting to two girls from Leeds when he stopped mid-sentence and caught Eva's eye. He smirked and carried on the conversation, which ended rather abruptly before he casually wandered over to her. "Hi," he began. Eva blushed. "Hi yourself." Dean guided her to my grandfather's chair, his fingers lightly brushing her lower back. As they leaned against the threadbare armrest, deep in animated banter broken by smiles and laughter, Jesse and I watched the closeness of their faces and the occasional touch. Eva wriggled in the sensuality of the moment, reddening at the unexpected attention, oblivious to the softening music and the occasional farewell around her.

The room became a jumble of blankets and pillows scattered amongst beer cans and party debris, tiredness and drunkenness, negating the ability to care. Jesse and I dimmed the lights and left behind a scene of slumber and emerging tranquillity, leaving also Eva and Dean absorbed in each other. It was then that I remembered that during our pre-party practice drinks, Jesse and I had agreed to share the attic and donate my room to Ben and Daniel. As we climbed the stairs, I paused at my open bedroom door, two elongated male bodies sprawled across my pale pink flowered bedding, motionless except for the occasional grunt.

As I stared at the king single in the cramped attic room, I quickly sobered up, unlike Jesse. He was attractive in both looks and personality, but I didn't want to risk our friendship by crossing the line into emotional entanglement. Underwear firmly in place and a borrowed T-shirt that, thankfully, due to Jesse's size, covered the important bits, I slunk into bed, keeping as close to the edge as possible without falling off. Jesse, wearing a very brief pair of boxer shorts, swayed and stumbled around the narrow space before falling headfirst into the middle of the mattress. His arms flailed wildly, then flopped to his sides, and much to my relief, all was still as he surrendered to an alcohol-induced stupor. Strangely comforted by Jesse's presence, I too drifted into sleep.

As night merged into day, I left Jesse mumbling incoherently and went downstairs. I crept past Ben and Daniel, oblivious to their spooning situation on my bed! I was greeted by a scene that resembled a mass casualty event without the bloodshed. Bodies were everywhere, pillows and blankets spread strategically covering sensitive spots. The smell resonated with a distillery; beer fumes trapped amongst humans and celebratory wreckage. I located Eva and Dean wrapped up in each other, partly under a very sticky trestle table. My grandfather would have approved of seeing a little wickedness from one of his angels.

4

The Rendezvous

James

On that first night Kate and I met, I watched as she slipped slowly away, not stopping or turning. As the front door clicked shut, I stood watching, wanting, needing to see her again. I drove home with the radio blaring, flicking channels as the picture of those blue eyes and pink lips became entrenched in my brain.

I arrived home to find Miles sitting on the couch, beer in hand and a cigarette perched precariously on his lips. Miles gave up smoking every second day, but as fastidious as he was in his declarations of quitting, he failed every time. He'd picked up the noxious habit about a year ago. Miles had just got his driving licence on his seventeenth birthday and had returned from London to celebrate a friend's 18th birthday. He and I were following our friends to the party; there was a convoy of cars, each with a designated driver for the night. The party was out in the West Pennine Moors, travelling along tree-lined narrow country lanes, the surfaces merged from tarmac to gravel to dirt. Tom, Matt and Lewis did not see the deer that leapt in front of them before it was too late. Swerving, flipping and rolling, the car careered across the dirt and tumbled down the embankment. Miles slammed on the brakes and came to a screeching stop. A few seconds of eerie silence followed before the air became charged with screams and shouts, chaos and panic prevailed.

The emergency services were soon on scene, and the flurry of activity saw Tom, Matt and Lewis extracted and safely on their way to the hospital. Miraculously, the injuries were serious, not critical, and even more miraculously, no one had died. The shock rippled through all of us. We sat stunned on the edge of the road. Residents of a nearby village arrived with blankets and sweet tea, and that's when it happened. Miles was offered a cigarette. Miles reached out his hand, shaking, drew the cigarette to his lips like it was a lifeline, spluttering at first, then inhaling and exhaling, relaxing just a little with each breath.

The effect of the events of that night stayed with us for many months. Tom, Matt and Lewis gradually recovered and were discharged from the hospital to recuperate at home. It took Miles several weeks to bounce back to my charming and charismatic friend. The persistent undercurrent of trauma caused smoking to evolve into a habit that proved impossible to break.

Miles guiltily stubbed out the offending cigarette.

"So?" he asked.

"So?" I replied.

For a man who could spin a yarn for the ladies, he, on occasion, used his words sparingly.

"You and Kate a thing?" he persisted.

"I hope so," I grinned in return.

As Miles lit up his next cigarette, I left him behind a cloud of smoke and went upstairs to my room.

The evolution of Kate and James' coupledom began slowly. Kate and I were very new to the dating game. I realised as I left Kate's doorstep amid a bubble of emotion, that I did not have her phone number. A problem for tomorrow. I continued to bask in the romance of the evening, the flirtatious conversation, her teasing smile, and the tiny touch of her hand. I smiled at the naturalness of that kiss and the craving for more.

The phone number issue was deliberated over for a couple of days. I was kept occupied sorting out lecture timetables and gathering textbooks and stationery supplies to fulfil the requirements of an LSE student. On the third day, no amount of creating schedules and organising stationery could stop the urge to see Kate. The solution to no phone number was stalking, not actual stalking of the cap and dark glasses routine, but more of the surveillance kind, sitting in my car outside her house. Kate eventually arrived on the arm of a male and female, Jesse and Eva, I presumed. I watched them playfully swaying, bumping each other as they ambled down the street, oblivious to my stares. I continued to watch as they jostled along, their close friendship evident. Feelings of jealousy surfaced, and the scary realisation of being smitten by this girl filtered through.

I waited until the threesome had disappeared into the house before venturing out of my car. My heart beat furiously as I slowly approached the front door, with sweaty palms, deep breaths, and nervousness. I silently questioned what I was doing. I had only known Kate for three hours, two dances and one kiss. The door opened, and six eyes were looking at me; four soon disappeared. Kate maintained a smile on her lips.

"Hi," I stammered.

"Hi," smiled Kate.

"Would you like to go for a walk?" I continued.

"Sure," Kate grinned.

As she grabbed her satchel, I noticed the four eyes were back hovering in the hallway. I tentatively waved and received non-committal nods. The eyes swept over me, assessing, judging. I was saved from the stares as Kate returned and we quickly left, closing the door firmly behind us.

It was a lovely, warm and sunny August day. A slight breeze periodically caught Kate's hair and blew it gently across her face. She was so pretty. I kept my hands in my jeans pockets as we walked, not quite knowing what to do with them. My fingers fiddling against the pocket lining, wanting to join Kate's, but I feared to. Kate likewise was a little shy.

We wandered down the street, flanked by rows and rows of Victorian terrace houses. The intricate brickwork and impressive stature of these buildings were akin to uniformed soldiers forming a guard of honour. Kate and I walked in silence, occasionally glancing at one another; the conversation that had come so easily a few nights earlier seemed to be temporarily lost. I thought frantically of something to say. Kate sensed my struggle and so began to explain the scrutiny of Eva and Jesse at the house. I knew that Kate and Eva had been friends since forever. Jesse's friendship, however, was very new, but a deep camaraderie had seemingly developed. The three, in a few short weeks of meeting, had developed a closeness that emulated mine and Miles' friendship many years on. Kate described the antics of their recent party and how the trio's bond had quickly developed. I nodded, inferring that I understood. I didn't. I never did accept the feelings shared by Jesse and Kate.

Kate seemed to sense my doubt and linked her arm through mine as we turned into a local café. London cafés, as I discovered, varied from the "café" variety specialising in fried food and homely meals to the modern-day cafés with trendy specialty blends and fancy pastries. We entered the latter; the coffee aroma filtered the air as the freshly ground beans were relentlessly pounded. We grabbed a table tucked in a corner surrounded by shelves overflowing with books and bric-a-brac. The noisy bustle of busyness provided the perfect backdrop. As the batch brews were delivered to our table, the momentum of the party chatter resumed. The excitement of our university studies propelled the conversation, and any awkwardness disappeared as Kate and I eased into a comfortable banter. Kate explained that she would have to do some theory before she would be "let loose" on real patients.

Her eyes shone as a kaleidoscope of emotions lit up her face. She described the intricacies of her nursing degree, the many subjects, and the opportunities, the prevention, management and cure of human illness. Her passion was palpable, drawing me momentarily into her world.

This soon came to an abrupt stop as the glass doors of the café swung open. I recognised Eva and Jesse as they burst through, but not so the male addition. Kate quickly whispered that he was attached to Eva, quite literally, as was apparent as time went on. Dean was a second-year medical student; he, too, was a native Australian, which was the catalyst for the friendship that had developed with Jesse. Eva met Dean at "the party", and the rest, as they say, is history.

Kate waved them over whilst I tried to hide my disappointment at sharing. Jesse and Dean portrayed the classic Australian look, carrying a tan, albeit slightly lightened, and wavy blonde hair. They both cut a fine figure with their tight shirts, hinting at gym-built muscles. I was a runner and was best described as lean. I did have a few ounces of muscle, mainly on my calves, from cycle cross-training. I, too, had wavy hair, but brown, with just a few strands dipping over my ears.

As the three ambled over, Kate and I moved a little apart, and an awkwardness returned quickly between us. Neither of us knew if we wanted the perception of togetherness. Eva, Jesse and Dean sat down with a varied selection of coffees, cakes and pastries. Eva led the conversation, or should I say friendly interrogation, directed at the life and times of yours truly. I indulged

Eva, Jesse and Dean with the tales of my life. Kate leaned back, quietly listening.

"Why accountancy?" was Eva's first question. I didn't really know. I explained that Miles was my best friend, and his dad, Nick, was an accountant and a decent chap. Jesse and Dean grinned at that description. I was not sure that the word "chap" was in the Australian vernacular. Nick was also very wealthy. Money was not necessarily the primary driver; I did like numbers, but also solving problems using statistics, strategies and economic theory. "Was I passionate about my chosen career pathway?" I was about to find out.

Eva seemed a little disinterested in the articulation of my life so far. She switched her focus to my love life, girls, dating and relationships. I felt uncomfortable disclosing details that I had not spoken about to Kate. I decided that the life history of James Davy would wait for another day. Eva conceded defeat. The topic turned to interests other than study and my love life, which, thus far, in my tender 18 years, was negligible. As we sat delving into each other's leisurely pursuits, I noted an ease had crept over the group. Jesse, Dean and I joined together in the discussion of sport, the NRL. Jessie and Dean favoured the Melbourne Storm, whereas I was a diehard Warrington fan; the international game of rugby league seemingly assured the finding of a common ground.

The ambush of the impromptu rendezvous with Kate was a catalyst to meet again, soon. We left the café together, retracing our steps back to the house. Kate and I lingered at the back, Eva and Dean just in front, giggling and holding hands. Jesse took up the lead. And that's pretty much how the next little while evolved, with Jesse content to play the wingman. On occasion, we were joined by Miles with various ladies on his arm, rarely alone. The awkwardness of new acquaintances soon disappeared as the relaxed trait of Jesse and Dean guided us into their Australian mate ship, which in turn filtered into a mutual acceptance of each other's quirks and idiosyncrasies.

Once back at the pillar box red door, Eva, Dean and Jesse disappeared inside. Kate and I stood. I quickly stepped forward and kissed her lightly on the lips. "Can I see you again?" Kate didn't hesitate; she slowly kissed me back and smiled a very definite yes.

5

The Boyfriend

Kate

The café excursion was the beginning of young love and an innocence of emotions that would spiral into so much more. Still standing on the doorstep, James reached for my face and gently pulled me close; his lips found mine. His gentle kisses teased, his fingers gently trailing my neck. My eyes closed as I felt myself melting under his touch. His kisses gathered in urgency, probing, searching. My mouth eagerly responding, the fervour of the moment sending an ache to my core. Innocence driving curiosity and the desire for more.

Then the intensity slowly lessened, the kisses lightened, and the breathing softened as James gently pulled away. We both stood, breathless. James slowly turned to walk away. My eyes followed him; I saw him turn. "I will call you," he whispered.

The giddy days of first dates were filled with the excitement of the unknown. James and I explored new beginnings, sensing an unspoken connection. We were smiling, laughing, sneaking little kisses, our hands joined as if never to let go. We met at both our houses, Jesse and Eva took great delight in teasing our obvious infatuation. Jesse extended his delight in repeating the teasing towards Eva and Dean. He, himself, seemingly content to stay single, keeping busy with his nursing shifts at St Barts.

Miles and I became firm friends, an easiness evident when the three of us were together. Miles often brought a lady home, but the relationships lasted no more than a few weeks. He would just shrug, light up the next cigarette and lean out of the window, "contemplating life" as he would frequently say.

The start of the university year came and went. James, Eva, Miles and I became students of a different kind. We embraced the novelty of student life, the endless studying, socialising and a little self-discovery. We became better versions of ourselves; Eva and I welcomed the opportunity to care, whilst James and Miles seemed a little more focused on the finance of the business world rather than accounting and numbers.

Eva and I had originally wanted to study paramedic science, but soon discovered that we needed the patient to be a little "sorted" before it was our turn to take over care. Horrific scenes displayed at our trauma lectures reaffirmed our nursing career choice.

We settled into a weekly routine of weekday learning and weekend get-togethers. Jesse and Dean, less so. Jesse was governed by shifts that encroached on drinks and dinners. Dean's medical timetable was relentless; flexibility was key. Catch-ups were often brunch or lunch; occasionally, there were six, but more often there were four, and of course, many times just two.

I had never been in a relationship before, and the boyfriend-girlfriend phenomenon was a little scary. I had no idea of the rules, who called whom, how long between dates, who paid for dinners, movies, and snacks, of which there were many. When did kissing and holding hands turn into considerably more? Eva wasn't much help, aside from octopus George; she had had little experience too.

James and I stumbled through the early days of dating, not really caring about the relationship protocols. Our first kiss evolved into increasing intimacy, very slowly. There were many moments of uncertainty and pure inexperience. We were blissfully immersed in each other, at times to the exclusion of others. Often, we would sit in one of London's many bars, The Founder's Arms was one of our favourites, overlooking the Thames. We would sit on the heated patio recounting our life stories thus far.

I knew bits and pieces about James. James grew up as the eldest of three. Alexander, or Alex, was the middle child, nearing the end of school, with Beth being the youngest, and according to James, the most troublesome. Barely a teenager, she thrived on pushing boundaries and engaging in risky behaviour, so far somehow avoiding serious consequences. Unfortunately, Miles was often to blame for some of the situations that Beth would find herself in. Miles enjoyed leading Beth astray; what Miles deemed to be mischievous often bordered on being brazenly bad.

James' parents were caring but not domineering, believing that life was for living and encouraged the siblings to be independent, an ethos Beth took a little too literally for her modest years. Linda and Peter were high school teachers and were very accustomed to the challenges of youth.

James' grandmother, Dorothy, known affectionately as Dot, was the family matriarch, admired not only by the Davy family but throughout Lancashire. Dot had been married to Arthur for 45 years until he passed away a few years ago. Dot was a no-nonsense woman, seemingly having no time for nincompoops, and certainly did not like to be treated as an old lady. Dot was, in her own words, "as sharp as a tack" and commanded respect.

James was Dot's favourite grandchild, as she would openly tell anyone who would choose to listen. James' relationship with Dot resonated with my relationship with my grandfather. James also had spent many weekends staying with his grandparents, mostly to avoid his younger siblings. His grandfather shared James's passion for rugby league and often they could be seen on a Saturday or Sunday afternoon at The Halliwell Jones Stadium watching the Warrington Wolves, hopefully thrashing their opponents. The passing of James' grandfather left a void, which Miles willingly filled, seeing it as an opportunity to pursue the fairer sex. Miles' captivation by a crowd of females amazed James. It seemed that Miles had progressed from being a boy to being a man and had missed many stages in between.

James' other sporting passion was running. James would immediately become visibly animated with excitement as he described the buzz, the runner's "high", a feeling of euphoria and most importantly, well-being. James was not super competitive; he enjoyed running. He enjoyed the sense of achievement of challenging himself and attaining personal goals of distance and time. His enthusiasm was contagious, and I found myself caught up in his flurry of running descriptions. I soon became accustomed to running terminology: carb loading, splits and warmups. James's training sessions were a mixture of pyramids, fartleks and reps of varying lengths; 500s seemed to be his favourite. Occasionally, he dabbled in cycling as a cross-training component to running, but running was his obsession.

James would turn the conversation to me, to my interests, my obsessions. I did not have an obsession as such and certainly did not share James' obvious passion for running. Eva and I had occasionally followed the Leeds Rhino rugby league team, for reasons not too dissimilar to Miles, but for the less fair sex. The standing in wind, sleet and snow at the hallowed Headingley ground quickly quashed that enthusiasm, so too did the realisation that 'beany' hair after the game did not achieve the glamorous look that we had intended.

I did enjoy walking; my parents had a beagle, Barney. Ben, Daniel and I would often trek along the Yorkshire moors, especially during school holidays. Barney would go off leash, bounding into the distance chasing rabbits and hares, and we would bound after him. Daniel and

Ben would collapse in a heap as they finally tackled him to a stop. My brothers were much faster than I, so as soon as I caught up, they would let Barney scamper off once more into the distance. Daniel and Ben thought it was great fun, me not so much. Eventually Barney the Beagle was leashed up, and we all trudged home, usually wet, muddy and very hungry. I smiled at the memory.

After school, walks were more common, the boys deferring the task to me. It was more of a sniff, being a hound, but Barney would have walked for miles. Eva occasionally joined us, insisting that she would take Barney's lead. The three of us could often be seen shuffling along, Barney's white-tipped tail wagging to the beat of our banter.

I admitted to James that I had a love of reading, more specifically a love of buying books and certainly a love of bookshops. This interest, unfortunately, was hindered by my current life of study. The constraints of time dictated that reading for pleasure would have to take a back seat while a nursing degree was attained.

James listened intently, memorising every detail, occasionally smiling but never interrupting, making me feel that at that moment I was the centre of his world. In a rush of emotion, I leaned over and kissed him.

6
The Graduation

Kate

James and I completed our studies in unison; both degrees had included practical experiences, mine included ward and the emergency department placements, where I put theory into practice, treating humans, sick humans. It had felt quite humbling to actually care for patients and to be a part of their healthcare journey; to be trusted and respected as a professional, to have my opinion valued, to be listened to and to be appreciated for simple actions that meant so much. I gained so much in life skills as a student nurse: the skill of communication, resilience, critical thinking, adaptability and most importantly, teamwork.

I had a variety of placements; medical wards, surgical wards and the emergency department, the latter known as the front door of healthcare, where patients presented at the very start of their journey, often unplanned and always unpredictable. My preference was the wards. I enjoyed the continuity of care that the wards allowed. The emergency department was transient care, a stepping stone to somewhere. The general surgical and trauma ward was my absolute favourite. The mixture of care, simple and complex, routine and variable, mingled with the joy of recovery and the heartache of loss, provided an all-encompassing nursing experience.

The student experience, on occasion, was as unpredictable as the patients. At the beginning of each student placement, there would be a feeling of fear and trepidation as to the nature of the welcoming party, aka the ward team. There were so many personnel involved in the care of a patient: doctors, nurses, physiotherapists, to name but a few, all had a hierarchy, all seemed to have a pecking order. As students, Eva and I soon learnt our place, not to say we became submissive, but we were respectful of experience and position. There were many an occasion when we would join the boys, usually James, Miles and Jesse, Dean as a medical student always seemed to be working or studying, to debrief about some mean nurse. Eva and I both succumbed on different occasions to Staff Nurse Melanie Wicks sending us halfway across a hospital for a long stand, when, of course, there was no such thing, much to the amusement of the ward nurses when we eventually returned. We decided that student nurses were expected to pass some type of initiation before being accepted into the registered nurse sisterhood. That initiation process seemed to occur regularly throughout our three years.

The study component was tricky; the main angst was the competing demands on time. As the years progressed, completing assignments and studying for exams, quite often whilst on prac, challenged Eva and me; often tears flowed in frustration and books were thrown at whoever happened to be near, at the sheer volume of knowledge that had to be acquired.

But we loved being nurses, we thrived on nearing that goal, to "getting our stripes", to being called Staff Nurse. Our patients, mostly, welcomed our presence and happily listened to our small grumbles, providing encouragement and winking when our names were hollered down the ward.

As Eva and I neared G Day, Graduation Day, the excitement amongst our student cohort was palpable. We had one more assignment and one more student placement to complete before our dream became reality. I was placed again at St Barts on a surgical ward, and Eva was at The Royal London Hospital close by. The assignment title was a little ambiguous: "Managing Complex Health Conditions". That was it, eight weeks, and we would be qualified registered nurses.

James and Miles had concluded their degree at LSE a little earlier. And as they basked in their glory of gaining a Bachelor of Science degree in Accounting and Finance, they visited many drinking holes, dragging Dean with them, avoiding the heightened behaviour of Eva and me. James had moved in with me, Eva sharing with Dean, so complete avoidance was impossible. Contact occurred only when absolutely necessary, the boys crossing off the days on makeshift calendars, one at my grandfather's house, one at Dean's, much to their amusement. Eva and I openly acknowledged the usage of James and Miles' newly acquired accountancy skills, our comments seemingly dampening their humour.

The final ward placements, as senior third-year student nurses, seemed to gain a little more tolerance from the ward team, and with the expectation that we were now competent, as we neared the completion of our training. We were graced with a little more autonomy, still under the guidance of a registered nurse, but Eva and I were both allowed to suggest more options in the designation of appropriate care. Neither of our hospitals felt the need for any more initiation activities, and maybe for the first time, Eva and I felt very much a part of our respective ward teams.

The final assignment was not so joyous. Eva and I needed a little guidance on two levels: firstly, on how to answer the question: from a patient perspective, how the patient managed their complex health condition, or from a healthcare perspective, how healthcare professionals manage complex health conditions. Jesse agreed it was a difficult conundrum, and the three of us decided to approach it from both the patient and healthcare professional viewpoints, in an interlinked manner. The second piece of guidance was how to focus on said assignment and not let our minds wander to a public house and the consumption of alcoholic beverages. Eight weeks.

Meanwhile, James and Miles became very comfortable in beverage houses, dissecting the last year of their accountancy degree, where they gained practical experience through working on case studies and real-world examples. The complex scenarios mirrored the problems that they were likely to encounter during their careers. Like nursing, James and Miles learnt that the development of key skills, teamwork, communication and critical thinking, are highly valued by potential employers. Dean still had a little way to go before qualifying as a junior doctor, but was happy to occasionally join James and Miles socially.

Jesse was busy at St Barts, and truth be told, Jesse enjoyed helping Eva and me solve our many assignment quandaries. We had to carefully ensure that they were different but had similar concepts. We addressed the management of different complex health conditions within different health population groups, which worked effectively. Four weeks.

Eva and I handed in the last assignment, which was on a Friday, two weeks before our nursing studies were officially completed. Then we awaited our results, graduation and official transcripts.

For James and me, this was a time to reconnect, to enjoy each other again, just the two of us. The previous six months had been dominated by study and placements; our relationship had drifted along, morphing into friendship, erasing any intimacy. The pressure of timelines and exams was not conducive to hanky-panky, as I jokingly voiced when James suggested putting the books away with a mischievous grin. But then the books were put away, assignments handed in, and placements finished. There was a brief pause, a small hiatus, before a renewed focus on jobs and career plans.

Lying together as James massaged the back of my neck, his hands swept around to fondle my breasts, and I smiled. I turned to face James. I took a second to recognise the person who had drifted away, now returned, facing me. James lifted my arms and slid off my nightdress, as it fell to the floor, he stepped out of his shorts, skin on skin, we came together, touching as our bodies became reunited. I felt him harden against me. I held his gaze as he leaned forward and kissed me, a little warily at first, then with intensity, his tongue owning my mouth. I responded, desperate to feel the familiarity of his touch. His mouth left mine, kissing my exposed skin; my neck, my breasts, still lower, his hands firmly gripped my buttocks, and an ache throbbed between my legs as my wetness yearned for him. James climbed on top of me, gently spreading my legs. My body trembled as I felt his erection enter, pulsating as he rocked back and forth. His mouth back on my mouth, his tongue slowly, gently flicking, sweeping, teasing. My hands were frantic, tightly holding his nakedness as we both exploded in pure ecstasy.

We lay panting, our hands holding. James drew the duvet up, and closing our eyes, we fell into the tranquillity of sleep. I awoke several hours later, hands still holding, I was content just to lie, smiling, thinking about the future of us.

Graduation week was crazy, as family and friends descended on London Town to celebrate. Mum, Dad, Ben, Daniel, and of course Lisa. James' family, including Dot, parents Linda and Peter, Alex and Beth.

Eva's parents and Miles' dad, Nick. Jesse had flown back to Australia to be with his dad and Luke, to commemorate the anniversary of his Mum's passing. He was sorry to miss the ceremony, to see us standing proud.

Eva and I started work as registered nurses, how exciting, on the wards where we did our final placements. Me at St Barts, and Eva at The Royal London Hospital. The application process was a little challenging, with resumes and interviews, of course, Eva and I had to shop for new outfits. We were both eager to begin our nursing careers, periodically hugging each other, as the thrill of what we had achieved overspilled into pure exhilaration.

Jesse had returned from Australia and had volunteered to be our photographer on our first day. No pictures on a mobile phone, Jesse decreed that this occasion called for a Canon 5D Mark III edition, of which Jesse just happened to have. Eva arrived at my grandfather's house polished and shiny in her uniform. I, too, showered and gleaming, like two schoolgirls on the first day of school. James, Miles and Dean, who had graced us with their early presence, stood watching the chaos as Jesse orchestrated the photo shoot.

The following week had been the boys' turn. James and Miles started at their accountancy firms. Eva and I had insisted on a repeat of our photo shoot. The boys had very reluctantly agreed to one photograph. Jesse had arrived home from a night shift, took out his Canon 5D, and took a photograph of the accountants, both in their uniform of beige chinos and white shirts, and then headed to bed.

7

The Shenanigans

James

I had enjoyed working at the accounting firm. As a first step in the field of accountancy and finance, it had been a great way to get on the ladder to success. It was a small company, some would describe as boutique, but it seemed to be thriving within a niche of a very broad market. I had formed some lasting friendships and found mentors among the older generation of employees.

Henry and Steve, whom I had met on my first day two years earlier, constantly challenged protocol and processes, testing the tolerance of Mr Samuel S. Dawson and Mr David P. Francis. I never did find out what the S or P stood for, the senior partners, to the limit. I, too, had to tolerate them both on occasion, as even though they were thirty years old, their maturity could be defined as possibly many years younger. As drinking partners, though, they excelled; like Miles, they had an eye for the ladies. The three of them would entertain Kate and me with their flirty antics and playful witticisms. Kate ensured that a degree of respect was always maintained.

Miles and I had always been drawn to the business side of our studies at LSE, and although we had both secured jobs in reputable firms as junior accountants, we were restless. Management consultancy was our dream, and at the tender age of twenty-three, we began to explore that career pathway. We were brazen in our applications, ignoring our own naivety in this part of the business world, carrying an air of confidence that, for the most part, was unsubstantiated. We applied to each of the "Big Four" consultancy firms. The application process was rigorous, aside from written applications, psychometric testing and interviews, there was also a full medical.

To my amazement, I received a job offer from ELT Finance and Consulting, starting the following Monday. All that was left for me to do was pass the medical, the final stage of the recruitment process. My fitness was unquestionable, although my running had been a little "off" lately, and I had struggled to maintain my pace over long distances, dropping a few seconds a mile. Kate gave me the excuse of stress from the job applications, but I wasn't convinced. At times, I found myself running out of breath and having to pause. I must admit, though, that as runners, if we felt our pace was on the slow side, we'd do some sprints to reduce the overall time, cheating, but not really cheating. I described it as fooling myself, though it did look good on Strava, my activity tracking app, for all to see. Lately, I'd felt the need to increase my sprinting. Maybe I was running too much; being a self-confessed obsessive, I needed to run every day.

The day of the medical arrived. I attended a medical centre near the ELT building in central London. Unexpectedly, I was a little nervous. My "off" running form had started to bother me. The doctor conducting the test seemed to have previously served in the Army Corps. "Dr Kelly," his name badge read, and I soon discovered he did not engage in small talk, or any talk at all. He conducted the medical by barking out instructions and grunting after each task.

I completed my vision and hearing tests, gave a urine sample, one I had prepared earlier, and then moved on to the overall fitness component. Dr Kelly asked me to run a mile on a treadmill; I earned two grunts for that. Post-run, he took my heart rate and commented that it was quite high. The fact that Dr Kelly actually commented bothered me. The final part of the medical was a general blood test.

When I got home from the medical, Kate had just finished her shift at St Barts. We had arranged dinner and drinks to celebrate my new job. Miles had so far failed to escape the grips of his accountancy firm, but true to our friendship, he was excited for my new opportunity, also using it as an excuse for a big night out. In true Kate and Eva style, dinner became an event rather than a simple gathering of friends. A traditional Italian restaurant was chosen, one that welcomed noise and mayhem.

As we got dressed, Kate, standing in her pink lingerie, asked me how the medical had gone. I described Dr Kelly, and she laughed at my comparison to an Army Major. Suddenly, I abandoned my chinos and white polo and pulled her into my arms. It had been so long since I'd felt her soft curves against me; my body immediately responded. Kate smiled as she felt me harden against her. I drew her closer, God, she felt so good. I felt an urgency to explore her body, to feel every inch of her, to lick and tease her nakedness.

Kate pulled away for an instant, breathless. "Dinner."

"Ten minutes," I replied.

I lay her down on the bed. I needed her, needed to be inside her. I pulled down her underwear; she immediately opened her legs, a dampness enticing my entry. I slipped inside her and was engulfed by an intense emotion of belonging. We moved together, quickening, faster and faster, until a crescendo of desire left us trembling in a tight embrace. The enormity of such passion I had never felt before. We parted, panting, glistening, and slowly our breathing settled.

I rolled over to her. I wanted more. I lifted the pink lace, exposing her breasts. I covered her nipples with my mouth, one at a time, sucking, tasting. My hands travelled down her body, slowly circling her naked flesh, smoothing over her stomach, lower and lower across her pubic mound. Still lower, until my fingers gently parted her folds and entered her. So wet, so soft, so warm. Probing, pushing, fingering in and out. Kate moaned and writhed to my rhythm, arching so I could reach deeper. My fingers slowly withdrew as I parted her legs wider, her wetness dripping around me. I entered her once again, this time slower, harder, pounding, climaxing into an explosion of raw desire.

We were late. We arrived at the restaurant to a standing ovation, slow clapping turning into cheers, back-slapping and smothering embraces. As we emerged from the clinches, I saw everyone: Eva, Miles, Jesse, Dean, Henry and Steve from work, and the bosses Samuel and David. Wives, partners, boyfriends, girlfriends, and a multitude of others I had briefly met and formed fleeting acquaintances with. The atmosphere was electric, the generosity so touching that, after such a short time at the firm, the send-off reached dizzying heights of acclamation.

I introduced Kate, looking ever so pretty in her pink floral dress, her curves accentuated. My curves. I watched as the tresses of her long black hair swished elegantly as she effortlessly slipped into the crowd. I saw her drawn into conversation, watched her eyes sparkle, her mouth never faltering to smile. I gave a silent thank you to whoever, whatever, for finding this girl I could call my own.

Eventually, the crowd settled into their seats. We occupied a long table down the centre of the restaurant, reminiscent of a medieval banquet. Kate sat to my right; next to her sat Eva, then Dean and Jesse, and then a multitude of others. To my left sat Miles, Henry and Steve, "the bosses", and again a multitude of others. The noise was deafening, the music blaring in the background lost to raised voices, exuberant laughter and the occasional eruption of cheers.

The food was typical Italian fare, bruschetta, pasta, gnocchi, pizzas, risottos, cheeses and cold meats, garlic oozing from every dish, infusing the air. Bottles of wine, too many to count, filled already near-full glasses, spilling unceremoniously onto the chequered tablecloth. No one seemed to mind.

Eventually, the feast was over. The food was cleared, tables shifted, and the dancing began. Italian and English music filled the restaurant, no discrimination of culture; tonight, everyone was one. I had never felt such camaraderie. The waiters joined in, as did the owner, Matteo, by the end of the night, Matteo was "Matt", and our friendship sealed.

Glasses clinked as impromptu toasts were made, hugs were given freely, as the evening slowly faded to a close. The two-kiss greetings turned into farewells as new friendships bid adieu. I found Kate giggling with Eva, eyes still sparkling, though her laughter was punctuated by the occasional yawn. Time for home. Despite a flurry of objections from Eva, we escaped into the night.

Once outside, we stopped and stood. I leaned forward and kissed her, my hand stroking her cheek, pushing a strand of hair gently behind her ear. I gazed into her eyes. "I love you," I said.

"I know," she replied. "I love you too."

We arrived home, exhausted but exhilarated after an amazing night. Kate was on a late shift at the hospital the next day, and I had a few days off before starting at

ELT, but tiredness swept over both of us. Thoughts of our pre-party shenanigans, Kate's word, not mine, deepened our contentment as we drifted off to sleep.

8

The Hardest Race

James

I awoke around 10 a.m. the next morning to a note from Kate on the pillow beside me, saying that she was meeting Eva and then going straight to her late shift at St Barts. I reached for my phone next to the bed. It was lit up like a Christmas tree, twenty or so missed calls from the medical centre. I sat bolt upright, my heart thumping. I called them and was told to come in urgently. I don't remember the journey into central London; I don't even remember getting dressed. All I remember is walking into the doctor's room.

There was a female doctor, the Army Major was nowhere to be seen. I remember her placing a blood test result, *my* blood test result, in front of me, her face ashen. My eyes were drawn to the bottom of the report; the words stood out: **ACUTE MYELOID LEUKAEMIA (AML).** In that moment, my world came crashing down.

I sat there stunned, the colour drained from my face as tidal waves of nausea hit me. I was going to vomit. Deep breaths, just breathe. Fuck, I was alone. The doctor came around from behind her desk and sat next to me. I put my head in my hands, closed my eyes and entered a world of nothing. I was blank. Somewhere in my clouded mind, thousands of questions whirled endlessly, circling chaotically, but I couldn't speak. The doctor waited. I slowly raised my head, my hands cold and clammy, fingers running through my hair. A single tear crept down my face.

I had no idea what AML was; I just knew it was bad, very, very bad. I stood up. I wanted to run. If I left, I wouldn't have to face the reality of this. I didn't even know what *this* was. I could pretend it was happening to someone else, that I hadn't heard the words, that I hadn't been told my life was about to change forever, and that this would be my biggest battle. My hardest race.

Then suddenly, Kate. Fuck. Fuck. I didn't usually swear. I was always of the opinion that the one million or so words in the English vocabulary would be sufficient, but the only word I could find at that precise moment was *fuck*, and I said it over and over again. It was the only way I could express my disbelief and fear.

I sat dazed as the words *blood cancer, chemotherapy, stem cell, and donors* washed over me. It was as if I were listening to a foreign language, one I did not understand. I tried to remember if I had heard Jesse talk about AML, and if he had, what had happened to his patients. I started trembling. Was I going to die?

The doctor had more patients to see, more people to tell that their lives would change forever. I stood. I had an appointment scheduled for the next morning, after I had "processed the news". She made it sound as though the Warrington Wolves had just lost the Rugby Football League Championship, not that my future was now unknown, uncertain at best. I had decisions to make and no time to make them; the treatment needed to start immediately.

As I turned to leave, the doctor got up and led me to the door. As she opened it, she briefly placed an arm across my back, in a sort of half-embrace. I appreciated the touch before stepping into the busy corridor, engulfed again by another world. I left under a blanket of hopelessness, wandering aimlessly along the London streets, watching people laughing, couples holding hands, babies being pushed in prams. Children were being dragged along by their parents on the promise of a treat; teenagers clumped together, looking for trouble. The city was alive with living, and then there was me. Confused, scared, and alone.

I tried to recall the conversation with Dr Death, or whatever her name was. I tried to decipher the words that had become jumbled in a mixture of catastrophic confusion. She had handed me a collection of booklets and pamphlets. I held them, too panicked to even glance at the front cover.

Then a new panic took over. Who do I tell? Kate, Miles, Dot, my parents, Alex, Beth, or even Jesse, the "cancer" nurse? I dropped onto a nearby bench, covered my face with my hands and cried. An overwhelming sense of powerlessness engulfed me. I wasn't a crier either. It seemed that in just a few hours my life was already beginning to change. My tears slowly subsided. I remained on the bench, a hollow feeling in the pit of my stomach persisted, accompanied by surges of nausea.

The light started to fade. Every now and again, I would sigh and wrap my arms around myself as a form of protection against the enormity of the unknown. I thought of Kate, now a qualified registered nurse, who had joined Jesse at St Barts. Her manager spoke highly of her, as did the rest of the ward team, although she had become a little restless of late, feeling drawn to the surgical patients with a twist of trauma. Kate had started to explore a transfer to The Royal London Hospital, a renowned teaching hospital specialising in trauma and emergency care. But for now, Kate was content in finally making a difference. I couldn't destroy her world. I decided, in that moment, I would tell Miles. I needed one person to help me not tell Kate.

Kate was on a late shift; I didn't expect her home until 11:30 p.m. I dragged my sorry self to the tube station. Catching the tube across London, I sat in a bubble of solitude among commuters on their way home from work. Fuck. I was due to start my new job on Monday, five days away. What was I going to say? *Sorry, I have to fight death first, then I can start. Or can you hold my job open for a few years? I'll be in touch, maybe.*

Anger seeped into my disbelief. I silently demanded, *Why me?* I oscillated between fear, rage and denial. The overwhelming feeling of pure terror swept over me as I got off the tube. I joined the tired throng of travellers exiting the station and trudged towards Miles's terrace home.

I collapsed into Miles's arms as he opened the door.

"Whoa, whoa," Miles said, gently guiding me to the couch and lowering me down.

Once again, I put my head in my hands. Miles was silent, too scared to ask what was wrong. I slowly began to tell my horror story, one in which I was playing the main character, the starring role.

The words came out in a jumbled mess. I was incoherent at first, then slowly the intent became clear. Miles stood and paced the room. He stopped and turned to me.

"Acute Myeloid Leukaemia, what the fuck is that?"

I tried to explain and soon realised I really had no idea. I could repeat certain words that Dr Death had told me, but most of the conversation had become incomprehensible gibberish. Two words had become embedded, *blood cancer*, repeated on constant replay in my brain.

Miles came to sit next to me, my best friend. I sobbed like a child, shuddering. Miles hugged me tightly, as if he could squeeze the badness away. Soon, Miles was crying too. I could feel the wetness of his face soaking my shirt. Eventually, we drew apart. It was at that point that our friendship reached a new height, our loyalty deepened, our bond stronger than ever. Miles stood again and said three words, "I'm with you."

Miles made me eat something. I realised I hadn't eaten since before my morning appointment, I don't think I ate then either; I couldn't remember. Leftover spaghetti bolognese was reheated, and to my surprise, I ate greedily. Then came the time to discuss my plan. I was leaving.

I sensed that Miles didn't agree with my plan, that leaving Kate, running away, was wrong. Miles questioned how leaving Kate could be better than telling her the truth. I gazed ahead, explaining in a monotone, seemingly detached from my words, not wanting to feel. I couldn't watch her crumble; I couldn't promise that I would comfort her tears, and I couldn't reassure her that I would be okay.

Because I didn't know.

I couldn't promise that I would be brave, strong and fight. I couldn't promise that I wouldn't dissolve into a shell of my former self, that in irrational moments I wouldn't blame her or envy her life. But above all, I couldn't promise that I wouldn't fade away, pass away, die. And because I couldn't promise these things, I couldn't promise that I wouldn't hurt her too much to ever recover. So, I couldn't tell her.

Miles never asked me again.

Sometime later, Miles drove me home. We sat in silence, too many thoughts racing through our heads. Once home, I showered and went to bed. Kate came home around 11.30 pm. I feigned sleep, mumbling only goodnight. Kate was on an early shift the next day, so she was keen to get some rest. Once I heard the gentle rhythm of her breathing, I opened my eyes and stared into the darkness. I was still staring several hours later when my alarm sounded, and I left to go for a run. I kissed Kate on the forehead and whispered, "See you." She stirred a little before returning to a deep slumber.

I loved her so much.

I silently wept as I crept downstairs. I left the house, closing the door gently behind me. I didn't run, I jogged to the end of the road and sat on the corner bench, thinking of nothing. I needed to take a break from reality, just for a little while. An hour later, knowing that Kate would have left for her early shift at St Barts, I returned home, packed a few things and left. No explanation, no note, no goodbye.

Tubing once again across London, I met Miles at my appointment. Dr Taylor, Dr Elise Taylor, as I discovered was her actual name, was waiting. I introduced Miles as my support person, my best friend. We sat. This time I listened carefully, trying to absorb details of leukaemia and the process from here. All the while, Miles sat next to me, his hand on my shoulder. Our eyes stared as descriptions of treatment spun around us. Chemotherapy was pivotal, but before that, there was a rigorous series of investigations: umpteen blood tests, including genetic testing to determine the protocol, bone marrow biopsies to analyse my blood cells, heart and kidney function tests to ensure my body could tolerate the assault of therapy. I was offered the chance to store sperm for later, whenever later may or may not be. We didn't nod; we didn't pretend to understand. Then came the side effects: hair loss, nausea, vomiting, mouth ulcers, oesophageal ulcers, fatigue, and so it went on. Dr Taylor began to describe the effect on blood cells. At that point, Miles interjected, "Enough," he shouted. "Stop." Dr Taylor paused and nodded, enough.

I stayed at Miles's house for the rest of the day. I sat, trying to navigate a cascade of emotions as Miles took over. He booked our train tickets to Warrington for some ungodly hour the next morning. Miles currently lived alone; his recent housemate, Colin, had left a week earlier. But being London, Miles knew a couple of friends looking for temporary accommodation. A few phone calls later, and two accountants from his firm would move in the following week. Next came an email to his boss asking, or rather informing him, that he was taking three months' leave for a family emergency. My heart leapt at those simple words. Then the realisation hit me, ELT. I would have to send an email rejecting their offer. A fresh wave of nausea washed over me. Miles drafted a short email, devoid of elaboration but to the point: due to circumstances blah blah, and I hit send. My dream career disintegrated in one sentence.

Miles's packing was as simple as mine, just the essentials, all focus on James Davy, or so it seemed. As he carried a single carrier bag into the living room, we looked at our two bags next to each other and shrugged in silent recognition of more important things in life than belongings.

Knowing Kate would soon be home from her early shift, I needed to text her. I kept it brief, saying I was going for drinks with Miles and others. I ended with a usual add-on, "don't wait up, I might even stay over at Miles", and pressed send. I hoped that my minimal packing wouldn't raise any suspicion. I remembered she was working another early shift the next day. My relief was soon replaced by a heavy guilt of lies and deception. In that moment, I had never despised myself more.

Dinner was a simple affair. Miles rustled up scrambled eggs on toast; we ate in silence, any small talk seemed useless. We both understood the gravity of the situation; we didn't need words. And so, to bed, but not to sleep. As dawn neared, I had dozed into a fitful dream. I got up to find Miles showered, dressed and ready. Miles steered me to the bathroom and ran me a shower. Toast and coffee greeted me from the kitchen bench when I emerged somewhat refreshed and looking a little more human.

We ate quickly. I had mentioned to Miles that I wanted to stop by Kate's terrace one more time to grab some books and maybe a few more items of clothing, knowing that Kate would have left for her early shift. Miles locked his terrace up and left the keys under a plant pot to the left of his front door. "Not very original," I commented. Miles replied with a cheeky grin, the first hint of a smile in over forty-eight hours.

We soon arrived at Kate's. We asked the taxi driver to wait just a few seconds while I raced inside, grabbed a bag of books and a handful of sweatshirts and tees, being careful not to take the ones Kate and I shared. I glanced around, my eyes settling on Grandpa Bob's chair. I fought back the tears and left, closing the red pillar-box door for the very last time. I, too, left my key under a plant pot. Miles nodded at the gesture, acknowledging the finality of this chapter in our lives. We headed to London Euston Station.

Then the fight began.

9

The Fight

James

My care would be transferred to the Clatterbridge Cancer Centre near Warrington. Dr Taylor assured me that this was a specialised cancer centre dedicated to haematology, including leukaemia, which, as I had discovered, was pertinent to my care. I was to present for admission the next morning, Dr Taylor was very clear that immediate treatment was critical as Acute Myeloid Leukaemia was a life-threatening disease, this was articulated at least three times during my consultation, each time Miles and I became a whiter shade of pale.

The magnitude of my battle ahead drove Miles' commitment to me. My fight was his fight. True to his word, he took three months leave and moved back to Lancashire. As he moved back to his parents' home, I moved into the Clatterbridge Cancer Centre.

I stood at the admission desk, I had my bag full of books, a love for which I had adopted from Kate. As she had tried to embrace running and failed, I had tried to embrace reading and succeeded. I would never have been more grateful for all the bookshops visited, the hours scanning shelves, and the pounds spent on building my collection. Dr Taylor had encouraged me to pack clothes to try and create some normality. I chose comfort; I resembled the fashion style of Kate, with tees, hoodies, and jeans. I left the chinos behind. I realised that Kate would be forever embedded in my being, I accepted this, shrugged and gave a wistful smile.

Miles raced in to join me. I was handed some paperwork and told to present to the reception desk of Ward 5C. We were briskly given directions. I heard go to the purple lifts, all else faded into oblivion. Miles followed me like a love-struck puppy close to my heels. The sign before us read *"Ward 5C Haematology and Oncology, Level 5"*; reality hit me like a truck. This was it, this was home for the next three weeks, at least. I answered a million questions, gave blood samples, sperm specimens and had a mass of investigations.

For the sperm collection, a nurse had escorted me to a private room where I was given a sterile jar. I looked around and saw some porn magazines lying on the table. It was reminiscent of a scene from a comedy, except I saw no humour in this. I sighed and questioned what my life had become. I had just been told that I had leukaemia less than 48 hours ago, and now I was expected to get horny and produce a sperm specimen. I had no such urge; the only urge I had was to survive this living hell and to be with Kate, and it was at that moment that I realised the importance of what I had been advised to do. So, I thought of Kate, I let myself indulge in a fantasy of lust and wanting, as I came, I felt my body shudder as tears of disbelief trickled down my face. I left the specimen on the table and went back to my room, where Miles was waiting. I could not look at him, I could not speak to him, I quite literally pushed him aside. I showered, standing under the hot water, trying to wash the feelings of humiliation away.

I sat in bewilderment on the bed. Later that afternoon, as tears tumbled down my cheeks, eyes blurry, swollen and sore, I sent one final message to Kate: "I love you. I am sorry", and with those six words, it was over.

The next few weeks were a blur of blood tests, bone marrow aspirations, chemotherapy, blood transfusions, anti-bacterial pills, anti-viral pills, anti-fungal pills, prophylactic antibiotics "just in case ". The trauma on my body was relentless. I experienced all that I had been warned about and more. The most devastating and confronting response was the loss of my hair. It was slow at first, just a few strands, then clumps on the shower floor. Miles visited just as I had got out of the shower, the red rims around my eyes alerting Miles to my misery. He immediately left my room and returned ten minutes later with an electric razor. Without a word, I sat in front of the mirror whilst Miles shaved my head, and then, still silent, he turned the razor to his own head. We sat there with two bald heads staring at the mirror. Over the coming weeks, Miles and I could be seen wearing an array of head attire, our favourite being the white, primrose and blue of the Warrington Wolves bobble hat.

I became submissive to the treatment, but not submissive to the leukaemia. I just accepted everything that was thrown at me, the tests, the infusions, the millions of pills, some of which smelled like poo, without questioning, trusting my life in the hands of strangers. And Miles was there, my punching ball, experiencing the rise and falls with me. The euphoria of a day without nausea and the ability to eat a few morsels of food, to the despair of crippling fatigue, and barely lifting my head off the pillow.

We learnt together. We learnt that the first round of chemotherapy was known as *induction*, as an inpatient for ten days, three and seven, three days intermittent and then seven days continuous. The chemotherapy hit the blood cancer cells in the bone marrow, and in doing so destroyed the white blood cells known as neutrophils, my body's immunity. The risk, as the doctors explained, was my susceptibility to infection. White blood cells, as these clever doctors went on to explain, are the first blood cells to respond to an infection, engulfing and destroying germs like bacteria and fungi. Miles googled fungi but did not divulge what he found. The doctors continued, even the common cold could have dire consequences. This explained the need for me to stay in hospital after the first round of chemotherapy had ended to monitor for signs of infection and provide my depleted body with blood products and thousands of tablets to support recovery.

The ability of the bone marrow to produce healthy blood cells or neutrophils, as Miles and I grasped, was pivotal to my remission and recovery. We became obsessed with asking "how they were" every day. They were measured in a ridiculously low numeric, and we soon realised that a 0.01 count was something to celebrate. We also learnt that nothing in this plan was guaranteed, and presumptions should never be made or hoped for. Our conversations featured terminology that had previously been unknown but became part of our everyday life.

I had one other visitor, Dot, who, at the mature age of 83 years, continued to be a grandmother of formidable standing. Dot did not engage in hospital talk. She would briefly ask how I was but would not be drawn into my woeful world. Dot would produce games to distract away from my reality, poker and gin rummy were her favourites. Dot feigned ignorance of my predicament; she wore a mask, too, as she informed me, to protect her from *my* germs. I craved her visits and the brief escapism that ensued. As Miles became a link to my friends in the outside world, Dot became my link to my family. Dot revelled in tales of my siblings, Beth still the rebel, although a little more settled and Alex seemingly sampling the delights of the female fraternity. My parents were unhappy about not visiting, but respected my wishes, for which I was grateful. Dot would often share tales of her own life, of how she met Arthur. Dot was my mum's mum; Arthur was her second husband. Dot refused to discuss her first marriage, aside to say that Mum's dad, Dot's first husband, left when Mum was six years old, never to return. I swallowed down a lump rising in my throat as I thought of Kate.

Dot met Arthur in 1972, on a blind date. I grinned at Dot's description, at the Grosvenor Hotel in Sheffield. Arthur was a Yorkshire man, but their courtship, another one of Dot's descriptives, frequently took him across the Pennines to visit Dot. Dot explained that the old Yorkshire/Lancashire saying of "never the twain shall meet" became obsolete as their relationship evolved into love, and they married on May 15th, 1979.

Arthur was ten years Dot's senior, but they complemented each other beautifully. Arthur was a gentle soul; he had three passions in life: rugby league, golf and Dot. As a Yorkshireman, he followed Leeds Rhinos, but as he became an adopted Lancashire citizen, his allegiance changed to the Warrington Wolves. But it was on the golf course where Arthur starred, winning many a trophy proudly displayed in a glass cabinet at their home. Arthur could often be seen playing in the snow with his yellow golf balls, still finding the hole to deliver birdies and pars. Dot could often be heard berating him for being outside in such inclement weather. Arthur would smile, do his famous wave, "cheerio", he would shout as he headed off into the snowy abyss. As Dot described their life, the deep love and obvious heartache of his passing, her eyes sparkled in a rare display of emotion.

There were days when I couldn't face any visitors, neither Miles nor Dot. Days when I lay curled on my side, lines hanging around me, fluids of various colours invading my veins, joining the war against disease. The nausea enveloped me, wrapping tightly around me so I couldn't escape. These were the days when the nurses knew to keep their interactions to a minimum, to avoid small talk, to just inflict the necessary and leave.

Miles hated these days. He still turned up, paced the corridor outside my room for a while, then left. I would often hear his idle chatter through my door to some poor unsuspecting nurse. One nurse seemed to be more of a focus than others, Ellie.

Ellie, I learned, had joined the team of Ward 5C earlier that year. She was very pretty, her curly red hair sat just above her shoulders, sometimes she would tie it up into a ponytail that would swish as she went about her cares. Ellie was Irish; the lilt of her accent often lulled me into a peaceful place away from the harshness of reality. I would often close my eyes as she spoke, the sea sawing of her voice seemed to rock me into oblivion, soothing and gentle. Miles did not describe Ellie as such, but his obvious fondness for that nurse became evident as the days passed. Dot noticed too, when she and Miles very occasionally visited together, she would comment on the gleam of his eye as Ellie left the room. Miles just smiled.

On my better days, I would let my mind wander to Kate. I missed her so much. There was a perpetual gut-wrenching ache deep inside me. I had sworn my family and Lancashire friends to secrecy and trusted them to say nothing. I hated myself for the way I left, I continually questioned my decision not to tell her. On these "good" days I thought maybe I should. Then on the days when I felt like I'd been through a holocaust, I knew that I was right not to.

I missed her chatter, I missed her kisses, I missed her touch. I just missed her. I was consumed by guilt at my inability to confide in her, to let her be there for me, to care for me as she was caring for others. But I couldn't, I couldn't bear to see her distress, her sadness, her pain at seeing me going through this. As I looked at myself in the mirror, the reflection of a stranger, bald head, dark sunken eyes, cracked lips within a pasty face, stared back at me. A shadow of my former self. I crawled back to bed, curled on my side and sobbed silently into the pillow.

On one such occasion, there was a gentle tap on my door. Ellie walked in, closely followed by Miles. Whatever conversation they'd been having dissolved at the sight of my crumpled body. Touching was discouraged as my ability to fight germs was depleted to non-existent, but in that moment, Miles rushed over and fiercely hugged me. Ellie hung back, then slowly I felt her, her arms tentatively surrounding Miles and me, her head resting softly on my shoulder. I melted into their touch. The door remained closed, hiding this breach in protocol.

And so, my good day had turned to bad and turned to good again. I looked between Miles and Ellie and sensed those unmistakable feelings of attraction. Miles had been there so many times before, but I sensed this time was different; maybe Miles had finally met *"the one"*. For Miles to find such obvious happiness at this time seemed strangely ironic.

I was coming to the end of the initial chemotherapy treatment, the induction stage, in what I called my fucked-up leukaemia journey. I had succumbed to oesophagitis, mucositis, and many more *itis's,* with fluctuating degrees of nausea and headaches, and fatigue. I continued to ingest upwards of twenty-two pills daily, my head still resembled a dinted bowling ball, and my body a stick figure. But according to my doctors, I was winning, and as my neutrophils crept slowly to the magic 2.0 number, home became reality.

10
The Feeling

Kate

The morning after the farewell dinner, I arrived at Eva and Dean's flat a few hours before our late shift. They lived on the top floor of a terraced house that had been divided into two separate living spaces, as was the approach of astute property owners taking advantage of the demand for accommodation in the centre of London. Eva and Dean had moved in shortly after Dean had qualified as a junior doctor, joining me, Eva, Miles, and Jesse in the realms of the gainfully employed. As Eva moved out to cohabitate with Dean, Eva preferred this description to "live with"; James moved in to live with me. James and I had no qualms using the words "lived with". Jesse continued to occupy the attic space. Life settled into a routine of catch-ups, as our conflicting work rosters would allow.

James and I became established, evolving quickly into girlfriend and boyfriend, successfully navigating the intimacies of togetherness. Our sexual exploits were simple by some people's standards, unadventurous, some might say, but we were content. Our inaugural romantic encounter, and ensuing loss of my virginity, was on the floor of his parents' lounge room. This impromptu event was punctuated not so much by fervent passion but by giggles and embarrassment. James, too, in his words, "was not very worldly".

Significant carpet burns were testament to the fumbling of activities; the afterglow of James and me, testament to the intense pleasure and the driver of many more escapades.

As I approached Eva's door, I was aware of the quietness from within. Eva peered through the peephole, then quietly opened the door. Dean had just come off night shift and was in deep slumber. Eva hushed me into the living room. The objective of this pre-work catch-up was to dissect the previous farewell evening at the Italian restaurant. We quickly realised that this was impossible to conduct in hushed whispers, so we decided to relocate to the nearest café and leave Dean to his peaceful snoring.

We grabbed our uniforms so that we could get changed at St Barts before our shift. Eva had recently joined Dean, Jesse, and me at St Barts. She had developed a passion for all things heart and had transferred to St Barts to pursue her cardiac interest. As the largest cardiac centre in Europe, Eva had found her calling. I was still looking for mine. Of late, I had been drawn to surgical and trauma nursing; consequently, I was considering leaving St Barts for The Royal London. Yet I had not spoken of these thoughts to the St Barts crew.

Eva and I decided to go back five or so years, to the café where it all began, where tenuous friendships had grown strong and resilient, personifying closeness and trust. So much had changed, yet so much had stayed the same. Eva and I were now fully qualified registered nurses. University had been fun for the most part, but we both basked in the joy of no study and an income to assure us of our independence. I was aware, and ever so grateful, to have been gifted my grandfather's house in his will, but it was a house in stature only, and a house, as I soon learnt, had to be upkept and maintained, and the demands of the windowed envelopes that regularly came through the letterbox had to be paid. Eva and I had umpteen bar and waitressing jobs over the course of our three years. The shuffling of work, hospital shifts, and study became a constant challenge; employers would soon lose patience with the chopping and changing of our availability.

The boys, James, Miles, and Dean, were now also ensconced in the workforce. Dean was the last to join, only recently becoming a fully-fledged doctor. James and Miles had both joined accountancy firms a couple of years previously, but like many of Generation Y, they had become unsettled and had begun to look for pastures new. Jesse continued to support and care for people living with cancer, having now risen to the position of senior nurse.

As we sat once more at the table amongst the shelves of books and bric-a-brac, blending perfectly with the raised voices telling tales the morning after of the night before, we dissected the events of the Italian farewell. I could not help dissecting the events prior to the restaurant shindig, reflecting on the bedroom activities that had blown my mind. A mischievous grin filtered across my lips. Eva knew better than to inquire into my thoughts but smiled in unspoken understanding.

Eva dragged me back to the restaurant scene of merriment. We both acknowledged that the farewell to James had become a subtext to the gathering and that the dominant factor was the assembly of an assortment of friends and acquaintances who had connected as one. The crescendo of music, the clatter of crockery, the clinking of glasses, and the slurping of pasta had empowered a commonality amongst the gathered guests. There was no room for assessment or judgment, just enjoyment of each other and the celebration of good food and wine. Much to our disappointment, Eva and I could not talk about who was with whom, or who was wearing what, we simply didn't notice. "Such a good night," Eva and I declared in unison.

Not so the following late shift. Busy was an understatement. One nurse had failed to arrive, so we were one staff member down, unable to be replaced at the eleventh hour. I began to regret not sleeping in a little longer after our night out. I didn't have much time to think about James, but when he briefly entered my thoughts, I imagined him having caught up for lunch with Miles, maybe going for a run, and indulging in a little nap. Meanwhile, I was answering the incessant buzzing of Mrs Appleby in room 19, who insisted on my attention every ten minutes or so. I offered her sleeping tablets early, in the hope of a reprieve from her demands. No sooner had she settled than Mrs Fredericks in room 20 buzzed, and so it went on. A medical emergency topped off my shift before I left, totally exhausted and ready for bed. I messaged James to let him know I was on my way home. He didn't reply. I sighed at the thought of him wrapped up in his duvet, sleeping soundly, where I so wanted to be.

I met Eva as planned so we could tube home together. Eva now lived just a few streets away from my grandfather's terrace. Tonight, however, tiredness overruled thrift, and we decided to taxi home, a rare extravagance. We leaned against each other on the back seat, enjoying the soft whirring of the taxi's engine, eyelids sinking, surrendering to an overwhelming weariness.

Once home, I clambered up the steps to the pillar-box red front door. Inside, the house was silent. Jesse was on night shift, and as I glanced into our bedroom, James was huddled tightly within the bedding and duvet. I quickly showered and collapsed into bed. As I kissed James lightly, he responded with a mumbled something before we both fell asleep.

I was on a morning shift the next day. James left earlier than me to go for a run. He placed a brief kiss on my partially exposed cheek. "See you," he murmured. My eyes flickered. I had no idea what time it was. I closed my eyes, ever hopeful of a few more moments of sleep.

My alarm sounded, and in what seemed to be a few short minutes later, I hauled myself to the bathroom, regretting swapping my afternoon shift for the morning shift, my late shift for the early shift, so early. I groaned. Charlotte, one of the senior staff nurses, had had a birthday function, not a party, as she was quick to clarify, to attend the previous evening and could not possibly rise for an early shift. Charlotte was a little odd and very wealthy; she mixed in the circles of the rich and famous, her narrative, not mine. On occasion, Charlotte was also happy to join Eva and me, although it always seemed that we were the consolation prize. Eva did not like Charlotte and would grumble when she arrived for drinks unannounced and often uninvited. I tolerated Charlotte; she seemed at times a little lonely. Socialising with the rich and famous seemed incongruent with true friendships, more resembling acquaintances, people that you are friendly with but not quite friends. I voiced my opinion to Eva, who was indifferent to my observation and neither agreed nor disagreed.

The ward was a little quieter that morning. Mrs Appleby bid me farewell, having only buzzed me once before she left at midday, Mr Appleby seemingly not in a rush to welcome her home. The remainder of my allocated patients seemed content not to impose too much on my time, requiring only the simplest of inpatient care on their short journey towards recovery and home.

I remembered that St Barts had recently welcomed an intake of new graduate nurses and that I had been given the task by my charge nurse to orientate them to the ward. I checked once more on my patients and then met two starry-eyed, very anxious young registered nurses at the reception desk. Lauren and Emma, I welcomed them warmly. I gave a brief background of my time at St Barts, now about to enter my third year. I explained that St Barts was renowned primarily for heart and cancer care. Once I provided the reassurance that the ward they were assigned to was a minor surgical ward, and subsequently, the patients were of lower complexity, many staying only two to three nights, I saw them visibly relax. I continued to describe the variances of care that were delivered. Of course, I mentioned the likes of Mrs Appleby and Mrs Fredericks, buzzer-happy but endearing in their own way, and I described the younger clientele, who could also have their challenging moments. I could not underplay my passion for nursing, and both Lauren and Emma absorbed my obvious sentiment; their excitement became palpable.

I went on to explain the staffing component, mainly females of all experiences, from the new and naïve to the older and worldly. There were a few males intertwined within the dominant female team, which I conceded added a bit of variety and spice. Lauren and Emma both grinned at this. Finally, I defined our fearless leader, the charge nurse, Claire Reynolds, Miss Claire Reynolds. I paused. Lauren and Emma waited anxiously for me to continue. I laughed, albeit very quietly. Charge Nurse Reynolds ran a tight ship, as many would comment, but was very fair. I, for one, was in awe of her capability as a ward manager; she not only cared for her patients but also her team, just not in a particularly warm and fuzzy way. Lauren and Emma seemed to grasp my meaning, seemingly comfortable in the knowledge that, despite maybe being a little scary, Claire Reynolds was a respected leader.

Orientation over, Lauren and Emma disappeared to complete some online training modules, and I returned to my patients, who seemed to be quite fine without me.

My early shift drew uneventfully to a close. Although the shift had been free of the dramatics of the medical kind, no medical emergencies had interrupted the day; it had been constant. I realised that I had not messaged James, a rarity; we normally "spoke" at least once during the day. I sneaked a look at my mobile phone, nothing. Strange. Being a man of leisure before commencing with ELT, he was probably out running ridiculous distances, trying to improve his times. James had recently voiced disappointment at his pace, frustration turning to irritability, which was very unlike him. I sent him a text just saying hi, that I would be home soon, and we could catch up then.

No bell as such sounded to signify the end of the early shift, but there was a crescendo of noise as the late shift nurses arrived on the ward. Work-wise, events of the day were discussed; life-wise, social and family occurrences and general chatter consumed the ward reception area. This was only a small window of time before work took over and patient focus resumed.

I noticed Charlotte looking a little less together than her usual polished self. She wandered over and asked if I could meet her after the patient handover in the locker room. I happily agreed, hoping for a titbit of gossip from the party function. Disappointingly, no titbits of gossip were forthcoming; what was forthcoming was a very nice bottle of sauvignon blanc as a thank you for swapping to the morning shift. As I thanked Charlotte, I sensed an unusual unwillingness to chat; she hesitated before returning to commence her shift. I shrugged, too tired to interrogate any meaning in her seeming avoidance.

I met Eva at our usual spot. Eva's early shift was more by poor roster management on her behalf than a shift swap; we were both tired and looked forward to a quiet night with the boys. Dean had finished his night shifts for a while, and James was biding his time awaiting ELT. I said goodbye to Eva as she turned down her street. I continued, very much looking forward to a warm hug from James. After nearly five years, I still yearned for his closeness.

I opened the door to silence. An uneasiness settled around me. I checked my phone, still no message. I tried to call him; it went straight to voicemail. I smiled at the message I had heard so often: "If you need me, you will have to wait." I briefly thought that he had better change that response before he joined ELT on Monday. Then my phone pinged with a message. James. I sighed with relief as his face and name appeared on my screen. Technically, it was not his name but letters: *MOMD*, Man of My Dreams, the consequence of many, many wines a few years ago. The text was brief: drinks with Miles and others, and the possibility of staying over. I had a mixture of feelings, relief that I had heard from him, but disappointment at not being wrapped in his arms. I wouldn't describe myself as being highly sexed, but the night of the farewell had left me craving more. I groaned, resigned to an evening alone with a glass of a very nice sauvignon blanc.

Just one glass; I had yet another early shift the next day, my last shift before a few days off. I was very excited to try and pin James down for some quality time together, or any time together. I became unexplainably sad, missing James so much for one night seemed a little extreme, but I could not escape the feeling of need. I showered, flicked on *Pretty Woman* and woke up sometime later to the rolling credits. I checked my phone one more time. Nothing. And so, to bed.

11
The Apology

Kate

I woke up to an inexplicable hollow feeling. I reached over to James's side of the bed and felt a cold void. Something was wrong. I had no idea how to articulate the feeling I had, but I knew. God, I felt sick. Once more, I looked at my phone, and once more it was blank. I didn't want to be that needy girlfriend who texted James's friends. I had no specific reason, just a feeling, not a reason, but a feeling strong enough to question, to ask why James had gone silent. I went on autopilot: showered, dressed, and choked down a sip of coffee and a bite of toast. Nausea kept rising; I was praying for a ping, a text, a call, but nothing.

I arrived at work under a haze of gloom, not remembering much about the journey; the only standout was that there were couples everywhere, all absorbed in looks of lust and post-coital glows, or so it would seem. Charge Nurse Reynolds was on a professional development day, and the ward atmosphere immediately took on an air of celebration, but this was soon quashed by the senior staff nurse, who decided it was her time to shine, and not in a sunshiny way. Rebecca Stanton was an unusual being, in her mid-thirties, and rumour had it she had never been kissed by male or female. No one dared to ask. Rebecca was one of those humans who, if she liked you, all was well; if she didn't, then heaven help you. I was lucky she seemed to like me. Actually, I would describe it more accurately as indifference, which today was fortuitous.

Staff Nurse Stanton turned her attention to the two male nurses on shift, Leo and Adam. The rest of us enjoyed escaping her scrutiny. I had the same patient allocation as the previous day, which again was very fortuitous, a light load, as it was deemed, and the "light load" patients were all being discharged. Four lots of discharge papers to organise, medication scripts to be filled, a few dressings to give and a wave goodbye. Then to the next four.

I functioned on memory, my thoughts preoccupied with James. I could not check my phone on the ward, a big no-no, so I had to wait until morning tea. I declined all offers of company and quickly left the building, something I never did. Once outside, I checked my mobile phone only to see the screensaver of James and me uninterrupted, again, no notifications of a text or missed call, nothing. Maybe he had had a big night with the boys and was sleeping, oblivious to the angst he was causing. I was conscious that maybe I was overreacting, dramatising, or overthinking. However, this rationale only lasted momentarily before a feeling of dread returned.

I made a pact with myself: I would not look again until the end of the day, not even at lunch. I needed to focus on work, and even though my four new patients would potentially be of minimal need, they still deserved one hundred per cent of me as their nurse, not someone who was distracted at best and absent at worst.

I decided to skip lunch. When asked, I stated that I had had an extended morning tea. No one challenged my response and were very happy to accept my offers of assistance. I had to keep busy. I loved nursing; the opportunity to do something for someone, no matter how small, was something I craved. To make a difference. And so, I kept on making a difference until the shift came to an uneventful close, and Senior Staff Nurse Stanton gave us a dismissive thanks for the day.

I left for the tube station; only then did I allow myself to look at my phone. A notification obscured James's face on the screensaver; one message received. Instead of a feeling of relief, I felt scared. A sense of foreboding settled over me. As my heart pounded, I put the phone back into my bag. I would soon be home. As I opened my door, I did not call out to James. I knew he would not answer; I knew he would not be there. I sat down on Grandfather Bob's chair and pulled out my phone. I breathed deeply and then opened the message, James's message, "I love you. I am sorry."

Somewhere in the distance, I heard Jesse bound down the stairs, his usual two at a time. He stopped dead as he saw the tears tumble down my cheeks. I was frozen, unable to move or utter a sound. My eyes were fixed, looking into nowhere. He tentatively crept towards me and crouched next to the chair, his arm resting on the warn armrest. "Kate?" I couldn't speak; I had no explanation as to what had happened. I tried to remember the last seventy-two hours, tried to find a reason why James would leave me. Had he not just told me that he loved me? What the fuck was going on? The silent tears turned into inconsolable sobs of confusion, and then the realisation that this was it. This was over.

Jesse took me into his arms, gently rocking me, trying to soothe away my tears. The power of his embrace tried to protect me against all things bad, except it couldn't. I was numb. In that moment, my heart was broken, leaving a hole of emptiness. Jesse broke away for a few seconds, and then he was back, holding me closer, before I realised a second pair of arms was tightening around me, Eva. The threesome back together, joined in my sorrow and bewilderment.

We sat there, the three of us. We had no words; we could find no reasons. We sat there waiting to wake up from this nightmare. But this wasn't a nightmare or a bad dream; this was real; there would be no happy ending. I tried to think of what I had done, what I had said. Had he met someone else? Was that why our lovemaking had been so different, so intense? I questioned over and over again. He told me he loved me, he messaged me that he loved me, but to love me, it seemed, was not enough. Eva and Jesse put me to bed, both sitting on either side, holding me. Exhaustion sent me into a restless sleep. They didn't leave my side, like shielding armour protecting me from hurt and pain. I remembered our pact, so long ago: "to protect and defend, to take care of each other."

I awoke to a different world, a world without James. I felt an overwhelming sense of loss, a gap where there were once such deep feelings. It felt surreal. I slowly got up. Everything looked the same. Looking closer, small amounts of clothing had gone, the odd T-shirt, sweatshirt, jeans. Some toiletries remained, and his chinos hung neatly in the cupboard. Several books had disappeared, but that was it. The sum of our life together packed into one measly holdall. I had so many questions and not one single answer. Where was he? What about his job at ELT? Did Miles feature in this nightmare? And then I came back to why? And the final question, what do I do now?

I wandered downstairs; nothing had changed. The birds still sang, the sun still shone, and the breeze played occasionally with the trees; life went on. My life had stopped, stunned into a stutter of unbearable sadness. I sat once again on my grandfather's chair. I wrapped a shawl around my shoulders, drawing my knees up to my chest in a cocoon of misery. I closed my eyes and entered a dark unknown.

Jesse slowly came down the stairs, one step at a time. He kissed the top of my head, wandered into the kitchen and made coffee. Silent, leaving me alone in my thoughts. Then Eva followed, another kiss. God, I loved these two people so much, my rocks. I uncurled myself and joined them in the kitchen. I suddenly needed to go out, to join some kind of normality. I needed not to think. I needed to escape torturing myself with the whys, with the questions that I could not answer. Jesse and Eva guided me upstairs; Eva forced me into the bathroom, turned on the shower and left me with strict instructions that we were leaving in ten minutes, giving me no time to reconsider.

We travelled into the centre of London, searching for a café with a very different vibe from our usual cosy couple setting. Café Anew was situated in Trafalgar Square, in the heart of the London tourist trap, very appropriately named and surrounded by more pigeons than people. We ordered coffees; Eva and Jesse entertained me with tales about their wards, patients and general events of their nursing worlds. Jesse was very excited to be a senior staff nurse and let slip that a fellow Australian registered nurse had caught his eye. He was very cagey, not wanting to flaunt his obvious feelings at this time. Eva squeezed my hand under the table and gave me a little wink.

Eva left our table to take a call from Dean. She had messaged him last night, had briefly explained, well, actually, Eva didn't know what she was explaining, and Dean was confused as to what had occurred, but he had accepted that Eva needed to be with her best friend. Finishing night shift yet again, he checked in before sleep. Eva and Dean's relationship had matured over the nearly five years since they met; they fitted like two halves of a whole. I had always admired their ability to be together but also to be happy apart. James and I resembled three-quarters of a whole, more together than apart, joined very tightly. Or at least we were.

Jesse and I reminisced back to the party days and pre-party days, how our friendship had evolved, the study nights, party nights and quiet nights, the nights of two, three and more. The squabbles over movies, board games and takeaways: *Pretty Woman* for Eva and me, *The Terminator* for the boys; Monopoly and Indian. Whose turn to cook, wash up, and put the bins out. Our graduation celebrations, yet more parties, our farewell party when Eva moved out and the welcome party when James moved in, and so it went on. Never a cross word, always the unspoken pact, always friends, good friends, never crossing the line to something more.

Eva returned to what was our second round of coffees. Dean would have a sleep, then meet us back at the house later, if that was OK. Off shift then for a couple of days. Of course, that was OK. Eva and Jesse continued with the chit-chat as we sat among a mixture of tourists and city workers. I kept floating in and out of the reality of my life.

How do I tell my family and friends? The narrative around relationship endings was always tricky, and the three of us were quite inexperienced as to what to say. Eva, Jesse and I agreed that less is sufficient, so the script was: "They/we are no longer together." Full stop. No more details, explanations, or information would be provided. I realised that I had no information to provide. I sat awash in coffee, eyes brimming with tears. It was time to go home.

Eva decided that she needed a little break from my relationship turmoil and went home for a much-needed hug with sleepy Dean. Jesse could not escape, as we lived together, although he seemed quite content to be my emotional crutch for a little while longer. We arrived home mid-morning. As I wandered from room to room, Jesse became my shadow, following closely, offering food and drink. I realised that I needed to be alone. I was desperate for time to reflect, to indulge in thoughts of James, to revisit our relationship one more time, to laugh and smile at the memories, to look at photos, breathe in shared sweats and tees, and to cry at the overpowering sense of loss. I needed to work out how I move on, and to where. I gently hugged Jesse and gave him a quick kiss on his cheek as I thanked him for being there for me. Then I turned and climbed the stairs to my room. I ran to my bed, buried myself in the sheets and ever so quietly wept.

It was near dark when I awoke sometime later. I heard muffled voices downstairs. I was surrounded by photos, scattered across my bed, among T-shirts and some very worn, misshapen sweatshirts. I held an *Accountants Count* T-shirt next to me and breathed in a lingering scent of Bleu De Chanel, my gift to James on his last birthday. I closed my eyes again; it was like the reels of our life together were passing before me.

12
The Rebound

Kate

I allowed myself to travel back through the passage of time. So many memories. Memories of trips to visit my parents, his parents, his Lancashire friends, my Yorkshire friends. Pictures of our Greek holiday, James, Miles, and I visiting the islands of Mykonos, Ios, Santorini and Halkidiki. Sharing a room with just James and Miles in Mykonos, morphing into sharing a room with twelve partying males in Ios. I remembered our trek each morning up the winding roads, avoiding speeding scooters to get to our oily tomato omelettes, which we shared every morning, recovering from too much Ouzo, and then lying on the white beaches under a clear blue sky until late into the evening. We then again visited bars and street sellers until the early morning hours, Miles being with James and me all the time. He was just there, and that was okay.

I remembered James and my impromptu trip to Amsterdam, this time, no Miles. We soon discovered why this capital of the Netherlands was known as the City of Sin. We spent the whole week trying to avoid the coercion of drugs; coffee shops took on a whole new meaning. We, of course, visited the Red-Light District; I laughed at James's reaction to the Ladies of the Night in windows and doorways. I remembered that James got his wallet stolen from our hotel room, and that during one particular disagreement, I stormed off in the middle of Amsterdam, back to the hotel, in completely the wrong direction. James rolled his eyes in exasperation and then ran after me.

Then there was the rugby league. Eva and I, diehard Leeds Rhino fans; James and Miles, Warrington Wolves. I would often persuade James to go to Headingley to watch Leeds, just me and James and eighteen or so thousand fans. Enduring the snow, wind and rain, no longer concerned about beanie hair. After the game, we would argue along the A660 about the referee, tries, conversions, penalties and the like, eventually agreeing to disagree. Or not, arguing persisted until we arrived home some hours later. We'd fall into bed; frowns would slowly turn into small smiles until our lips touched, our tongues found each other, and our impulses took over. Night attire was discarded, our naked skin touched, our lips left each other's to kiss everywhere, the rugby soon forgotten.

I then remembered one time when Leeds were playing Warrington at Headingley. We had taken the train up to stay with my parents. After the game, the usual discussions arose, but I was aware that it was only a short journey back to my parents' house, not the usual drive back to London, and there would be little time to quell any disagreement. The Rhinos had won, of course, and to say that James was unhappy was an understatement. The disgruntlement continued long after we had left the Headingley bar, and as we arrived back at my parents' house, James's frustration was very apparent. I was a little uncertain if the source of the frustration was due to my arguing or Warrington for losing. Either way, as we opened the front door, my ever-faithful beagle bounded towards us, sensing something was not quite right, another protector, and knocked us both over, landing on top of James, who had landed on top of me. Needless to say, frustration turned into amusement, turned into apologies, James's, not mine, which eventually turned into sex. Very quiet sex.

I lay there just for a few moments, no more reminiscences, no more reflections, no more looking for the why. As I descended the stairs, Jesse, Eva, and Dean turned, anxious to see how I looked. A puffy, blotchy face returned their gaze. Dean stood and wrapped me in a heartfelt hug. I sank into his unexpected embrace, holding tight, absorbing his sweet gesture. Then I saw the table overflowing with Indian takeaway, tequila, and Monopoly. *Pretty Woman* ready and waiting on screen.

Eva and Dean vacated the couch, moving to Dean sitting on my grandfather's chair with Eva on one of the many scatter cushions on the floor, leaning against his legs. Jesse shuffled along, patting the now-empty space next to him. I wearily curled up next to him, my head against his shoulder. I needed just a little contact to quell the feeling of loneliness, the constant circle of comfort now replaced by nothingness. Jesse sensed my need and gently leaned in and rested his head against mine. Eva and Dean, silent, not knowing what to say. *Pretty Woman* played softly in the background to the occasional sound of a poppadom. The Monopoly was left untouched, as was most of the curry. I stared at the tequila; this was not a night to drink, the thought of being an emotional and irrational drunk was not appealing. I just needed to be quiet. So, as Richard Gere and Julia Roberts indulged in flirtatious innuendo, I leaned on Jesse and closed my eyes. Eva and Dean crept away, whispering "I love yous" as they went. Jesse moved closer, looping his arm around me into a guarding hold. I was trapped in a bundle of friendship from which I never wanted to escape. I slowly slipped off to sleep. Jesse scooped me up and took me upstairs.

I woke a little while later in my bed, Jesse next to me. We were both fully dressed, although intertwined. I looked at him, staring at his face. I smiled, my broken heart bursting with love for my special friend. Jesse had always been there for me, for us, Eva and me. Through those study days when assignment deadlines loomed, when exam questions seemed impossible, to our student placements when we dealt with bossiness, bitchiness, and the insecurities of entering the unknown. Jesse listened to our relationship dilemmas, as our innocence and inexperience often caused catastrophes and the occasional meltdown.

I leaned forward and softly kissed him. Jesse stirred and ever so gently kissed me back. We stopped and stared. His hands caressed my face and brought our mouths together, his lips warm and soft, parted slightly to allow my tongue to slip inside. As our eyes held each other's, we slowly undressed, all the time staring, not wanting to lose each other in this moment. Until, naked, we held each other tight. I felt Jesse's arousal against me; we kissed, the urgency of wanting each other driving uncontrollable desires. Jesse paused and held me away from him, looking, my nakedness open and bare. I pulled him back towards me, hands exploring, then lips, as he drew my nipples, one at a time, into his mouth, teasing and tasting. As Jesse lowered his body to cover mine, my legs opened, a dampness inviting him to enter. His erection smoothly driving back and forth, in and out, until we both came to a shuddering climax, collapsing into a confused oblivion. We didn't speak; there were no words.

I woke the next morning wrapped in Jesse's body, his legs over my legs and his arm draped loosely over my breasts. I could feel his breath brushing against the back of my neck. I wriggled and turned to face him; he groaned as he released me from his grasp. He reached out to me; I edged closer to him, yearning for his embrace. He rolled me onto my back, his body hovering above me, fingers stroking my curves, his lips dipping to my nipples, hardening under his touch, and then lower, covering my skin with flirty kisses, still lower until he parted my legs and licked between, deep inside, slowly, gently at first, then harder and harder.

I squirmed in response, trying to ride his tongue, then his fingers, pushing, playing in my wetness. I squealed as Jesse straddled me, manoeuvring so his erection slowly penetrated my opening, back and forth, all the while butterfly kisses fluttered over my neck and breasts. The intensity was unbearable as we exploded together.

We lay there, not wanting to break the fantasy, scared that if we spoke, reality would come rushing back. Jesse squeezed my hand, kissed my forehead, grabbed his clothes and left.

Then the bubble burst. What the fuck had I done? I had only had sex with two men in my whole life, one was my true love, my soulmate, and one, my best friend. I became consumed by a mixture of guilt, regret, and uncertainty.

I could hear Jesse clattering and banging in the kitchen. I clung to the duvet, pulling it up to my neck, suddenly feeling vulnerable and exposed. I tried to process what had happened. Was I just deflecting the pain and hurt to Jesse, or were my feelings for Jesse real?

I decided to go for a run. I needed air, to escape the rollercoaster of emotions swirling around me. I showered quickly and dressed in an assortment of running paraphernalia. I crept out of the house, avoiding Jesse still clanging in the kitchen. I got outside the front door and stopped. I could not leave without talking to Jesse, even if only briefly. I was conscious not to emulate James, not to just go. I went back inside. Jesse was humming, absorbed in some egg concoction he was creating, totally unaware of me standing next to him. I blurted, "I'm going for a run." Jesse jumped, tossed the pan into the air, scrambled eggs flying everywhere, the pan ricocheting off the floor. Momentarily, we stood startled, staring at the eggy mess, and then dissolved into laughter.

"OK." Jesse managed to stifle his laughter, gave me a quick peck on the cheek, and I left.

I wasn't a runner; that was James's domain. I jogged awkwardly, feeling, and presumably looking, ungainly, limbs flailing in all directions. Then I seemed to get into some kind of rhythm. Gosh, it felt good. It was a cool, sunny morning, and a hint of a breeze brushed away any threat of tears. I jogged for a little while, my mind drifting aimlessly, then my thoughts came abruptly back to the here and now, to the chaos of my life. Should I be grieving the loss of James? Fuck James, I didn't know how I was supposed to do this. I didn't know the rules around being left. What was the being-dumped etiquette? And where was James?

I realised that I had not tried to contact him, I had not texted or tried to call. In my disbelief at receiving his text, I had lost all ability to think. Thinking now, as I pummelled the footpaths of my neighbourhood, I questioned if I should. Anger became the reason for my answer, no. How dare James throw away nearly five years of our life together with six words? Tears started to trickle down my face; this time no breeze was able to brush them away.

I kept jogging, no idea how far I had gone or where I was going. The vision of Jesse and me wrapped around each other invaded my thoughts. I had crossed the line with Jesse, and not once, but twice, albeit at the same time, if that made sense. Nothing made sense to me at that moment. What did I do now? Continue to cross the line or stop and try to re-enter the friendship zone? I had no idea. I loved Jesse, but that was a friendship love, not a love-love. Or was it? Comfort sex or not?

I stopped and turned around. I needed to go back home. The original good feelings had dispersed, replaced by first anger and then, once again, confusion. The premise of running to clear my mind had failed to eventuate, and I was as muddled as when I had left. Jogging back, I decided that I had to talk to Jesse. He deserved my honesty, even if my honesty might not be what he wanted to hear. As I turned the corner to my house, I realised I could not commit myself to Jesse when, despite my anger, I loved James.

I got home to be greeted by Jesse, Eva, and Dean, sitting in the kitchen amongst a mass of resurrected eggs and bacon; the smell was amazing. I suddenly realised I was very hungry. I said a very brief hello, avoided penetrating eyes, and headed to the shower, promising to return soon.

The jets of hot water pelted my bare skin; I could not shake the feeling of misery. There were three people downstairs who so obviously loved me, but there was not the one person I actually needed, and I realised in that moment, there never would be. How could James re-enter my life when he had left it so abruptly?

I turned off the water, shivered as I got out of the shower, and dressed unceremoniously in sweatpants and an oversized sweatshirt. In the realisation that it was one of James's, I immediately took it off and flung it across my bedroom. It landed on the floor, then, like a crazed woman, I stomped on it, repeatedly stomping, jumping up and down, until I collapsed on my bed, crying.

Finally, I stopped. I lifted my head and saw Jesse, Eva, and Dean, looking fearful as they stood motionless in the doorway. In that instant, I declared, no more crying, no more tears for James.

13
The Match

James

I sat on my hospital bed; it was discharge day. I still had so many questions; I realised that the words *Bone Marrow Transplant* had been bandied about since my diagnosis, but I did not know what the determining factor was, what the outcome was if I didn't undergo a Bone Marrow Transplant, or what the likelihood of finding a match was. My focus had been, so far, on getting through the induction chemotherapy and now the consolidation phases. I had not thought about my future after that or how precarious that would be. The clever doctors' focus, however, was on a Bone Marrow Transplant.

As I sat waiting for my discharge papers and a thousand pills, a trillion outpatient appointments, dietary booklets, exercise booklets, *staying away from infection* booklets, *what to look for if you got an infection* booklet, and so on, I asked to see one of the clever doctors. Miles arrived, his timing impeccable as always. Dr Wilson, aka my clever doctor, aka my haematologist, entered my room.

I had my questions written down; I had learnt this strategy along my fucked-up leukaemia journey to ensure that if I became a blithering mess, Miles could take over asking the questions for me. I felt quite calm today, dare I say even a little excited to be going home.

My questions were pointed; I took the no-bullshit approach, which Dr Wilson agreed with. "I will cut to the chase" was often how he started his consults with me, good or bad or indifferent, he was a straight talker, and I became a fan of this technique. My first question was: what if I chose not to have a transplant? Dr Wilson said that I might get a couple of good years. I had achieved remission through induction and hopefully would continue through the two consolidation rounds. However, there was a likelihood that the leukaemia would come back and an unlikelihood that he would be able to cure me.

I then flipped the focus. How long would I be off work post-transplant? The reply was very non-committal; it could be six months, a year, or the rest of my life. And the final question, for now: what was the life expectancy post-transplant? Twenty to thirty years was Dr Wilson's response. My decision was unequivocal; the major snag, I needed a donor. The search for a match began.

I had been at the Clatterbridge Cancer Centre for three weeks and four days when I was given the news that my neutrophils had reached the magic 2.0 number, ensuring that the next part of my journey, fucked up or otherwise, could continue, the consolidation phases of chemotherapy as an outpatient. There were countless outpatient appointments, days spent at the cancer day therapy unit for the chemotherapy, blood tests, bone marrow biopsies, and of course thousands of pills. I was advised that gentle exercise and nutrition were major factors for my wellness and well-being.

My parents doted on me, as did Dot in her not-so-obvious way; the words *tough love* sprang to mind. Alex and Beth tried hard to carry on as normal, Beth from her ever-changing European hideaways, but I caught a glimpse of pity every now and again. Miles was Miles, although a certain registered nurse with red curly hair had seemingly captured his heart.

It was three weeks and four days since I sent the text to Kate; since then, I had heard nothing. I was surprised that she had not tried to call me or send me a text, but silence. Kate seemingly had disappeared from my life. Miles reminded me that that's what I had wanted, what I had intended the outcome to be; now I was left alone with the consequences of my actions. I was still in love with Kate, with or without her.

I turned my focus back to myself. The conversation with Dr Wilson on the day of my discharge kept echoing in my brain, a twenty-to-thirty-year lifespan post Bone Marrow Transplant. Obviously, there were numerous caveats around this prediction. The risk of infection was the highest risk, but so too was the "graft versus host" scenario, or, put simply, rejection, with quite possibly dire consequences. Small steps. Predominantly, the priority was to find a donor, starting with family members, siblings first, Alex and Beth, and then my parents. That search was unsuccessful, so the next step was the British Bone Marrow Donor Registry, and that also failed. My last hope was international searches, which were conducted through a global network of registries. I remained positive, I had to.

Meanwhile, I continued my fucked-up journey. My gruelling regime continued, although the side effects, at times, did not seem quite so onerous. Still bald, still stick-like, maybe not quite as many bony prominences on show, shadows around my eyes more grey than black, and the nausea and fatigue not as crippling. The fresh air on my daily ambles felt amazing. I had to hide from the sun, but the warm air was still able to permeate my bones. The appreciation of all things simple was very humbling.

Infection at this point was still enemy number one, and my visitors were contained to parents, Alex, Miles, and Dot, more the latter two. Oh, and occasionally Ellie. Beth remained on her European pilgrimage, as she liked to describe it.

Miles and Ellie, I struggled to define their relationship. Miles's obvious aversion to commitment was evident throughout their very early days. He said very little to me; he assumed that I would not be interested and would not want to hear the specifics of his love escapades, my words, not his. He was wrong. I needed any distraction away from this continuing trial of endurance. Ellie was not so protective of my feelings and, on a rare occasion that we were alone together, would tell me stories of Miles's bungled romantic gestures. Her summation of Miles at the end of such a story would leave me very amused. I appreciated Ellie's candid approach and wished that others would not tiptoe around me, especially Alex.

Alex had just finished his teaching degree at Edge Hill University, following in the parental footsteps, which of course made them delighted, the prodigal son as opposed to the prodigal grandson, the honour bestowed on me by Dot since the day I was born. Family dynamics aside, I was actually very proud of my little brother, and I respected his ability to control thirty or so hormone-enraged teenagers whilst imparting knowledge at the same time. Very commendable. I did not share my thoughts with Alex; our relationship was punctuated by grunts rather than words, which, as a teacher of the English language, I found quite worrisome. Since my leukaemia diagnosis, Alex had become more tactile, with pats on the back rather than sounds. I made no judgement none of this fucked-up journey was easy for anyone.

Beth had decided to take a gap year, travelling around Europe, waitressing in bars and restaurants. Occasional communication assured us of her well-being, and frequent pleas for funds assured us that Beth would return home eventually. Career-wise, Beth had always favoured the arts, floating between graphic or interior design and fashion. Beth's personal style throughout her teenage years had been both interesting and shocking, depending on the impression Beth wanted to create. Beth was petite, blonde and, by most people's definitions, adorable, which softened the shock of the looks that she occasionally portrayed. It seemed that Beth's signature look in her gap year mostly incorporated bikinis and sarongs.

I loved Beth dearly. I admired her free spirit and non-conformist attitude; above all, I admired her freedom and often whimsical ways. Her carefree life was so opposite to my grave circumstances. I was desperate to experience her fantasy, even just for a moment. Beth was sometimes heard to be described as "the non-achiever of the family". I disagreed. As I sat in my often-solitary confinement, Beth was achieving all that I wished I could.

Beth, in her unique way, decided that my cancer thing, as she described it, was too sad; she admitted to an uneasiness in the notion that her eldest brother was very sick. It simply did not fit in with her idealistic perspective of family life. I agreed. We decided on one of our rare FaceTimes shortly after my diagnosis that she would not come home to visit and that she could get updates through Miles. As my sister, I was hellbent on protecting her from my gruesome situation. We ended the conversation when Beth admitted that she had no idea how to talk to someone who was potentially dying. I had no answer to that.

I continued on the wheel of hope, going round and round from one treatment phase to the next; five days of chemotherapy, then a rest for three or so weeks, repeat, ensuring all the cancer cells were eliminated and my body stayed in remission. All the time anxiously waiting for a donor.

The day came when I attended the outpatient department to again get my blood results. I had just completed round two of consolidation. This round felt like weeks in a boxing ring, punctured, bled and knocked around. My main complaint on this day was my headache; the pain was excruciating, the vice-like pressure unrelenting. A crescendo of nausea kept sweeping over me. I clung to Miles, both literally and metaphorically, as we entered the waiting room.

I was called into the consult room and was surprised to see Dr Wilson, my clever haematologist from the Clatterbridge Cancer Centre, looking as serious as ever, his brow knitted together in deep thought. I flopped onto a chair, relieved to sit down and prop my head up with my hands. Dr Wilson noted my distress and buzzed for the nurse to bring me some painkillers, more pills, but I did not recognise these. He nodded reassuringly as I gulped down the pills with a glass of water. He let me sit quietly for a few minutes before he spoke. I sensed a flicker of emotion, maybe even a hint of a smile.

My clever doctor went on to inform me that not only was I still in remission, but that they had found a possible bone marrow donor, a young man from Germany. Miles leapt up and screamed, "Yesss!" Then, remembering my exploding head, quickly sat down next to me. The emotion I felt at that moment was indescribable. Four or so months on from my initial diagnosis, there was a chance that this nightmare would end. Miles hugged me, glancing at Dr Wilson, fearful of a reprimand for touching me; no reprimand was forthcoming, just a smile for two men who now had a chance to continue to be lifelong friends.

And so, to what was next.

Dr Wilson was aware of my pounding headache and asked if I was OK to proceed to the next chapter of this evolving voyage through the turbulent waters of my life, or as Miles and I defined my "how to stay alive plan". Dramatic but accurate descriptions.

The glimmer of hope lifted my headache considerably and again changed my mindset. I had always fought, but I had not envisaged the savageness of the next stage. Dr Wilson explained that the Bone Marrow Transplant needed to follow the consolidation treatment as closely as possible to maximise the effectiveness of the transplant. I was very keen to accept this plan; this required another stay at the Clatterbridge Cancer Centre, Ward 5C, to commence the preparation of my bone marrow for the new cells. Exciting but scary.

Dr Wilson considered my blood results carefully and reflected on my leukaemia pathway so far. He decided that I could have two days of freedom before I had to commence the pre-preparation for my bone marrow transplant. Two whole days to try to feel a little human whilst still pill-popping and resembling an escaped prisoner of war.

First came sharing the exciting news of my Bone Marrow Transplant donor, Mr German man, to whom I was incredibly indebted. Miles proposed that we organise a party, not a party in the true party sense, as I was now even more paranoid about germs and potential infection, so we suggested a park, an open area, and everyone would have to mask up when close to me. We mentioned our idea to Dr Wilson before we left his consultation rooms, and he conceded to give his cautious consent.

The gathering, a more appropriate word, was set for the next day, the obvious choice of the two days that I had in this blip of normality. Miles took over the organisation of food and drink. I was still feeling nauseous, although my headache had improved to a dull thump.

The invitation list comprised a select few: my parents, Dot, Alex, Miles and Ellie. Beth had politely declined, citing the short notice and the fact that she was about to set sail waitressing on a private yacht for a Tuscan winemaker. I did a video call with Beth, and although visibly shocked by my appearance, the news of a donor brought a rush of joyful tears. Between sniffles, we blew each other a hundred kisses and promised to talk soon.

It was unseasonally warm, and so we set up under the shade of an enormous oak tree. Miles and Ellie had decided on a simple fare, respecting my sensitivity to almost every food group that existed, so non-fragrant was the rule: sandwiches, potato crisps and the like. I indulged in what had become my staple diet of yoghurts and smoothies. Food was no longer a priority; survival had taken over. My parents and Alex had joined Miles, Ellie and me. We all turned and were stunned to see Dot crossing the grass, accompanied by a suave-looking gentleman, appearing very much together. Dot smirked at our obvious gawping, enjoying the shock waves that she had created. Grinning, Dot introduced Martin Bell as a dear friend.

Miles approached Martin, Mr Bell, or however we should address him, and warmly shook his hand. Ellie, Alex and my parents followed. I hung back; I sensed Martin understood my hesitancy and gave me a warm smile, which I returned. The arrival of Martin Bell took the attention away from yours truly, for which I was grateful, as Martin, whom he was happy to be called, fielded a bombardment of questions. I looked on, feeling an overwhelming love for these people, my family and friends, who had been my unwavering support.

Miles tapped a stick on the table to gain everyone's attention. Martin was visibly relieved at a reprieve from the spotlight. The reaction to my donor news was a rapturous applause followed by a myriad of questions. Everyone put on their masks and came closer, just needing a little part of me to touch, just quickly, just very gently, just once. Miles stood in position by my side, bodyguard-like, monitoring the moment. We both sighed when, once again, a distance was created between them and me.

The attention quickly turned back to Martin, the new kid on the block in the Davy family clan, happy to divulge a little of his life to his captive audience. Dot wandered over to me, put a mask on for her protection of course, and we sat down on a nearby park bench. I had missed Dot's one-on-ones since I had been at home; I had been preoccupied with a paraphernalia of treatments and follow-up appointments. Our catch-ups had been fleeting, with barely a hello and goodbye. Dot, so it seemed, had been busy with her own life. Dot seemed keen to provide me with her own version of Martin Bell, and I was keen to listen.

Martin had arrived in Lancashire over thirty years ago, landing from Edinburgh. He had previously lived in Scotland, where he was born some 81 years ago. His strong Scottish accent defied the thirty or so years living in England, and even Dot acknowledged that she had difficulty understanding what he was saying and on occasion risked just nodding. Dot had mellowed; Dot never just nodded. They had met in the local library, where Dot was a frequent visitor. Martin was not and had popped in to do some research on something or other. Dot couldn't quite decipher his explanation and didn't feel comfortable asking Martin to repeat what he had said, very unlike Dot.

She went on to explain that Martin had invited her to join him for afternoon tea; she enjoyed his company, and that was that. I sensed there was more to "that was that." Later, Miles filled me in on a little more about Martin Bell: how he was a football supporter, not rugby league, how he now supported Celtic and Liverpool, and how he used to work in finance, the details of which were a little sketchy, but he was financially comfortable. I liked Martin, and more importantly, Dot seemed happy to welcome this companion into her twilight years.

Dot rejoined the others. Martin gave her a peck on her cheek. I sighed. I realised that I had not experienced the female touch in so many months; every now and again, I missed that contact, that affection and tenderness. My thoughts strayed to Kate. The perpetual ache in my heart resurfaced as I stood watching Miles and Ellie, and now Dot and Martin. I suddenly felt the emptiness of where there had been so much. I said aloud to no one, "Kate, I will never not love you."

14
The Frenchman

Kate

After my few minutes of rage, Eva, Jesse and Dean pulled me into a group hug, Dean effortlessly blending in. I sank into the strength of their arms, lost in a moment of friendship. Finally released from their hold, I sent them away. I got dressed in clothes that were definitely mine and hurried downstairs. We sat eating reheated bacon and eggs, which tasted surprisingly good, doused in tomato ketchup. Not much was said; we were lost in our own thoughts, sitting in comfortable silence. Camaraderie was enough to negate the need for conversation. I appreciated the silent space to think whilst in the company of my friends.

Eva and Dean soon left, mumbling something about grocery shopping, housework and some other undefinable chore that needed to be done. We hugged again quickly, as they were obviously eager to escape the moroseness of my grandfather's house, which left Jesse and me enveloped in awkwardness. Jesse inched closer to me and tentatively put his arm around me; I rested my head on his shoulder and groaned. Flashes of last night invaded my thoughts. I was lost in the memory of Jesse's body seamlessly joining mine, the craving of being comforted turning into an insatiable desire.

Jesse kissed the top of my head and began, so quietly, so gently. Jesse was candid as he explained that he did not know how he felt right now, but he loved me as a friend. He admitted he was not totally convinced that that was the only love he felt, the friendship love, but he did not want to promise that it was anything more. He went on to mention the feelings he had developed for Isobel, a fellow cancer care registered nurse, although nothing had eventuated from these feelings so far. Jesse paused and sighed. I lifted my head, gave him a little kiss on his cheek, and I too sighed, but I also smiled as a feeling of relief swept over me.

I loved Jesse, at times over the past five or so years, as a little more than a friend. He was attractive both in looks and personality; he exuded charm. His preference for wearing minimal clothing around the house, regardless of the season, central heating in winter on high to accommodate the "freedom" he needed in his partial nakedness, evoked an occasional spark of longing that I was quick to dispel. But I had had James, and I was happy. Now I did not have James, but I had only just not had James, if that made sense. I reflected on the grief process; I had propelled through shock and denial, but was now entrapped in pain, anger and misery. Rebuilding and hope were not on my horizon; it was far too soon. Jesse and I mutually agreed to be as we were. No more sexual encounters, as tempting as they were. Just friends.

Another elephant in the room reared its head. Work. I was due to return to St Barts on a morning shift the next day. Jesse and I dissected options regarding the best tactic. We opted for a say-nothing approach. Jesse firmly articulated that what happened in my private life was just that, private. I agreed but remained anxious about questions and the inevitable nosiness of my team. Jesse reminded me that less is sufficient and the script "we are no longer together" needed to stand firm.

The rest of the day, Jesse and I spent in our own company. I decided to put James' stuff, clothes, shoes, random toiletries and a few remaining books in a tea chest that I had used in my London move. I labelled it simply *James*. Jesse was happy to store it under one of the eaves in the attic. I cried a few tears. I accepted that the proclamation of no more tears for James was a little premature. It had only been 48 hours since I had received that text, a minuscule time in comparison to the years that we had been together.

Having packed James away, I focused on my return to work. Groceries bought, meal prep completed, as I was working five shifts in a row, uniforms ironed, and an alarm set for tomorrow morning. Finally, I glanced at my phone; I saw several texts from my mum and my brothers, just the usual enquiry as to how I was, what I was up to, and the usual nag from mum, when we were, as in James and me, visiting home. There was even a very short text from Dad saying hi. I suddenly felt homesick. Maybe I should go home on my days off. I planted the idea in the back of my mind as I continued in my pre-work mode.

Talking to Eva that night, I mentioned the idea of going home on my next days off. Eva was keen to join me as Dean had several nights rostered. Jesse welcomed my idea; he also had night shifts, so the plan was set. Home for a couple of nights on the weekend. Eva and I shot off texts to our families. Then, of course, Eva began planning the entertainment schedule, whilst I fretted about how I was going to spill the news of James and me.

The rest of the evening continued to be spent separately; both Jesse and I needed a little alone time. As it neared the time to call it a night, Jesse knocked on my bedroom door. I paused before opening, clad only in very dishevelled night attire, my heart racing. I slowly peered through the slight opening I had carefully created. Jesse stood there grinning. He blew me a kiss and left. I shut the door and slumped down against it, not sure whether I felt disappointment or relief.

I awoke the next morning, and the world remained unchanged. I was still expecting everything to become different, altered now that James had disappeared, but the house did not seem to notice. The gap that James had left in my heart had not been replicated; there were no new spaces, no yawning openness. The void I felt was mine alone.

I quickly showered and dressed, slurped kettle coffee, grabbed my lunch bag and left. I was envious of Jesse, rostered for a late shift, sleeping on.

The tube was the usual busyness with early morning commuters in various stages of awakening. Many held coffees, most seemed to rock to the motion of the carriage, no one spoke; it was too early to form the spoken word and too much effort to engage in superficial conversation. All eyes conveyed the same message, daring others to talk.

The ward was busy; the only person to ask about James was Charlotte, which was strange. Charlotte had only met James on a couple of occasions. James, like Eva, disliked her affiliation with the wealthy and influential, or, as James would describe, the café society. Charlotte appeared shallow to James. He would often say to me that he found he had very little in common with Charlotte's subject matter, making me laugh at his choice of words. Charlotte appeared not to be surprised that James and I were no longer together. I felt an uneasiness at her reaction but quickly pushed it aside. Charlotte, in her inimitable way, quickly changed the topic to the opening of a new club by some celebrity at the weekend, asking if I would like to attend. I smiled at the word *attend* and was thankful to have the excuse of going home to decline. Charlotte shrugged and went off to find my replacement.

Registered nurses Leo and Adam were extremely sweet. Sensing I was a little sad, they kept checking on me throughout the shift, never making a comment or pressing for information. Their day was spent side-stepping Senior Staff Nurse Rebecca Stanton, who seemed intent on providing supervision to my male counterparts, who were clearly competent in providing excellent patient care without the scrutiny of a micromanager, albeit not the manager. I was again thankful for her indifference to me. Lauren and Emma were also on shift, and I was grateful for their demands on my time. They had settled into the ward but still had many questions, and I was happy to provide the answers to such enquiring minds. My patients were less demanding but still required my attention. I was careful not to allow James to invade my thoughts as I kept busy doing what I did best, caring for others.

I arrived home to an empty house; Jesse was on his late shift. I showered and ate a just palatable microwave meal. I was going to watch *Pretty Woman* but then decided that Julia Roberts splayed out on a piano was a little too much to bear. I curled up under one of my many throws, flicked through channels until I fell asleep.

I was awoken by Jesse just after midnight, home from his late shift. There had been a medical emergency on the ward, which had ended badly, so Jesse had stayed behind to lead the hot debrief with his staff. He was visibly shaken. I gradually regained consciousness and began to process the trauma he had observed.

The passing of Jesse's mother, Julia, was never far from his thoughts, as every day he preserved her memory in his cancer care work. Sometimes, as in that moment, it all became too much. I reached out to him and pulled him close, fleetingly aware that I was barely covered by a very flimsy nightdress. Jesse welcomed my embrace, his breathing steadied as he gradually became calm.

Jesse wriggled closer to me. I sensed my nipples hardening under the closeness of his body, and a warm, damp feeling evolving somewhere very low down. Jesse lifted his head and lightly traced the outline of my face with a finger; what little resolve I had disappeared in an instant. I closed my eyes and surrendered to him, his kisses on my lips, his tongue sweeping over my breasts, his hands touching. Clothes lost in the entanglement of us. Jesse and I, again naked, again in need of each other. This time driven by Jesse's emotion, his need. I opened my legs. God, I wanted him. My wetness dripped around his hardening. He let out a groan and thrust deep inside me, with a fierceness that was uncompromising, relentless in his wanting. I responded, riding his erection, the crescendo of feelings driving him deeper and deeper. We came together in a rush of longing, Jesse not wanting to release me, still holding me tight, as I felt a warm tear trickle down his face.

We stayed holding each other until the small hours of the morning. Gradually unfolding myself from his grasp, a muddlement of feelings washed over me. I tried to decipher what I felt, but I could not define my feelings for Jesse when I couldn't define my feelings for James. I was desperate to travel back in time to be wanted, to be needed, to be loved. But I had to stop, to pause. I had to have time to process the abandonment and hurt of James, to allow myself to be angry, to grieve my loss and be miserable, just a little while longer. To not have expectations of others, either in friendship or more, to just be, to just live. I sighed. I looked at Jesse. I did not want to hurt him; I loved him, but was I in love with him? Probably not.

I focused once again on my pre-work routine, showered, dressed, sipped kettle coffee, grabbed my lunch bag and left. I hesitated to look at Jesse sleeping on the couch, to kiss or not to kiss. Not to kiss. I did not want to stir any feelings, or anything else, so I crept to the door.

The tube journey was much the same at this inhumane hour as any other day. Sleepy commuters with a common goal to survive the journey, barely acknowledged the humans surrounding them. I would have succeeded if I had not been sitting next to a strikingly handsome gentleman who smelled of a fragrance that was simple, elegant, and classy. I tried not to breathe aloud, but amongst the mixture of aftershaves, this was an absolute standout. The handsome gentleman grinned at my obvious captivation. He leant over and whispered, "Prada Amber Pour Homme," in a very sexy French accent. "Bon," I replied in my non-existent French. He stood and reached out his hand. "Dion." I took his hand. "Kate," I replied, and watched him disembark as the tube pulled into the next stop, cursing that I was on a late shift the next day. The realisation that I could do that, that flirting was allowed, further confirmed that now I was not half of two, but one of one.

That day was different on the ward. That day, I became restless with the routine of lower care patients. I sat on my own at morning tea; I needed a change, a challenge, a distraction, something to fill the void of James, who was not a male, English, Australian or otherwise. What I needed was a drama that was not mine. I needed the trauma of others that would test my skills and capability as a female and as a nurse. To meet new people, to make new friends, to be a part of a new team. Just thinking of the possibilities and opportunities to make a difference of a different kind stirred an excitement within me. I remained pensive as I walked back from my break.

The shift continued much like any other. Following the afternoon handover, Charge Nurse Reynolds had organised an education session on a new medical emergency procedure, specifically focusing on bleeding in the post-surgery patient. I was surprised that it included a component of trauma response, piquing my interest. The sun and moon seemingly aligning, further creating a catalyst for a change.

The tube journey home was consumed by thoughts of the complexities of trauma patients, the acquisition of specialised skills and the provision of trauma-focused care. The excitement was occasionally overshadowed by the realisation that I would not be able to discuss my ideas with James. I had always welcomed his opinion as someone outside of the health field. I hypothetically questioned what his advice would be, a ridiculous game to play. The James I knew would be encouraging, enthusiastic and supportive, but the James I knew is not the James I thought I knew. Within my jumbled thoughts, I did know that he would be proud of me, taking a leap, trying something new, and strangely, despite the hurt and pain that he had caused me, that mattered.

I had three shifts before Eva and I returned to Leeds for the weekend. A late shift, a short late shift finishing at 9 pm, and an early shift. Eva had the same. Eva was busy trying to organise our social itinerary for our two nights away, whilst I was trying to organise some sort of explanation for the absence of James in my life. I was looking forward to the company of Eva, just Eva.

The next three days were busy at work; I was a little preoccupied with thoughts of The Royal London Hospital, famous for its trauma and emergency care. I was fastidious in my research. I needed to make an informed decision before I leapt into foreign waters. I chatted briefly with Eva, Jesse, and Dean, who gave positive vibes to my choice, although Jesse and Eva would be sad to see me leave St Barts. I decided that I would think some more once home and would decide soon. I had to admit that applying for a new position and attending an interview was very daunting.

I did not see much of Jesse over the next three days. He had days off before his night shifts and had been engrossed in a cancer care workshop that he was coordinating. Our paths seldom passed, each of us preoccupied with our careers. We respected each other's space; any contact that we had was as it had always been. There was no awkwardness, no embarrassment, no regrets, for which I was glad. As Jesse put it, "It was what it was." Very profound, but also true.

15
The Visit Home

Kate

Eva and I caught the train up to Leeds on Friday afternoon after our early shift. We had a selection of cars available for us back home, so we decided to enjoy a couple of hours chilling in economy class on the King's Cross city train to Leeds, with hundreds of like-minded individuals. The carriage was full of various types of travellers: tired end-of-the-week corporate beings, elderly couples visiting families, young mothers with husbands trying to ignore their fussing babies with squabbling siblings, and the likes of Eva and me looking to escape the bright lights of London for a little more subdued Yorkshire. Although Eva was evidently keen to hit party mode, subdued was not often a word in her vocabulary.

Eva and I were a little quiet at first. The past week had been hectic. Eva had been a little more dramatic in her description; tumultuous was the word she used. I tended to agree. It was a week when friends and relationships had changed in a blink, when six became four, not even five, as James and Miles vanished. Silence where there was conversation, joviality, and opinion. Two friends who had decided, for whatever reason, to be our friends no more.

We stared out of the windows, watching the passing blur of suburbia becoming countryside becoming suburbia.

Eva caught my eye. We had been friends for an eternity, and it bothered Eva to see her friend hurt and confused. James had been my true love; neither Eva nor I had lost a love before. Eva reached out and squeezed my hand as the train darkened under a tunnel; the dimness matched my mood. Eva's immediate solution was food. We headed to the buffet car, navigating random legs, feet and abandoned bags as people spilt into the aisle. The Friday rush hour personified.

The buffet car was surprisingly a little quieter. I grabbed a couple of seats whilst Eva raided the hot food cabinet, returning with sausage rolls, meat pies and the compulsory can of Coke. So much food. I jokingly looked around to see who else was joining us. Then, out of the corner of my eye, I saw Mr Frenchman, Dion, the amazing cologne man from the Tube. He glanced my way and gave me a brief wave. I smiled back. Eva noticed the brief interaction and began an inquisition, beginning with her own description of this very handsome male. We were too far away to catch his signature fragrance, but as he steered towards us, narrowly missing two small children who had decided to have a picnic on the floor of the buffet car, the scent of Prada Amber Pour Homme filled the air. Eva visibly swooned as she inhaled the captivating aroma. I laughed; it seemed Mr Frenchman had a secret weapon in relation to women that was not so secret.

Eva was just able to compose herself as Dion outstretched his hand towards her. "Enchanted," he soothed. Eva giggled, "Likewise." We invited Dion to join us, which he readily accepted, and to share our questionable cuisine, which he politely declined.

Dion was a Professor of Language and the Arts back home in France and was based in London for six months, teaching PhD students at the University of the Arts London. Eva and I were very impressed with this suave professor, whose speckled grey hair completed his distinguished look and stylish demeanour. Pushing the sausage rolls, pies and ketchup discreetly aside, we sat mesmerised, listening to little glimpses of his life in France. Dion was only in Yorkshire for the weekend, catching up with his brother Jean, pronounced John, and his English wife Lucy, who lived on a sheep farm situated between Leeds and Harrogate. I occasionally had to nudge Eva so she changed her stare to a more just-interested guise. Although I had to admit his manner was very bewitching. Dion enjoyed imparting some of his personal history to Eva and me, without the need for ours in return. I was happy to skim over the fact that we were nurses and now lived in London.

Our interlude with this stranger, although not such a stranger anymore, occupied the remainder of our journey, and we were soon pulling into Leeds City Station. As we stepped onto the platform, members of the Dixon and Douglas clans surrounded us. Eva and I arranged to catch up later for a quick drink after going to our respective homes to shower, unpack and have dinner. We were aware that the families needed some one-on-one time with their elusive daughters.

The dinner table was laden with my favourite foods: lasagne, garlic potato bake, tossed green salad with a vinaigrette dressing and warm bread rolls. The air was abuzz with family anecdotes, stories and the usual recalling of embarrassing moments, with Kate Rose Dixon as the main focus. The atmosphere was almost festive, the celebration of the youngest child returning fleetingly to the fold. Then one question brought the festive mood to an abrupt stop. Mum innocently asked how James was. The clank as my cutlery dropped on my plate caused all eyes to be on me. I had planned on trialling responses to this question with Eva on the train, but unfortunately, the unexpected encounter with our cultured professor had hindered that plan. I floated off momentarily into a land of hurt and pain, unsure of how to describe the end of something so certain. I sensed a hushed stillness, a waiting, an expectation of something bad. "I don't know," I replied.

Dad stared at me puzzled, waiting for an answer. There was none. I did not know. Mum put her hand gently on mine. Ben and Daniel went into brotherly protective mode, fists clenched, simmering under a cloak of irritation; they deserved something. I attempted to explain the events of the last week or so: the excitement of James gaining a position at ELT Finance and Consulting, the big dinner farewell, James's night out with the boys, the staying over at Miles's and then the text, the six words, then nothing. As I told the story, I remained calm, trying to stay detached from the cruelty of those final words. I held back tears and pretended to be brave; I did not want my family to share my sorrow.

Watching my family's faces, I realised the brutality of what James had done. My anger was soon overshadowed by Dad and my brothers, who articulated revenge in various forms of physical harm. I appreciated the sentiment of retribution on my behalf, but I could not endorse violence, tempting as it had been. I assured all three males that I was OK.

I made it clear that I did not want to discuss James for the remainder of the weekend; that declaration impeded all other conversation, so I excused myself and met Eva for a drink. Daniel kindly offered to drive me. We travelled in silence, and as we saw Eva waiting, Daniel leaned over and whispered, "I'm here for you, sis." Holding back tears, I nodded, "I know."

I felt exhausted as Eva and I sat in a booth away from the gathering crowd. The raw emotion of detailing the finality of James and me, watching the distress and worry on the faces of my family, had broken my heart. Whilst we sat in the Dexter Arms, sauvignon blancs in hand, Eva prattled on about the arrangements for the next night. A sublime feeling of reality swept over me. It was no longer James and me, the boyfriend and girlfriend, the partners, the cohabitors; now it was just me.

I sensed that Eva was getting a little disgruntled by my lack of contribution to the planning of our night out. I took a deep breath and focused on my friend. We decided on a jaunt into the city, a public house in the centre of town, which offered a live band for dancing options should the night progress, which my friend Eva assured me it would. Eva had organised the guest list, at which point I had to clarify that this was just a night out with a few friends. Eva flashed me a cheeky grin. I said no more.

Ben, hero brother number two, messaged me and offered to drop Eva and me home. Cognisant that we had a very big day the next day, we gratefully accepted. I did not ask why Ben was awake at 11 pm and willing to drive around Leeds rather than be in bed with his beautiful, now fiancée, Lisa. I appreciated the gesture and loved him even more.

Eva safely at her parents' house, I arrived home to see Mum in the kitchen nursing a mug of cocoa. She immediately poured me one. I was not sure of the combination of sauvignon blanc and cocoa, but I gracefully accepted and sat down. Mum filled me in on all the family updates: who had got married, who was about to be divorced, who was sleeping with whom. I nearly choked at that little titbit and finally to Dad. Dad had seemed to have mellowed; Mum said that he had had a bit of a health scare. She did not elaborate. He was all good now. And then to me: she pushed my hair behind my ears, as she did when I was five years old, and drew me into a hug.

I woke early the next morning to text messages from Eva confirming the day's plans. We were meeting to go clothes shopping for the big night, Eva's words, not mine. Eva had deemed that I needed a new outfit, something different, whatever that might be, something to signify the entering of a new era, singledom, an era which, truth be known, did not seem wholly inviting to me. At times, it was easier to just go with Eva's ideas, and this was one such time. So, I got dressed, ready for the day.

Several hours later, with a brief pause for lunch, Eva declared the mission a success. Laden with bags, I arrived home exhausted but happy, sort of. Mum insisted on a fashion show of my buys and was impressed with the colours and textures of the two dresses that I had chosen. Dad passed wolf-whistling at one point, which made me smile.

And so, to turning a gloomy girl into Leeds's life of the party. Eva insisted I go for a vibrant, eye-catching look: red or pink. Both had an off-one-shoulder neckline that allowed my long black hair to fall over bare skin and for a little cleavage to be on show. Short but not too short. Tight but not too tight. Figure-hugging was how the sales assistant had eloquently described the dresses, which pleased Eva, who was aiming for sophisticated and chic. I decided on the red, with strappy black heels. Mum had insisted on her friend Fiona doing our makeup, a little over the top, but Eva and I were happy to indulge Mum a little in contributing to the night. Eva looked stunning, her long dark hair complemented an emerald green dress, tight also, highlighting her slender figure. The dress had a halter top neckline, showing off both her shoulders and a tease of skin at the crossover. Eva chose silver-heeled sandals. Perfect.

The boys, Ben and Daniel, were joining the night out. Mum drove us into the city, laughing at Eva and me bickering with the boys. Eva was especially vocal, trying to protect her dress from getting crumpled, sitting between two hulks of men. I rolled my eyes as I sat very comfortably in the front.

The night, I had to admit, was a little fun. It was a "welcome all" get-together: school friends, neighbourhood friends and university nursing friends who were now nursing in Leeds or the surrounding areas. Ben and Daniel had invited some of their friends too, some of whom Eva and I knew, some we didn't. Raucous laughter interrupted boisterous chatter. Conversations were fractured, as occasionally the use of single words had to do; the evening was abuzz with the reunion of old friends and the forming of new.

Eva and I were the recipients of many compliments, which we graciously accepted. Our red and green dresses were stunning; Eva especially strutted a striking pose. Everyone gathered around us, jostling for our attention. I felt like I was swaddled in friendships, shielded from harm. Eva periodically glanced over, checking, watching, daring a wrong word or comment to be voiced. I smiled at her to reassure her that I was OK.

I tried to immerse myself in my new era: the time in my life where I was now single and free, the time to explore relationships, although it soon became clear that that time was not now. I felt detached from the crowd like a voyeur, observing. I smiled a lot, but my smile was a mask of betrayal to my true feelings, hiding a sense of sadness lurking within me.

As I was handed yet another glass of an alcoholic beverage, the name of which I had not heard above the hubbub of music and chatter, I saw that the bearer of the drink was Professor Charming, Dion. Eva had also been captivated by Dion and had extended an invitation to him, Jean, and Lucy, who were excited to have a big night in the city, entrusting the sheep to a neighbourly friend. Dion accepted the seat recently vacated next to me, miming, "May I." I smiled, "Bien sûr," of course. Dion seemed extremely impressed by my French response; I hoped he did not expect more. Dion sensed my hesitancy in my commitment to the party scene before us, accepting my hesitation, not knowing my circumstances and apparently not inquisitive enough to find out. I found his air of not needing to know pleasing.

Dion, occasionally mixed with others, but his focus seemed to come back to me. I was flattered. I liked Dion; I found his obvious charisma intoxicating. I was happy to bask in his attention, finding that my contribution was only a tiny part of our conversation. I liked that I could just listen.

Eva was concerned that Dion had totally hijacked me, and she swooped over to me, insisting that I mingle with others. I assured her that I was quite happy talking, or more accurately, listening to Dion.

I did concede to Eva later that evening that, in time, Dion's dominance in a conversation could prove annoying, as it did seem to be all about him, but in these early days of being acquainted, I was happy for him to dominate our liaison, allowing me to stay in the shade just a little while longer.

As I became absorbed in Dion's vibe, the night drew to a close. I conceded to Eva's wish and extracted myself from Dion's hold. I circled the crowd, thanking them for being there: so many hugs, so many fleeting kisses, so many kind words; people knew, but they also knew not to say. It was humbling to have so many people care. I looked for Eva; she too was bidding farewell to all, flamboyant in wine-soaked goodbyes.

Finally, I said goodbye to Jean and Lucy and then to Dion, who swiftly moved in for an embrace, his mouth nearing mine. I quickly deflected his lips, turning a cheek. Dion seemed annoyed at my avoidance. I mumbled, "Sorry," and ran out. I simply was not ready. Jesse had been Jesse, but Dion and others were simply no. I felt tears welling as I ran out into the cool air, as Lisa arrived, another hero, just finishing her paramedic shift, to take us home. We piled into her car, Eva, Ben, and Daniel in obvious merriment, slurring recaps of the last few hours. I sat quietly, thinking; I was not ready to move on, not yet.

16
The Changes

Kate

The morning after the night out, I awoke to the familiar surroundings of my childhood bedroom: the pink and purple décor, flowers and love hearts swirled around me. Rag dolls and teddy bears sat, still waiting for someone to play with. I looked at my mirror, bordered by lights as if I were about to star on Broadway. I smiled as I thought of those simple days when life was just family, school, and Eva, oh, and the beagles, first Barkley, then Barney. How did life get so complicated?

The simplicity had continued for a while: moving to London, meeting James, completing my nursing degree, commencing the career of my dreams, living with the man of my dreams, MOMD. Not too many dramas. Then everything changed. James disappeared, I had sex with Jesse, more than once, and I met Dion. Dion, whom I had innocently, naively thought of as a new friend, until he assumed more.

I wanted to close my eyes to my new life, to not face the reality of change. As I lay hiding amongst my pillows, I became aware of voices coming from downstairs. I listened carefully: Eva, Ben, and Daniel chatting to Mum, doing a postmortem on the previous evening. The trio a little subdued, I surmised the remnants of too many drinks influencing their hushed voices.

Dressed in a questionable choice of night attire, themed pink and purple, that I had grabbed in the darkness of my bedroom, I added an equally garish purple dressing gown, the questionable fashion choice of my early teenage years. I glanced in my Broadway mirror, I winced at my reflection, shrugged and headed downstairs. I entered the kitchen, all three; Eva, Ben and Daniel groaned and buried their heads in their hands. The kitchen table was littered with water bottles, cups of weak tea, and dry pieces of toast. Mum fussed in the kitchen, trying unsuccessfully to find a remedy for three sorry individuals. I sat down feeling not too shabby. Mum offered me breakfast: bacon and eggs. I replied to further groans. I was joking, of course. Coffee and toast were fine. I insisted that Mum sit down as I reoriented myself in the kitchen.

The reflections of the night continued as I joined the table. Eva focused on the charming professor, Dion. I recapped the final scene of my night, the non-kiss, as I referred to Dion's attempt to plant his mouth on mine. Eva, Mum, and the brothers were aghast at his audacity, Mum's term for his behaviour. I realised that in the many hours since his audacious behaviour, I had become indifferent to the advances of the amorous Frenchman, as he now would be known. After a little more thought, the table of judgment decreed that his behaviour had possibly been driven by alcohol and the party spirit, not by me. I was a little unsure of how to view this sentiment; agreement seemed the easiest option, and the subject was closed.

We chattered a while longer. Dad joined for a few minutes; he was keen to revisit the topic of James, after being shot down by Ben, Daniel, and Eva, which was a mighty effort considering their wilted faces, he conceded defeat. My new, mellowed Dad swept me into a brief hug and left.

The train left Leeds City Station at 2.15 pm. The journey back to London's King's Cross was noticeably quiet, both from a passenger perspective and from Eva and me. We were both tired, and Eva was still a little queasy; the motion of the train caused her to turn many shades of grey, a paper bag close to hand. Eva and I decided that napping was the best way to fight the nausea, so scrunched-up sweatshirts were placed against windows mimicking pillows, and we dozed the trip home.

Dean was at King's Cross to welcome us. "Welcome" was a little understated. Eva flew into his arms, buried her face in his neck, and squeezed him tight. I stood watching, unaware that I too was being watched. As I stood alone, consumed by an emptiness, driven by the sight of pure, undisputed love, I felt a gentle tap on my shoulder, and I turned to see Jesse grinning from ear to ear. The ability of this man, this friend, to be there at just the right time, I could not thank him enough.

The following weeks saw many changes. I left St Barts, having been successful in gaining a registered nurse position at The Royal London Hospital on a general surgical and trauma ward, and I loved it. It was a big learning curve, but I embraced the challenge. Leaving St Barts was bittersweet; I had made many friends in the two years that I had worked there. The farewell drinks, Adam and Leo had insisted, were low-key as per my request. We gathered one Saturday night at the local bar; it was a good turnout. Of course, Eva, Dean, and Jesse were there. Adam, Leo, Charge Nurse Claire Reynolds, Senior Staff Nurse Rebecca Stanton; it was very entertaining watching Adam and Leo skirting around the edges of the group, trying to avoid Rebecca Stanton's glare. Lauren and Emma arrived with a huge hamper full of wines, sauvignon blanc of course, and a tiny bottle of tequila. And then there was Charlotte.

My interactions with Charlotte had continued to be weird over time, since James had disappeared, and any communication had left me feeling unsettled. On the night of my farewell drinks, I decided to confront her. I invited her over to a table in the corner, hidden from prying eyes. I did not want to leave my drinks for too long, but I needed to know the reason for her recent behaviour towards me and her obvious avoidance of any interaction between the two of us.

Charlotte reluctantly sat opposite me, trying unsuccessfully not to meet my eyes. I waited. Charlotte knew why I was waiting; I needed an explanation of the strangeness, the one-word greetings, and the eagerness to leave my presence. I took a deep breath as once again a feeling of foreboding washed over me. Charlotte's explanation featured James, of course. Charlotte went on to tell me that she had seen James many, many weeks ago at the medical centre near the ELT building with a woman who had her arm draped around him, and then she had heard that we were not together. She paused. I breathed. I had nothing to say; I just nodded, got up, and walked away. I felt Charlotte's eyes bore into me as I joined the others. I would process that conversation later, when I was alone. For now, I had the responsibility to be present for the team that had supported me for the past two years; they were my focus for tonight.

It was a lovely night. I successfully pushed the conversation with Charlotte to the back of my mind, something I was getting quite used to doing: shutting out the rawness of James until I had the space to tackle my emotions. I knew that my astute friend Eva sensed an undertone of something, but knew better than to respond to her instincts at that time. Dean and Jesse were very much absorbed with many young female nurses to notice anything, and, of course, Eva was a little preoccupied watching Dean, much to my amusement.

Close to midnight, as I sat on my bed, showered and in pyjamas, a classy white and light grey ensemble, respectable too, no flimsiness tonight. I contemplated the Charlotte conversation. I had so many questions mixed up in my thoughts; why was Charlotte at the medical centre? Why was James back at the medical centre, or was he there on the day of his medical? When exactly had Charlotte seen James? Was it the morning before he sent me the final text? And lastly, who had her arm around James? But then I realised that none of those questions, or the answers, would make a difference to where I was now.

I had moved on, finally. I still missed James. I would always miss James; maybe a part of me would even still love James, but he was gone. I suddenly realised that the reason for leaving me didn't matter anymore; it was of no consequence. He was once a part of my life, and now he was not. I lay back on my pillows and closed my eyes. I did not cry.

17
The Hello and Goodbye

Kate

Some aspects of my life continued as before: Eva was still madly in love with Dean, Jesse and I were still trying to avoid having sex with each other, sometimes successfully, sometimes not, and Dion seemed to have slipped away into oblivion.

I settled into The Royal London Hospital quickly, adapting to a very different pace on a busy surgical and trauma ward. The ward culture was a little different to St Barts: there was less emphasis on hierarchy and more focus on team spirit. There was a definite feeling of interdependence, collegiality, and collaboration. The complexity of the patients drove the need to respect each other's capabilities. There was a lot more socialising away from the ward, modest get-togethers often after the late shift that finished at nine, at the public house across the road, called, aptly, The Florence Nightingale, or The Flo, as it was more commonly known. The Flo became the scene of reputable and occasionally disreputable liaisons. There was another pub around the corner called The Dock, which was for more established relationships.

It was at a Christmas ward party at The Flo that Sarah and I became acquainted. Sarah was a general surgeon at The Royal London; our paths sometimes crossed on ward rounds. We became friends that night after we had escaped the clutches of a couple of junior doctors, running, quite literally, from The Flo to the more respectable surroundings of The Dock. Sarah and I had the commonality of singledom: Sarah being a little jaded from the events of a failed marriage, me still trying to compute my life without James. Sarah looked like she had stepped off the front cover of Vogue; I looked like I had stepped off the cover of a Dolly magazine, sophisticated versus primitive, although that maybe was a little harsh. Sarah wore a classy look and turned heads as she walked into a room. I hoped that they stayed turned as I quickly followed behind her. Eva liked Sarah; she aspired to her elegance and her effortless ability to look "so put together." Eva and I could only occasionally achieve some semblance of togetherness. Sarah's chic persona did not detract from her openness and genuine caring demeanour, which ensured her popularity with both staff and patients. Sarah was lovely.

After that night at The Flo and The Dock, Sarah and I would often meet for drinks. Eva was excited that I had found a single comrade to peruse the eligible bachelor scene. Eva likened Sarah's and my situation to having a box of chocolates, as in available men, at our disposal, and we just had to choose our favourite. Sarah and I referred to Eva's analogy and replied that they all seemed to be coffee creams, and so far, our favourite, chocolate caramels, were nowhere to be found. Maybe we needed a different box of chocolates and to leave The Flo and The Dock behind.

Chocolates aside, I enjoyed Sarah's company, a little older than me and a little more worldly, having experienced marriage and a near-completed divorce, we complemented each other nicely. Professionally, we respected each other's opinions and enjoyed discussions on best care, often finding common ground.

Personally, Sarah did not minimise the effects of my relationship with James; I did not pretend to comprehend the enormity of a marriage ending in divorce. We both accepted that we were now single, for whatever reason, and enjoyed the fallout: the opportunity to pursue personal goals, a period for self-reflection and growth, and maybe the chance to find our chocolate caramel.

It was on one night, I had been out to a fancy London bar with Sarah and Eva, that I found myself lying in Jesse's arms, having once again failed not to have sex. Jesse propped himself up on the pillows and looked very serious. I had been expecting, for a while, the conversation that followed. Jesse had, of late, been restless at work; he had organised the cancer care workshop, for which he had received many accolades, but he appeared to be searching for something more, still in the cancer arena, but more in the research field, perhaps. Jesse recognised that he was lost as to which direction he was headed. His personal life, excluding our occasional rendezvous, was mundane; the relationship with Isobel had fizzled out before it really began. He had a circle of male friends, but they were all coupled up, and Jesse was a little tired of being the third wheel.

And, it was a big and, he missed home. Jesse paused and looked at me. He tightened his arms around me, leaned over, and kissed me softly on the lips. I closed my eyes and took a deep breath. Jesse and I both knew that what we had was a friendship love: a shared emotional understanding and a mutual loyalty, but so many times we had hovered on the very fine line of so much more. Friendship love, according to the expert's definition, does not include sex. Friendship love should not have a desire for intimacy or romance. We therefore agreed that we did not have or need a label per se for what we had; we knew we had each other, and that was what mattered. Now, we didn't.

Melbourne was 10,534 miles away. Across the other side of the world, and no matter how strong whatever friendship or love we had, it would be forever changed. But I knew Jesse had to go home, to be with his dad and brother Luke. To be close to where his mum, Lisa, would have been. I understood. I hugged him so tightly; I did not need to speak. He reached out to me one more time, the last time, and as our bodies became one, as he entered me, desperate for one last touch of all of me, our tears silently fell.

Jesse moved out to home, Melbourne, Australia, a couple of weeks later. There was no planned party, no planned drinks, no fanfare. Jesse wanted to slink away in his own time, in his own way. The night before

Jesse's departure, Eva and Dean arrived, arms laden with Indian takeaway, Monopoly at the ready, and *The Terminator* on standby. After more than five years of friendship that we treasured so much, we knew that our pact would stand firm, albeit across two continents.

We did not promise to keep in touch, but we knew we would. No matter how infrequently, we knew that we would be a part of each other's lives. As we sat reminiscing, there was a knock on my pillar-box red door. I prised myself out of a very comfortable cushion at the feet of Jesse. Opening the door, there stood Sarah, Ben, and Daniel, waving tiny Union Jack flags whilst grappling with a few assorted bottles of alcohol. Sarah had not met my brothers; she had decided to farewell Jesse, whom she had met at various drinking holes that we had visited over the last few weeks. Ben and Daniel, in London on business, had the same idea: to bid Jesse goodbye. They had become quite fond of the Australian, as had I.

Jesse, who did not want a party and definitely didn't want drinks or fanfare, was super excited to see the unexpected guests. Introductions were made, and Sarah very quickly became part of the clan. The Indian was eaten, Monopoly was attempted and abandoned, as the abundance of alcohol made purchasing houses and hotels, and negotiating getting out of jail, a little tricky. We watched *The Terminator* and *Pretty Woman* before we conceded that the night would have to end, and the day of Jesse's departure would inevitably arrive.

And so, to bed, for all seven of us, no one wanted to leave. Alcohol ensured all inhibitions were forgotten, and, together with the need for sleep, the beds and rooms available were quickly allocated. Eva and Dean would share Eva's old room, Daniel and Ben could share my room, and Sarah, as the newbie, was happy to take the couch, which we could all testify was very comfortable, leaving Jesse and me in the attic, together in one bed, which no one questioned.

The melancholy mood hung over Jesse and me as we climbed the stairs to the attic. Our thoughts went back to our party all those years ago. In Jesse's bed, I wore one of his shirts, just covering my important bits; Jesse wore his brief shorts, sleeping. Here we were again, maybe for the last time, me in his T-shirt, Jesse in brief shorts, not sleeping. Jesse lay staring at the ceiling. I shuffled over and crept on top of him, lying there together, joined in sadness, my head on his chest, arms wrapped around each other, hugging tight. I could feel his erection pushing against me, but we did nothing; we said nothing. Finally, I lifted my head and kissed him, so fleetingly, so tenderly. Jesse whispered, "Can we just lie here?" "Of course," I replied.

Jesse left the next morning. He insisted on getting a taxi, no airport scenes. We all stood at that red door, waving. Eva and I wiping tears as they trickled down our faces. I knew he had to go; he needed his family, he needed to find his way, how to continue his mother's legacy. I knew that I loved him, in what way, I had no idea, but I knew more than anything that I was going to miss him.

18
The Stranger

Kate

A few months after meeting Sarah, her divorce from Michael became finalised, their apartment in central London was sold as part of the settlement, and Sarah, after a couple of seconds' deliberation, gratefully accepted my offer and moved in with me. My grandfather's house had been screaming out for the sound of more than one voice; I had been screaming too, rattling around in that terrace, alone and lonely.

Sarah's planned move was without major incident. Removalists were hired, and Eva, Dean, and I were on hand if necessary. Five years of marriage were summed up in half a dozen tea chests, a few plants, and several miscellaneous pieces of furniture. It transpired that most of the furnishing had belonged to Michael, and those that were jointly owned, especially the king-size bed, Sarah was happy to let Michael keep, very happily, which suggested a hint of infidelity, but I said nothing. Sarah was going to move into Jesse's space, the attic, and was to inherit his king-size single bed. I did suggest Eva's old room, but Sarah was content at the top of the house; the ensuite and a smaller room suited her just fine.

Memories of that bed, Jesse and I, triggered thoughts of the times we had spent together. At first, Jesse picked up the pieces of a shattered heart and then became my cornerstone, where once James had been, giving me back my self-worth, believing in me, being there for me. I missed Jesse, I missed that hunk of an Aussie swanning around the terrace, sometimes barely clothed; I missed our chats, our camaraderie, and yes, I missed the sex. Most of all, I missed his manliness, the male opinion, his understanding. He got me, and I missed that.

Sarah and I were content to enjoy each other's company, being mindful that we both needed space to rediscover the next chapter of our lives. My shift work and Sarah's unpredictability of her on-call ensured that we had time to be together and to be alone.

On the male front, to be honest, neither of us was keen to jump out of the frying pan into the fire, so to speak. My brief liaison with Dion, if you could even call it that, a chat might be more accurate, but that does sound a bit flippant, affirmed that I was not ready to dive straight into another relationship, and Sarah agreed. Michael had been her second love, Steven being her first. Sarah did not provide me with details surrounding the Steven relationship. Suffice to say, they were both young and naïve, and what they thought was going to be forever was not.

Michael was a little different; he was older by five years, mature in Sarah's eyes, experienced in many ways, details of which would only emerge after a few sauvignon blancs had transitioned into tequilas. Michael was also a surgeon, which is how they met, whilst Sarah was at medical school. Michael was everything that Sarah wanted to be: smart, accomplished, and recognised for his skill and precision with a blade. Sarah loved performing surgery, loved helping her patients, and loved Michael. Michael loved Sarah, just not enough.

Sarah and I were content in each other's company; occasionally, we would join Eva and Dean, frequenting bars that welcomed the single population as well as loved-up couples, which suited both Sarah and me, and Eva and Dean. We missed Jesse; our communication was minimal, shift work and the time difference was a nightmare to navigate. We believed he was looking for a nursing position at Melbourne's The Alfred, but were unsure of the outcome of his quest. Sarah and I also socialised with work colleagues from The Royal London. These evenings usually meant the sampling of many beverages in numerous bars and inevitably finished with two miserable friends, Sarah and me, reflecting on our failed relationships. We thought very carefully before embarking on those nights out.

On a night out, just the two of us, we enjoyed male company and even practised a little flirting; it was flattering to be wooed. Sarah's effortless ability to be noticed ensured that we were very often pursued by a 'brotherhood' of men. We indulged in their company but always observed boundaries of our fraternisation; we were careful not to tease, to mislead, or to give the impression of something that was not. On occasions when we felt a little sad, we both enjoyed the escapism of menfolk vying for our attention, all in good fun, of course.

Sarah and I acknowledged that men were always going to feature in our lives, either as acquaintances, colleagues, or a little more. We both knew that at some point we would be ready to take a step a little further than friendship; the timing, however, was unknown.

A nudge in that direction occurred sooner than I thought. I had returned home after an overtime shift to the sound of a voice I did not recognise, coming from the living room. I paused to hear male Scottish tones talking to Eva and Dean; Sarah was nowhere to be seen. I went in search, and I found Sarah crouched down behind the kitchen table; she whispered for me not to say a word. We both sat there listening to what seemed to be a superficial meet-and-greet conversation. I quickly realised that the visitor was not going to leave anytime soon, so I left Sarah hunched in her temporary hideout and ventured into the living room.

The male stood up as I entered and walked over to me. "Neil Doyle, remember me?" I didn't.

It turned out that Dr Neil Doyle was a baby doctor at St Barts when I was a student nurse. We had met very briefly, apparently, when I had attended a professional development day in the operating theatres. Neil was camouflaged in scrubs, a hair net, eye goggles, and a face mask. There had been no face, as such, to remember, although the Scottish twang was a little familiar. I queried why Dr Neil Doyle was sitting in my living room in my grandfather's chair and why Sarah was hiding in the kitchen.

Eva stepped in to answer my questions whilst Neil sat there listening intently, ready to pounce on any deviation from the truth. It transpired that Neil had just arrived home from the golden land of Oz. I sensed that Eva was going to enjoy telling this tale, and I also sensed that Neil was a little apprehensive about the storyline. Eva continued: whilst in Australia, Neil had worked at Melbourne's The Alfred, and had met none other than Jesse, who was working in the emergency department, having decided to take a break from the trials of cancer care. So, the Scotsman had met the Australian.

Neil had planned to return to London, having finished his fellowship year, specialising in general surgery, as a consultant surgeon back at St Barts. Jesse, being Jesse, put on his matchmaker hat and suggested that Neil should seek out yours truly, brazen, even for Jesse. As Eva paused, Sarah appeared from her hiding spot; Neil visibly paled as their eyes met. Eva, Dean, and I waited, looking from Sarah to Neil and back again as if watching a tennis match that was stuck in a tie break. Finally, Neil broke the silence and muttered an awkward "Hi". Nothing followed Neil's awkward hi. Sarah's response was a silent stare. Neil, who was starting back at St Barts the following week, quickly bid farewell, mumbled that he hoped he would see me again, and stumbled out of the house, bumping into a picture that now hung very precariously on the wall. All eyes turned to Sarah.

Sarah sat in my now-vacated grandfather's chair, composed herself, and explained. Neil had been a groomsman at Michael's and her wedding. Sarah did not want Michael to know of her whereabouts and so was not happy to find her ex-husband's groomsman, aka his best friend, sitting in my grandfather's chair in our living room. To be fair, neither Neil nor Jesse knew that Sarah had moved in, and Jesse was absolutely not aware of the specifics of her wedding or wedding party.

It was decided that I would contact Jesse so that I could then contact Neil, to ensure that Sarah's whereabouts did not filter through to Michael. Convoluted, maybe, but a plan that would reassure Sarah that she would remain hidden from her ex-husband. Sarah did not allude to why this was so important. I did understand that Sarah needed to move on from Michael and did not need any reminders of him, virtual or otherwise. Sarah successfully avoided Michael at work. Michael was now focused on his private practice patients and only operated at The Royal London once or twice a month.

Sarah's mood became a little pensive; she sat quietly. Eva, Dean, and I discussed Jesse's career detour. All agreed that he would be well-suited to the drama of The Alfred emergency department. We then verified the plan: I would contact Jesse to get Neil's contacts, then I would contact Neil, meet, potentially, to ensure that the secrecy of Sarah's whereabouts remained intact. Sarah was very appreciative of my help. I was very appreciative of the opportunity to see Neil again. I was quite drawn to the tall Scotsman, but that declaration could wait for another day.

We had planned a home-made pizza night; Dean was a self-proclaimed pizza dough expert. The inevitable squabbles occurred over the choice of toppings, and Sarah soon became relaxed as all four of us were covered in flour and dough in the spirit of the culinary arts. Tomato sauce dripping from our chins, Eva was a little overzealous with the margherita topping, we mopped up pizzas with a light red wine, Dean's suggestion. He not only described himself as a pizza dough specialist, but also a wine connoisseur; we were impressed with both qualities. The pizza was delicious, and the wine a perfect choice.

With the mood considerably lighter and our uninvited visitor momentarily forgotten, the evening inevitably flowed into Monopoly. We had swapped Richard Gere for Hugh Grant as *Notting Hill* took to the screen, before pizza-laden, we called it a night.

Propped up by multiple pillows, waiting for the pizza to dissipate before I could lie down, it was the perfect opportunity to call Jesse, hoping that he was not at work or sleeping after a night shift. Jesse answered on the second ring; it was so good to hear his voice. We chattered about his new role in The Alfred's emergency department and a new lady friend, Bree. It was very early days, but Jesse seemed smitten by this young veterinary nurse. Jesse was living with his brother Luke. Bear, the golden retriever, was the other inhabitant, and Jesse had been tasked with the yearly vet visit for Bear.

Bear was not a fan of a vet visit, and a simple check-up with a vet usually resulted in a vet and at least one veterinary nurse, as occurred on this occasion. Bree came in to assist with this very non-compliant hound; a combination of multiple dog treats and Bree's soothing voice achieved success. As the vet went to the next patient, a more compliant feline, Jesse and Bree struck up a conversation over the now-settled Bear, a coffee date followed, and then drinks. I was very happy for my friend.

I then gave Jesse a quick synopsis of what had occurred that evening. Jesse became quite amused, but amusement soon turned to horror as I further described the tangled web of Sarah's previous life and the role of Dr Doyle. Jesse stayed quiet whilst I told him of our proposed plan to ensure Sarah's ex would stay in the dark regarding her living arrangements. Jesse agreed to give me Neil's contact details, for which I was very thankful. I paused; Jesse jumped in to enquire, potential disaster aside, what did I think of Neil? Despite 10,054 miles between us, Jesse had sensed that I might have some feelings for Dr Doyle. I had to admit I felt a little attracted to the Scottish doctor, with a beard that was little more than a 5 o'clock shadow; he was not openly handsome, but had a certain je ne sais quoi, I think it was his eyes. Jesse laughed. "Careful," he said. I rolled my eyes, which was pointless as Jesse and I had decided against a video call, a tad inappropriate as I was in bed. We chatted some more.

Jesse was happy to be back home; his dad and brother welcomed him warmly, and he had found solace in visiting his mum's grave. Jesse was unsure about his ongoing cancer care nursing; he and I both agreed that all aspects of nursing travelled down the same path of caring for others. The constant demands and ever-changing environment of a major emergency and trauma hospital, The Alfred, unquestionably gave Jesse every opportunity to care. It was getting late; Jesse was on a late shift, and I had an early shift in the morning, so we reluctantly said goodnights and I love yous, promising to be in touch very soon.

It was a full moon. My room became bathed in moonlight as I switched off my light; a soft shine settled over my bed. I lay there thinking. James, Jesse, Dion, Neil, ugh, thoughts of all these men, all these conflicting emotions, it was exhausting trying to understand my feelings. Did I have the space to welcome someone else into my life, into the gap left by James? I missed that specialness of being in a relationship, but I knew it had to be the right person at the right time. Was that time now? I wasn't sure. Muddlement remained as I gave in to sleep.

19
The Meeting

Kate

I messaged Neil during my morning break. I kept my message brief, asking if we could catch up quickly to chat about yesterday evening. Neil messaged me back straight away, asking if I would like to meet for a drink after my shift. I suggested The Dock at 7 pm, if that suited. Thinking I would have time to go home, shower, and prettify just a little before we met, Neil agreed. Sarah was on call that night, which meant she would stay at the hospital, grab any sleep she could in a recliner chair with a lumpy pillow and a minimalist blanket. Often, she would not sleep and, fortified by questionable coffee, would spend the night operating.

My shift was busy, and it seemed that every foreseeable barrier popped up to delay my ability to leave: a medical emergency, a visit from the hospital hierarchy, and last but not least, a missing scheduled eight-drug, one of those special lock-away medications, which caused everyone to remain on shift until it could be found. It wasn't found, because it wasn't lost; someone had miscounted. Finally, I was able to escape. Once home, I showered, and then came the tricky bit: what was I going to wear? The weather was surprisingly warm; I needed to go for the effortless look which Sarah always achieved; my effortless look seemed to take a lot of effort. As I decided on a simple pale blue dress, complemented by tan sandals, a shoulder bag and plain gold necklace, bracelet and small gold hooped earrings, understated but classy was the aim. The dress was one of my favourites; it had a fitted, ruched bodice that ended just under my breasts, with a long, flowing skirt that skimmed my body as it fell. Sarah and Eva likened me to a character in *Jane Eyre*, the lighter colour, as Eva informed Sarah, signifying the upper class or the privileged. I gently reminded Eva that the novel was set in the 1830s, I was not sure of the relevance of that snippet of information now, interesting as it was. Eva sighed at her attempt to bring some culture into my life.

I took a second look in the mirror and decided that jeans and a floaty white peasant top would be more suitable; the accessories could remain, the tan sandals and shoulder bag complemented outfit number two beautifully. So, I discarded my dress and several other try-ons on my bed, settling on cute and casual rather than classy and chic. I quickly applied a subtle touch of makeup, including my signature pink lipstick, and left to meet Neil.

The Dock was its usual busyness. I spotted Neil dressed in jeans and a white linen shirt, also conducive to the casual theme, sitting, beer in hand, at a table half hidden, half not, private-ish. I grabbed a wine from the bar before wandering over. Neil stood up as I approached and pecked my cheek. I hid my surprise at the unexpected show of affection and the stirring of butterflies that had ensued. A little flustered, I took a sip of sauvignon blanc to buy a couple of seconds and resume the persona of calm.

I sat opposite Neil and explained that Sarah was concerned about Michael knowing of her whereabouts. Neil listened. He told me that he was not as close to Michael as he used to be and hadn't seen or spoken to him for a little while, even before he did his year of doctoring in Australia. He went on to say that they had drifted apart as friends. He reassured me that Sarah's personal circumstances would not be disclosed to anyone by him. Relieved, I thanked him.

We sat for a little while longer, engaged in general chit chat, mostly about our careers, occasionally dipping into likes and dislikes. Small awkward pauses occurred when the conversation seemed to drift towards a more personal level. Neil offered to buy me another drink. I was enjoying his company, so I happily accepted. The replenishment of drinks saw the awkward pauses disappear, although we both tiptoed around our relationship status. Neil was being deliberately vague; I guessed that he did not have a girlfriend, but I wasn't entirely sure.

Newly single, I also did not elaborate; suffice to say, I was not looking for a relationship and did not give any more details. Someone that I had known for only a few hours, in my opinion, should not be privy to my personal story, not yet, anyway. Neil seemed content with my minimal information, accepting that what he saw on the surface would have to be enough for now.

I did like Neil; he had a wicked sense of humour, and I found myself smiling and even laughing as he told anecdotes of his life. Tales of Australia were particularly amusing, especially when Jesse entered his story. He had only known Jesse a little while, but as he told of a couple of their adventures, it became clear that Neil had been drawn to Jesse's endearing traits. We both agreed that Jesse was affable and easy-going. I was careful not to be exuberant in my agreement with Neil; I did not want to cause him to question the extent of Jesse's and my acquaintance. Neil was especially appreciative of Jesse's friendly, outgoing personality; even though he had been nearing the end of his year in Australia, he welcomed new friendships to maximise his Australian experience.

It was getting late, and I was struggling to stifle a yawn. Neil dropped me home, refusing to let me tube at such a late hour. The shift from The Dock to Neil's car broke the momentum; we mostly travelled in silence, with just the odd comment regarding London's nightlife. His car pulled up outside my terrace. I thanked Neil for meeting me and for a lovely evening. Neil was about to get out, and I presume walk me to my door, but I did not want the awkwardness of the doorstep farewell, so I insisted that I was fine to see myself inside. Neil wound down his window and asked if he could call me. I closed my front door without answering.

It was so quiet; Sarah was in the throes of being on call, so it was just me alone with my thoughts. Even though it was late, I showered quickly before bed. The hot water hit my skin as I tried to decipher the evening: the peck, the conversation, the laughter and, finally, my avoidance to commit to anything further.

Sex had not really been a big deal with James, but now that it wasn't on tap, so to speak, I found I missed it, even craved it on occasion. Jesse had fulfilled that need for a while. I thought of Neil; I would like to see him again, but I had no idea what I wanted from him: a relationship, I doubted; friendship, possibly; sex, maybe. With all these differentials playing in my mind, I turned off the shower, put on some very sensible non-sexy pyjamas, and crawled into bed, being careful to move my night try-ons to the side. I resolved not to have any more thoughts of Neil, and as sleep took over, I tried to convince myself that he probably wouldn't call.

I awoke at 9 am to a missed call from Dr Doyle. I wasn't sure whether I was flattered or annoyed at the pure arrogance of calling so early. I was on a late shift, so I tried to grab a little more sleep. I would listen to the voicemail later, but curiosity took over and, sighing, I listened: "Thank you for a lovely night, I would love to see you again." That was it. No "call me" or "text me," or "I will be in touch." Vagueness again from Dr Doyle. I sighed and tossed my phone across my bed to join the jumble of clothes and rolled over to sleep.

Sarah was pottering in the kitchen when I finally emerged from my bedroom a little while later. She'd had a little sleep after her on-call and was scrambling eggs, looking very dopey. I sat down at the kitchen table and filled her in on my evening with Neil. She was very happy to hear that Michael, Mr Ex, would not learn of her whereabouts. I gave her a little insight into my evening, but sensing her need to eat and sleep, I gave her a very short version. Sarah listened, plonked some scrambled eggs on a small plate for me, kissed the top of my head, and went back to bed. I sat pondering. I decided that I would park Neil to one side and resume my day.

Neil was all but forgotten amidst work and catching up with Sarah, having some much-needed ladies' time. Sarah had been a little rattled since finding Neil in the living room, even though her marriage was over and the divorce was settled; something was bothering her. Sarah and I had become close friends, but we did not share the life experiences that Eva and I had. I was wary of intruding on her previous life, but I did make it clear that I was here to listen if she wanted to talk and left it at that. On that phase of her life, Sarah remained mostly silent.

20
The Electrician and The Builders

Kate

Sarah and I were excited to enjoy some female bonding, to get back to the London nightlife. On occasion, Eva and Dean joined us. It was nice to see a couple so obviously in love, if not a little infatuated. Sarah and I were certainly not in a position to judge, although we did enjoy teasing their obvious compatibility. Sarah and I described Eva and Dean as two peas in a pod. I reflected that their compatibility was not dissimilar to James and me, James and me, past tense. Sarah did comment that she and Michael were never truly compatible. Sarah was gorgeous, the type of female that, when she entered the room, people, men and women, would stop and stare. Sarah confided, in a rare moment of sharing, that Michael, although esteemed amongst his profession and quite handsome, did not have that wow factor, and that it seemed that that was hard for Michael to live with. Michael liked to be the centre of attention, and when Sarah was around, he was not.

The sad thing was that Sarah was unassuming and unaffected by her looks. She knew the effect that she sometimes caused, but it was not orchestrated; it just was. On those rare occasions when Sarah opened up a little, I listened, I would squeeze her hand or give her a tiny hug. I sensed that even with the little disclosures, there was still something more.

Very occasionally, only Eva would join Sarah and me. These would turn into super fun nights, full of giggles and laughter. Eva would be intent on finding Sarah and me "hook-ups" and often referred to the chocolate box analogy. Sarah and I insisted that our "favourites" were nowhere to be found. Eva would huff in total disagreement and scan whichever drinking venue we found ourselves in, which often resulted in hilarious male potentials. On the odd occasion our interest was piqued, the gentleman in question was soon swathed by a female, who would often shoot us a deadly glare. The three of us replied with big cheesy smiles and moved on to the next unsuspecting victim. To be fair, we innocently picked men who appeared to be alone before it became obvious that they were not.

Nothing ever eventuated, except on one occasion Eva did spot this gentleman who seemed to be alone. We smiled over to him, and he smiled back. We were a few drinks into the night; consequently, our inhibitions had long since gone. We enthusiastically waved him over. His smile grew wider as he moseyed over to our table. He was actually very nice; his name was Jack, and he was totally absorbed by Sarah, of course. He was soon joined by three friends, male friends, who were equally as charming. Jack was an electrician by trade; his friends were builders; they worked for a London construction company. Scott, one of the builders, seemed to have taken a shine to me. I did not have the headspace or heart space to welcome another male into my conundrum of men, but I was very happy to enjoy his company.

Later that night, I glanced over to Sarah; she was quite animated in her chat with Jack. I smiled as I saw a blush creeping over Sarah's cheeks, as they gradually turned a soft shade of pink. It was lovely to see her relaxed and flirtatious, her face lit up as they chattered. Eva and I seemed to have become a little separated, as we enjoyed the company of Scott, Rhys and Chris.

It was such a good night. The men were very entertaining. It was refreshing to get away from healthcare workers and to realise there was another world out there. The friends worked for a construction company specialising in high-end residential projects, linking strongly into design-led work. Eva and I were fascinated as they described their work as part of a company within a company. They had worked together for several years, and it was obvious they had an unspoken bond. They bounced off each other as they spoke; it was amusing to listen to their witty repartee. The conversation was mainly about life as a builder and interests outside of the company. All three were active sportsmen in the amateur arena, being members of local football teams. Scott described himself as a keen runner as he went into the hilarious details of his recent adventure, where he got lost and ended up running around in a very large circle. Eva put her hand on mine, just for a second. I gave a tiny sigh, took a sip of wine, and refocused on the here and now.

All too soon, it was time to bid farewell to our newfound companions. Scott, Rhys and Chris all had to work the next day. We agreed to keep in touch and to meet again for drinks. Scott was content to say goodnight. He gave me a little wink as he left. I smiled warmly. I appreciated him not venturing for anything more. Eva and I finished our drinks. It was late, and we were tired, so we splashed out on a taxi. Eva and I never got used to the feel of London at night; home in Yorkshire had a very different vibe, and we often felt a London cab was a safer travel option. Sarah remained being charmed by Jack and insisted on meeting me at home later.

Jack slowly became a feature in Sarah's life. Sarah would occasionally slip out and meet him for a drink or a bite to eat, happy to keep it casual. Now and then, we would all catch up, and on a couple of occasions, Dean would join us. Eva and I laughed at Dean's facial expressions as he listened to building site escapades. We all agreed that Jesse would appreciate the humour and would gel with our new friends. It wasn't all building site work. Very often, they would be asked to give their opinions more in the design realm; they were recognised for their experience on site, but also for their knowledge of the logistics of design being transferable to projects and business plans. Dean was a little less impressed than Eva, Sarah and I, but then Dean was more focused on the content of the conversation, not on who was doing the conversing.

21
The Scottish Doctor

Kate

Neil re-entered my life one afternoon when I was sitting on the tube, homeward bound after a ridiculously busy shift at The Royal London. It was several weeks after we had met for drinks, the phone call and voice mail message had been left hanging, but that was ok.

I had enjoyed reconnecting with Sarah and Eva and spending time with our new construction buddies. Scott and I had continued down a purely platonic path; there was a mutual attraction, but neither of us had felt the need to explore a romance. We both engaged in the occasional innuendo; little sparks would fly, and we would grin slyly, enjoying a small moment of temptation. I enjoyed the feeling of being wanted, but enjoyed even more that I did not have to give.

Neil's text was a little less vague. He apologised for not being in touch; he had started back at St Barts and was being kept busy. Neil would like to meet for a drink tomorrow night. He suggested a bar in the city, but wanted to avoid The Dock or The Flo. Wow, from not contacting me for weeks to wanting to meet tomorrow night. It seemed that Neil did not understand dating etiquette, and although I did not want to feign disinterest, I was not going to meet him as requested. I thought carefully before responding; I was in no rush, as it was evident he hadn't been either.

Sarah was at home, busy beautifying, not that she needed to, before meeting Jack for drinks and dinner. She looked amazing in a short, clingy, black dress with black leather knee-length boots and gold accessories; her blonde tresses flowed in waves over her shoulders. I sat on her bed whilst she completed the look with the application of makeup, just a wisp of mascara, a bit of blush, and a shimmer of lip gloss. Simply gorgeous.

Sarah saw my troubled look and asked if I was ok. I told her that Neil had messaged me and that I was unsure of my response. Sarah understood my dilemma, and wisely she advised me that if I wanted to meet Neil, I should. I agreed, the question was when. Again, my wise, beautiful friend advised when I wanted to. Helpful, but also not, as the decision was still mine. Sarah stood back from the mirror, obviously happy with her look. She packed away her makeup, kissed the top of my head, and left me brooding. Two seconds later, she returned and gave me a little hug before disappearing into the night.

I trudged downstairs from the attic and showered. Adorned in an interesting assortment of nightwear, even though it was barely 6 pm, I flopped onto the couch for some serious deliberation regarding Dr Neil Doyle. Unfortunately, the craziness of my shift saw me doze off into a deep sleep, to awaken several hours later. It was pitch black and a bit chilly. I flicked on the television for light and a bit of background noise, pulled up one of my hundreds of throws, and compiled a message to Neil.

Sensibly, I had decided to be governed by my roster. I was rostered off on the weekend, so I plumped for Saturday night, hoping it would suit. I fired off the text and settled down to wait. Only a few minutes later, my phone lit up with a message from the elusive medic, agreeing to meet on Saturday night. Neil suggested a bar in Brixton. James and I had not frequented Brixton and South London, so I readily agreed. I messaged back straight away. I wanted to see him, and I was too tired to pretend otherwise.

That done, I searched the fridge for leftovers, finding a very sorry-looking lasagne, unsure of when Sarah or I had ventured into the realms of cooking. I realised the unlikelihood of that happening, then remembered Eva and Dean had brought it around on some night in the near distant past to have with drinks. Not wanting to risk the possibility of a foodborne illness, poisoning seemed a little dramatic, as I had an early shift the next day, I had cheese on toast, a cup of weak black tea, and headed to bed.

The weekend soon arrived, my shifts continued to be nonstop, it was as though The Royal London had a big sign shining out the front of the hospital, "All Welcome, the sicker, the more broken, the better." My week was spent shuffling patients to try to accommodate the endless arrivals to my ward through the emergency department that required surgical and trauma care. The constant need to think, adapt, and respond caused a buzz of anticipation, an adrenaline rush, which manifested into a sense of achievement and satisfaction in the ability to perform under such pressured circumstances. This was acute tertiary care, providing care to the most complex and severely injured patients, and I loved it.

Saturday morning, I had a little sleep in. It was a beautiful sunny morning, with a sneaky chilly breeze, the sort of morning that called you to the outdoors. Having spent most of my week in the confines of a hospital ward or travelling on the tube, I needed to feel the fresh air on my face and the breeze blowing in my hair. Sarah had had a sleepover at Jack's, a recent development in their relationship, so, disturbing no one, I pumped up my music, dressed appropriately in black leggings, grey sweatshirt, and white joggers that were leaning more towards a motley grey, I slurped my kettle coffee, and entered the outside world.

I didn't run; that venture had not progressed, but I did walk swiftly. It felt so good to be away from walls and people. A few joggers flew past, red-faced and puffing, occasionally glancing at their Garmin, or some other trendy device. I frowned a little as I allowed myself to think of James. The same repetitive questions reared, as to why he had left me and where he was now. The same overwhelming feeling of hollowness and even a little wave of nausea swept over me. All these weeks, months on, I still had no answers, and still deep down, I missed him, but I was meeting Neil that evening. I stopped, I took a deep breath, gathered some inner strength from somewhere, and as I had done so many times, I blocked James from my thoughts and walked on.

I arrived home an hour or so later, having detoured to a café to grab a batch brew. My mood improved. Sarah and Jack were at home creating some breakfast concoction in the kitchen. I waved as I ran upstairs for a shower. The day stretched out in front of me. I was not meeting Neil until 6.30 pm; he had suggested that he pick me up, but I was a little wary of him seeing Sarah, so I said I would meet him at the bar.

I had a constant niggle since I had agreed to meet with Neil, suddenly, as I dressed in some outlandish combination of black sweatpants and a lemon sweat shirt, looking a little like a bumble bee, my black hair topped off the similarity perfectly, I realised that I did not know what the relationship had been between Neil and Sarah, as in friendship or not. I knew that Neil had been Michael's best friend, but where did Sarah fit in the puzzle?

A little while later, having decided to rekindle my love of reading, I ferreted out a romance by Jojo Moyes to while away the hours, being careful not to linger on the sexual references, although her books were described as having muted sex scenes. I was interrupted by Sarah tapping on my door. Jack had left to play in a football game with Scott, Rhys, and Chris, and as much as Sarah professed to liking Jack a lot, it was apparently not enough to sit on the sidelines for 90 minutes cheering him on.

I gently broached the subject of Neil and her. I was mindful that I did not want to create any angst between us by seeing Neil. Although I did not know if I would be seeing Neil, as in continuing to see Neil, I certainly did not want my life to become more complicated by seeing someone who would cause Sarah any anguish or hurt.

Sarah curled up on my bed and drew some pillows to her as though protecting herself from her previous world. I sat quietly. She began by describing men friends in general terms, having a sort of unspoken kinship, like a masonic hood or brotherhood. She went on, as it became obvious that her and Michael's relationship was deteriorating to the point past reconciliation, Neil's loyalty and camaraderie to Michael kept Neil firmly in Michael's corner. I silently made the comparison to James and Miles. Sarah explained, Neil never openly professed to be for Michael and therefore against Sarah, although Sarah admitted that against was pretty strong and probably not the right word, but Neil didn't actually profess to anything and became a pawn in their game of human emotions. Did Sarah mind me seeing Neil? No, but she was honest in saying that she could not help being indifferent towards him. I admired her honesty, although it did cull my feelings a little.

Sarah pushed the pillows away, seemingly becoming more comfortable, dipping into the past. She continued. In the beginning, the very beginning, when she started dating Michael, Neil was stepping out, she stopped, as we both laughed at her reference to times gone by. Neil was seeing, she corrected, a girl called Ruby. This time,

I grabbed a pillow, feeling a little uncomfortable but also very interested. They had met at The Dock's trivia night, where all the central London hospitals entered a team of health professionals; doctors, nurses, physiotherapists, the denomination was irrelevant. General knowledge was the key, and the ability to drink copious amounts of alcohol and still be coherent and provide an answer, preferably the correct one. The competition was fierce and entertaining; it was fascinating watching normally quiet professionals become spirited in the quest to win.

Ruby stood out from the crowd. She possessed an ethereal air, petite, very pretty, beautiful, some would say. Sarah stuck to pretty, her dark brown hair framing her face in a bob, which she occasionally tucked behind her ears, successfully portraying a look of innocence. Ruby favoured clothing that was flowy in fabrics of satin and silk, soft colours, and white lace. Overall, her look was delicate with makeup of soft tones and shimmer, finishing the look. Sarah and I both looked at my "bumble bee outfit' and sighed.

Ruby was not in healthcare; at that time, she was finishing her studies to become a lawyer, specialising in family law. Ruby frequented The Dock with her mixture of friends that were from all walks of life, from medical to law, diverging to engineers and accountants, mostly friendships that had continued from school. Sarah liked Ruby; for all their apparent differences, they seemed to find a common thread. She enjoyed her company and her take on life. Ruby came from a large family, the youngest of many siblings, and would have to be assertive to be heard. This was apparent in all aspects of her life, career-wise and with Neil. Sarah liked that Ruby had a voice, but did feel on occasion that Neil became irritated by this. Sarah herself recognised that sometimes it was better to remain quiet.

Occasionally, Sarah, Michael, Neil, and Ruby would go out as a foursome. Michael confided in Sarah that he endured Ruby's company out of loyalty to Neil. Sarah questioned Michael's obvious dislike of Ruby. Michael described Ruby as often self-opinionated, and he was not a fan of her 'floaty' look. Michael did not have to endure Ruby for too long; after several months, the relationship fizzled to a natural death. Neil was philosophical when asked about the relationship ending, stating that Ruby was the wrong person at the wrong time, and just left it at that.

Sarah and I sat quietly for a few minutes, both absorbing the tales from the past. Sarah retreated to the attic for some much-needed alone time whilst I contemplated the evening ahead. What to wear was easy. I would wear the pale blue dress that I had abandoned for the previous meeting. I felt that tonight was more of a date than a meeting, so I would dress accordingly. It was a cooler evening, so I toned down the look just a little with my short denim jacket. A high-end denim jacket, with intricate stitching, technically, Sarah's not mine.

I arrived at the fancy Brixton bar, Neil had messaged me the address but not the name, and half the letters were obscured by a leafy vine. I didn't even try to guess, although I could just decipher something 'ola'. He had messaged that he would be in the courtyard. As I entered, I saw him sitting at a table a little more in the open than at our first rendezvous. He looked quite handsome in dark blue jeans and a white buttoned shirt, his 5 o'clock shadow a little more established and nicely trimmed. He rose to greet me, again a little peck to the cheek, which I received graciously. As he leaned in, he smelled amazing, a waft of a light spicy fragrance, with a hint of sweetness, permeated the air over me. I later discovered it was a very expensive unisex perfume by Christian Dior, aptly named Spice Blend, very nice. A glass of sauvignon blanc was waiting for me on the table, next to his near-empty beer.

We sat talking about the happenings of the previous few weeks. I told Neil about our new builder friends; I am not sure that Neil was all that interested and was certainly not enthused at my reference to Scott. Neil chatted mostly about starting back at St Barts as a consultant surgeon; he said it felt strange being a very senior member of the surgical team and to have a bed card on the surgical ward, so that his name appeared below a patient. He gave me an example of Mr Bloggs under the care of Dr Doyle. His whole being illuminated with pride, I leant forward and gave him a little kiss. I acknowledged that it was a very big deal.

We explored each other's interests. I declared my love of books, both reading and buying, mostly the genre of romantic fiction; although I was often time poor to indulge in my love of books or bookshops, which were my absolute happy place; browsing shelves, reading descriptions, and discovering a new release by a favourite author.

Neil's passion was travel, although he admitted he would have to stay put for a while. Whilst in Australia, he travelled up north to explore the Barrier Reef, travelled to Sydney's Harbour Bridge and Opera House, he took advantage of medical conferences in Perth and Canberra, and of course, was based in Melbourne. He loved Melbourne, especially the food and the coffee. He indulged in his newfound obsession with the Australian Football League, or AFL as it is known. At this point, he lost me. Awash with alcohol, I had difficulty understanding Australia's national sport. I tried to liken it to rugby league, much to Neil's frustration; he abruptly changed the topic. Maybe Jesse would teach me the rules.

Neil's other sporting interest was golf. Neil was relieved that I knew the intricacies of that sport and didn't liken it to hockey or some other inappropriate comparison. I knew a lot about golf; James would often tell me stories of his grandfather Arthur's golfing trophies proudly on display at his and Dot's, James's grandmother's, house. I did not disclose this to Neil. It was my turn to be vague. Neil was just happy to chat about his handicap, birdies, and pars, and I was just as happy to listen whilst sipping my wine.

As darkness fell, the courtyard became alight with coloured lanterns hanging from the wooden and glass roof, and purple and gold illuminated the tables. Music piped at just the right volume, adding to the atmosphere, a live band was due to play later. Neil informed me that this venue was famous for its cocktails and that it would be a crime not to have one. I laughed at his idiom; two or three sauvignon blancs into the night, I was not going to argue.

The cocktail bar was a little to the side of the courtyard, so we decided to relocate, leaving the noise and bustle. We were greeted by a different, more stylish décor; the sophisticated surroundings were a complete contrast. Soft music surrounded us, cushioned low armchairs, and dimmed lights completed an intimate feel. Neil bought the cocktail list over, so many to choose from, with many names and blends that I had never heard of. I told Neil to choose, and he came back several minutes late with what looked like a tropical garden in a glass. It tasted delicious. Neil had a very conservative margarita, but it was beautifully presented with salt and limes adorning the glass. I eased slowly into tranquillity, as Neil amused me with more stories of his life. As Neil spoke, he held my hands across the table, never leaving my eyes, his face so animated as he described his past.

Reluctantly, my cocktail quota was finally reached, I could not look at another garden in a glass, and I certainly could not take another sip of gin, vodka, or tequila, which I guessed had featured in one or more of my delightful concoctions. Neil agreed, and so to home.

We decided to go back to Neil's, avoiding any awkwardness with Sarah. Neil lived in much the same living arrangement as Eva and Dean, except he occupied the bottom level of a terraced house. I silently offered thanks for not having to negotiate stairs; the walk from the taxi to the front door was a little wobbly, at best. He opened the door to a beautifully presented bachelor pad, as he had described his living quarters. It was a combination of old meets new, very tastefully manicured; it exuded a cared-for look but was just haphazard enough in the odd mix of furnishings to be inviting. I shivered, like most old English houses without central heating, it felt cold. I took a little wander around, steadied on occasion by Neil's arm, peering behind what I presumed to be the bathroom door. I gasped as I saw the most beautiful while and gold claw-foot bath. Neil came up behind me, leaned over, turned the taps on, and poured some exquisite-smelling lotion into the now steaming hot water. "Care to join me?" "Oh yes", came my immediate reply.

He stood facing me, slowly he lifted my dress up and over my head, before reaching to unclasp my bra, exposing my breasts, my nipples erect and hardened under his gentle touch. He stepped back and pulled his shirt off over his head to reveal an impressive torso, harbouring a nicely sculptured six pack. Standing naked except for my tiny lace g-string covering my lady bits, Neil hooked his fingers under the side ribbons and watched as it fell to the ground. I trembled in my nakedness; he gently lifted me into the bath. Stepping out of his jeans, I glanced at his nudity. He grinned. Lowering himself into the mass of bubbles, facing me, he took the soap and began to wash me, slowly. He lifted my arms, then washed my neck, down to my breasts, caressing my nipples with his fingertips, then lower, circling my stomach, before soaping my pubic mound. Then he placed the soap on the side of the bath, and as he parted my legs, his fingers felt inside. My eyes closed, I moaned, and melted to the pressure of his thumb against my sweet spot.

Then he stopped, turn around, he whispered. I stood and sat back down into the bubbled water, my back to him. He soaped my neck and my back, moving further and further down, stand-up, he commanded. I stood, the soap travelled over my buttocks and then in-between, I caught my breath as I felt first the soap and then his fingers between my buttocks, touching, teasing. He stood, lifted me out of the bath, and carried me to his bed. Naked and dripping, he lay me down, kissing me, licking me, touching me, fingering me. I was mindless with desire. I opened my legs wide. He stopped, looked down at me, smiling, then he held my arms above my head as he glided his erection inside me, his hardness thrusting in and out, his hands freed my arms as he gripped my buttocks, lifting me up to him, faster, harder, he surged into me; I whimpered as I exploded with a wild frenzy of emotion. Neil kept thrusting, as he soared to a climax, hands and kisses touching me everywhere, one final entry and a shudder of release. Duvets and blankets appeared from nowhere, covering our nakedness. Neil pulled me towards him, kissed me softly as we succumbed to sleep.

Neil and I started seeing each other, not too often, but enough to qualify as some sort of relationship according to Eva and Sarah. I enjoyed his company; his humour would have me curled up in laughter. I am not sure if it was the Scottish tones, but some of his phrases were comical. Neil left Scotland for London when he was five years old with his parents, who returned a few years ago, and now lived in Fife. Neil promised to take me one day to the land of haggis and bagpipes; he was especially excited to take me to the famous St. Andrews golf course on the East Coast of Fife. I remembered James telling me how Arthur's face would beam as he told of one of his proudest moments there, competing in a pro-am, professional, amateur competition.

Neil was attractive in looks, his trimmed beard suited him, and his hazel eyes were a little mischievous, subtly changing colour from more brown or green depending on the light. Neil's personality also had a hint of mischievousness; the sex was adventurous; I forgot my inhibitions as Neil tempted me to explore a little sexual deviation. Sometimes I was hesitant, and every so often he would search my face for permission, waiting for my small nod of approval.

Sarah continued to be indifferent. I missed being able to share tales of Neil with her. Occasionally, she would ask how my date was, but I could detect a disinterest in my reply. Eva, though, wanted every intricate detail of my sexual exploits; she was provided with an abridged version, and would sit wide-eyed, listening. We often collapsed in girlish giggles as I recounted the tales of the previous night. Very occasionally, Neil and I would tag along with Eva and Dean to a bar or out for Chinese or Indian. Neil and Dean had the medical profession in common and would exchange gory details of various patients. Eva and I did not visit the nursing world; we, instead, focused on who met whom, who was not seeing whom, and other important topics.

Eva provided the St Barts update, including Adam and Leo, who were now both working on Eva's cardiology ward away from Senior Staff Nurse Stanton. Charlotte, who had stayed on my old surgical ward, was still the same, as Eva had observed from afar. Charlotte, mixed with the rich and famous away from work, but did not really mix with anyone at work, except when she needed to. Eva never did consider Charlotte as a friend. Lauren and Emma had moved to nursing in the operating rooms, mostly scrubbing for surgeons, looking after the doctors, more than the patients, in Eva's and my opinion, as the patients were generally asleep. I must admit I was surprised to hear that they had left the ward environment. Neil asked Eva to describe their appearance so he could look out for them in the operating theatres. I felt a tiny twinge of jealousy at his enquiry.

The weeks rolled by; I kept seeing Neil maybe a little more frequently. We rarely met at my house, as the atmosphere between Sarah and Neil remained frosty. Neil tried to engage Sarah in a conversation, but Sarah would usually provide single-syllable answers before either meeting Jack or retiring to the attic. We went out for drinks, indulged in the occasional cocktail, went out for dinners, and had nights in, mostly at Neils. We caught up with Neil's friends and, of course, saw Eva and Dean. The sex continued to be varied and still with surprises, but all the while, something was missing.

One evening, Sarah was on call, and we were in my kitchen, cooking up some culinary delights, well, Neil was, I was supervising, slurping on wine, when Neil suggested that this coming weekend, we were both rostered off, we should go to Scotland and visit his parents. My face went grey, my heart started racing, I felt sick, sweating my wine glass fell to the floor. Neil stopped and rushed over to me. I steadied my breathing and reassured him that I was ok. Neil hovered for some sort of explanation; I murmured some non-committal response as I suddenly realised that I couldn't do this. How could I love someone when I was still in love with someone else?

22
The Night Out

Kate

The relationship ended, not straight away. Neil insisted I needed time. I did not need time; I needed James. It had been over a year since James had left. Why was he still a part of me? I insisted that Neil go to Scotland on that weekend; I needed to have time to think, to try to process where I was at. I liked Neil a lot, a very lot, I did not want to hurt him by promising something that I could not give.

Eva and Sarah were insistent that I would not spend the weekend moping. They quickly organised drinks; Jack rallied the boys, Eva decided to invite the Barts crew, and in Eva's usual way, Saturday night turned into a mini party, of sorts. Eva decided to come over to get ready with Sarah and me. Dean was on call overnight, so Eva decided to bunk down with us, too. She arrived with a suitcase, in true Eva style, which included a bottle of sauvignon blanc. The subject of Neil was not addressed, both my friends realised that I needed to work out what I was going to do by myself. We opened and sipped on the wine as we dressed. Eva, despite the suitcase, borrowed a dress from Sarah, much to our amusement. We decided to all wear dresses of various colours and designs. Overall, we looked very stylish and elegant, maybe a little over the top for a bar, but we hadn't partied together for a while, so gorgeous, Sarah, stunning, Eva, and pretty me stepped into the night.

The bar had just opened in London's West End. It was quite fancy, so we fitted in nicely in our classy attire. The St Barts clan must have sussed out the bar's style, as everyone looked pretty special in their trendy outfits, even the builders, as they were known, looked very handsome. Scott greeted me with a hug, lingering just a little. I gave him an extra little squeeze as we came apart. I had missed the boys and the special connection that I had with Scott. It was fun to be back in the realms of innuendos and suggestive comments, safe in superficial remarks, both knowing there was an unspoken something between us. Scott and I had not become involved in each other's private lives; we knew that if we wanted to, we could deepen our friendship, maybe going to the next level, but it was clear that where we were was where we both wanted to be.

Much had changed at St Barts over the few months since I had left. The more we drank, the more exaggerated the stories became. Only Charlotte remained with Charge Nurse Claire Reynolds and Senior Staff Nurse Rebecca Stanton. I was told that Charlotte might drop by later after her late shift. I felt a little uneasy at the thought of seeing her again. The others had flown the coup. Adam and Leo had found their niche with Eva in cardiac surgery and all things heart; Lauren and Emma, as I had known, were now in the operating theatres. Both were unsure if that was the right fit for them, but they were happy to try a different aspect of nursing. All four had love interests of sorts, although on that night they had decided to fly solo. The night progressed into a scene of raucous laughter and shrieks of expletives as new discoveries were made about old acquaintances. It was all harmless fun, and the wine and spirits that were consumed ensured that the memory of specifics was unlikely to occur.

As the night ended, I perched on Scott's knee, surrounded by Eva, Rhys, and Chris. The atmosphere was a little more subdued; the nurses had flocked to Charlotte on her arrival, looking exquisite in an electric blue off-the-shoulder figure-hugging top, complemented by a very tight pair of white jeans. She was the centre of attention, just where Charlotte liked to be. I had offered her a slight smile and had received a flicker of recognition in return.

My perch transitioned into me being draped over Scott, my head resting on his shoulder, suddenly heavy due to the combination of alcohol and tiredness. Scott put his arm around my waist to steady me, as my eyes blinked rapidly, resisting the urge to close, I glanced towards the door and saw Neil staring back at me.

Why wasn't Neil in Scotland? I leapt off Scott's knee and ran over to Neil. In a cloud of alcohol, I couldn't gauge his mood. He briskly offered to give me a lift home, obviously sensing that my night was over. I gratefully accepted. Eva, not reading the vibe, came over. Neil, of course, offered Eva a ride too.

Eva, devoid of any inhibitions, demanded to know why Neil was not in Scotland. I sank deeper into the passenger seat as Neil explained that he had been asked to cover emergent leave as a consultant on call. He had gone up to Scotland early on the Friday morning to see his parents and so agreed to come back. The residual ward staff back at St Barts were quick to tell Neil about the night out. He peered over to see that Eva was gently snoring against the car window on the back seat, as he finished his explanation. I pretended to sleep, not wanting to explain why I was sprawled all over Scott.

Once home, Neil carefully helped Eva and me out of the car and assisted us up the steps inside. Eva settled on the couch, encased in throws and cushions, and fell into a deep sleep. I started to climb the stairs, a little precariously, gripping onto the bannister. I turned to see Neil walking out of the front door.

We saw each other a few more times after that night, but the feelings between us had changed. Neil's love for me was unrequited; hard as I tried, I could not love Neil as he needed, deserved to be loved. We met for a drink one last time. I knew that I was the catalyst in the ending of our relationship, and I was so, so sorry. Neil listened as I tried in a mumbled way to explain. Eventually, I stopped my garbled excuses, I got up, kissed him very gently on his cheek, and walked away.

23
The Curry House

Kate

Back home, sitting up in bed, knees drawn to my chest, my face blotchy, my eyes stinging and swollen as tears streamed down my cheeks. Confusion crippling my thoughts; how do I shake this all-consuming love for James? Every time my heart started to heal, the wound broke down again. Every time I thought I had conquered the heartache it rose from the depths of me. I needed to stop looking for relationships and focus on my friends and my career. I could not risk hurting people, playing with feelings, anymore.

My thoughts rambled on, gnawing inside of me. I did not want to hurt Neil, but I had, and because I couldn't work out my own feelings, I had hurt a person whom I really cared for. I had tried to explain, to use excuses, but the reality was I couldn't feel what I so desperately wanted to feel, I couldn't be a part of a relationship that I so needed to be a part of, and I couldn't love the person who so wanted my love. I was so very sorry, but sorry wasn't the word that Neil wanted to hear. Sorry was a word that was empty, that was left dangling. Sorry did not make things right. It was a word that was useless to those who wanted more.

I realised that Sarah had come home; I quickly turned out my light. She paused outside my door on the way up to her room. I did not breathe until I heard her footsteps on the stairs up to the attic. I had not shared the evolution of Neil and my relationship with Sarah, respecting her past; I was not going to share the demise. This was my situation, my mess, a puzzle of feelings that needed a solution, my solution, one that I did not have. Not yet.

I threw myself into my career, the easy bit of my life. I was proficient in caring; I had mastered complexity, negotiated challenges and succeeded in embracing opportunities. The ward was relentless in its busyness; there were so many competing priorities, but the patients would always remain the primary focus. I applied for a Senior Staff Nurse position, and to my surprise, I was successful. I was now in my third year post graduating, I felt thankful at being recognised for the contribution I had made to the surgical and trauma ward at The Royal London, as I had demonstrated to Lauren and Emma all that time ago at St Barts, I was passionate about nursing, the ability to make a difference, every day, to someone's life was indefinable.

Of course, Eva wanted to celebrate my promotion. We had already planned a small party for my 24th birthday, looming not too far in the distance, I suggested just a few drinks with the builders at a bar, nothing too extravagant, maybe a quick curry to follow. Eva reluctantly agreed to a low-key affair. Sarah was a little hesitant; I had sensed, of late, that things were not all rosy in Sarah and Jack's Garden of Love.

Jack wanted more than what Sarah was prepared to give; no, they were not going to break up, neither of them wanted that, but Jack was getting too demanding of Sarah's time. Jack needed to chill, as Eva and I expertly concluded after listening to Sarah's relationship update. Sarah was not confused as to what she wanted; she was very clear; she was happy as things were, girlfriend and boyfriend, a little more than casual, she could not commit to anything more. Sarah had been very open from the outset; she was not saying never to commitment, just not now. It was up to Jack to decide if that was ok or not.

The night out was perfect; it started low-key as suggested, even quiet, but just right. Jack was there, so obviously infatuated with Sarah, definitely not chilled, Eva and I smiled. Scott, Rhys and Chris were also at the bar. Rhys and Chris were joined by two lovely ladies, Georgia and Belle. Scott awkwardly introduced me to Maya, a beautiful young woman, very young, I surmised, who clung to Scott's arm, looking nervous, her grip tightened to vice-like when Scott gave me a tiny kiss on the cheek. Dean was joining us later.

The chatter was mainly about my up-and-coming party in a few weeks. It wasn't a milestone birthday; my grandfather's house had hosted several mini parties, as Eva had described the celebration of auspicious occasions over the years, but only one "big" party. A lot had happened since that party, so long ago, so much had changed. Eva sensed that this party would be like transitioning into the next stage of our lives, so very dramatic, so very Eva.

The builders and their lady friends seemed immersed in each other, and of course, Jack was under Sarah's spell. Eva and I, sauvignon blancs in hand, reflected on where we were in life. Eva loved dissecting the lives of others, especially mine and Sarah's. Eva and Sarah had become close friends in the 18 months or so that I had known Sarah. We had our differences, Sarah knew that Eva and I had been friends since the beginning of time, our time, but had been very happy to join our party late, as it were, and we were very happy that she did. More sauvignon blancs were placed in our hands as we continued. Eva and I decided that we approved of Jack, not that Sarah was asking.

I then moved on to Eva and Dean. I said very seriously that I approved of Dean, to which Eva laughed and leaned forward to hug me, causing wine to spill down my pale-yellow dress. The same yellow dress that I had worn all those years ago when I first met James. We both quietened in the realisation.

Eva quickly resumed the examination of the relationships of others. We deliberated as to what Jesse and Bree were up to. When we last spoke to Jesse a few weeks previously, all was going well, and Jesse seemed to be falling for the pretty veterinary nurse. We briefly touched on Dion, both agreeing that he would still be making women swoon with his tantalising cologne and sexy French accent, although we presumed he was probably back in France, where his accent would have less of an effect. We knew Neil was still single, Eva would occasionally see him at St Barts looking very handsome in pale blue scrubs, he always smiled at her and said hello.

And so back to me. I was ok, any thoughts of romance were paused. I was content being amongst my friends, I thrived at work, and at home, well, I continued to fumble through my life one day at a time.

The London Curry House was anything but low-key, as we were to find out. It was pumping, with the strains of melodic music competing with the noise of many, many people from all nationalities and ethnic communities. Dean had become the designated driver; as many as legally allowable squashed into his car. We spilt out to be greeted by a maître d on the footpath, welcoming people inside. It was as colourful as it was noisy, vibrant shades of reds and golds sparkled, textured silks and cottons decorated walls and tables, exploding with bursts of colour, the dimmed lighting added to the mood. Eva, Dean and I were mesmerised by the crowd. Fortunately, we had booked a table, and as Sarah, Jack, the builders and their ladies arrived, we sat. The authentic aromas of India wafted around us; the food was amazing. A banquet of samosas, naan, roti, curries, dahl, rice, and papadums covered the table, interspersed by wines, spirits and beers. Eva grinned as low-key had turned into a festivity of food, wine and music. No one complained as we were drawn into the ambiance. The builder's ladies became instant friends, Maya, Georgia, and Belle dipped their naan and roti, scooped up curries and joined the consumption of various alcoholic beverages as Dean looked on in amusement.

It was always at the end of such a night, when I crawled into bed, overcome by the need to sleep. I'd slip between the cold cotton sheets and draw the duvet up to my chin. I would instinctively put my hand out to touch the expanse of emptiness next to me, no Jesse, no Neil, and of course no James, that's when I felt so alone.

24
The Sighting

Kate

The planning for my party began. Eva and Sarah went into bossy mode. They were excited to organise everything and did not require my input. I was told quite firmly that I was to turn up like the guest, and the only reason why I was privy to some details was because I lived where the party was taking place, which was a big disappointment to Eva, who loved organising surprises. I had to smile as Eva and Sarah plotted the events of the night; voices dropped to hushed whispers when I entered the room. Dean oversaw the food and wine, as he was a self-professed expert on both. Jack was given the task of lighting, which made me nervous, just how big this "little" party was going to be. I jokingly asked if the builders had been allocated a task. I immediately regretted my question when I saw the deliberation on Eva's face.

On party eve, as Eva insisted on calling the day before, I was tasked with gathering the last-minute incidentals, as Eva and Sarah called them, bits and pieces of little relevance from my viewpoint or how to keep Kate out of the house. I had already decided that I would spend part of the day in my happy place, my favourite bookshop. To have the whole day ahead of me with very little to do felt quite luxurious. I could, in hindsight, which was a wonderful thing, have picked up an overtime shift on the ward for a few extra pounds, but a few hours to myself sounded much more appealing. I munched on a piece of toast and gulped down a kettle coffee as Eva arrived and, together with Sarah, shooed me out of the house.

The bookshop wasn't too far away; I stopped for a batch brew on the way. I decided to sit and enjoy rather than get a takeaway, a luxury in itself. People-watching was another one of my favourite pastimes. I settled at a corner table, grabbed a magazine as a prop, and spent a while criticising and judging the blend of young and old, singles and couples that drifted in and out. I recognised a few nurses and doctors from St Barts with a red-headed Irish girl whom I had not met before; her accent was like a breath of fresh air amongst the English drones. I was thinking that I might go over and say hello, but they appeared deep in conversation, and I didn't want to appear rude by intruding. I unashamedly tried to eavesdrop, but the hum of the café thwarted my success.

It was time to move on. I smiled towards the table as I walked past; only the Irish girl smiled back. Back out on the London streets, I still felt a genuine warmth from that smile. I pondered who she might be as I headed towards my bookshop. The bookshop, in contrast, was very quiet. The owner, Jeff, nodded as I walked in. We had known each other even before I had moved to London; when I would visit my grandfather, he would often sneak sweets when my grandfather was busy researching something or other, usually related to finance. I had grown a little too big for sweets, but I remembered those days and so was always mindful to give Jeff a little time out of my day. He was always interested in my nursing career and boyfriends; today I was only happy to indulge him in the former.

I was soon browsing the shelves. Romantic fiction was usually my choice of genre, but today I felt a little disinterested in the heartbreak of others. I wandered over to crime, light crime, if there was such a thing. I picked up a book by Liane Moriarty. I had heard of the three Moriarty sisters, Australian authors, but had not read any of their books. Jeff appeared over my shoulder and seemed pleased by my book of choice, *Big Little Lies*; he explained that the writing of Liane Moriarty was generally classified as domestic or psychological thrillers.

Perfect, I thought, a long way away from romance. I continued to browse some more. I was in no rush, and I found the crime thriller section quite captivating. I was excited to broaden my reading ethos. I was interrupted by a text from Eva; would I like to have a little pre-birthday celebration and meet for lunch? I had been so busy, in my self-indulgence, that I hadn't realised it was close to lunchtime. Eva explained that the party preparations were ahead of schedule, so she and Sarah would like to take me to lunch. She promised nothing extravagant; she had been recommended a no-frills café, as it had been described, that had opened a little while ago. Looking down at my no-frills jeans and T-shirt, I hoped that was true.

My scepticism was unfounded; it was a very quiet, unassuming eatery with a friendly atmosphere and just busy enough to reassure the three of us that the food was good. The menu was limited; we all selected burgers and shoestring chips, and we were not disappointed. The conversation was unusually stilted, as Eva and Sarah tried to avoid all reference to the party. I became quite animated regarding my new reading genre; Eva and Sarah laughed at my avoidance of romance, even in the text of a book. We left, not before Eva had given me an updated shopping list which seemed to have grown quite considerably. Eva was going home, as Sarah deemed the party preparations could be completed during the day tomorrow, before the actual party. Sarah had some study to complete, so I continued with my me time before I grabbed the groceries.

I tubed home; my me time had taken me a little further afield than I had planned. I disembarked with my arms laden with groceries, my *Big Little Lies* purchase somewhere within one brown paper bag, nestled in with lemons, Himalayan pink salt, tomato ketchup and other life essentials. The other bag contained beef goulash dinner ingredients. Struggling down past the terraces in my street, I was relieved to see the pillar-box-red door coming into sight. As I started up the steps, I had a strange feeling that someone was watching me. I turned, and there I saw James standing, staring.

The brown bags fell to the floor. I watched my groceries hit the steps, then turned to look again. He was gone. Scrambling up the remnants of the beef goulash ingredients and the essential accompaniments to the tequila lip, sip and suck, I stumbled through the front door. The rest of the night, Sarah and I, once Sarah had recovered from my look of a very pale ghost, tried to make sense of James's reappearance.

25
The Birthday

Kate

Early the next morning, before Eva arrived, Sarah and I had revisited the sudden appearance of James. Eva had stood aghast at the snippets of conversation that she had overheard. Of course, I had to provide a full recap to Eva, who appeared lost for words, very unlike Eva. Both Eva and Sarah asked me what I was going to do. I had no idea. I had spent most of the previous night in a fitful sleep, trying to decipher the reason why James would return to my life, to stand staring for a few seconds and then leave, as he had done so many, many months ago. He had again stirred so many emotions, the same disbelief and confusion. I had been so desperately hurt, my heart had been so badly broken, I questioned if I was willing to endure that heartache again.

It was party day, my birthday, which Eva and Sarah had momentarily forgotten amidst the deliberation of another chapter of my life and James.

Hugs and kisses, and a very noisy tuneless rendition of Happy Birthday, filled the terrace. Sarah rushed up to the attic and brought down two bags full of wrapped parcels in various pastel shades, very chic, beautifully presented with ribbons and bows. Pink twine added a little rustic look. Eva ran out the front door and returned with a bunch of pink helium balloons that she had left tied to the gold-plated door knocker, then she ran back outside and returned, placing a pair of knee-high tan leather boots, nearly concealed by wrapping paper, on the kitchen table. I absolutely loved them. I immediately put them on; they were gorgeous and so in trend. Next, to Sarah's parcels, classy was the word that sprang to mind, beautifully individually wrapped items of underwear, or lingerie, as was the more appropriate word, silks, lace and sheer, that oozed delicate, sexy extravagance.

Birthday breakfast was provided by Dean and Jack, who arrived with arms full of coffees and pastries. Dean also gave me a stunning bunch of pink and red roses. Thoughts of James were paused as I immersed myself in the love and affection of my friends. More renditions of Happy Birthday followed, and smatterings of pastry splayed everywhere as we laughed at the jarring sound of inharmony.

A little later, I was to be banished for a few hours and could only return to glamorise. More me time, I smiled. First, I disappeared to my bedroom as I had received messages from Ben and Daniel. I had not seen them for a while; I missed my big brothers. I called them together. Ben was bursting with excitement as he and Lisa had finally set a wedding date. I was so excited. Daniel also had some news; he had been courting. I laughed. *Courting?* I questioned. Ben affirmed that Daniel was obsessed with the notion of courting someone. Daniel ignored Ben's and my jibes and told me that her name was Ivy, and she was also in the music industry. In Daniel's obtuse way, no other details were provided. I told Ben and Daniel about my party, and we chatted for a little while longer; both enquired after Jesse and Sarah. I didn't mention James; I was not sure what to say, so I said nothing.

Mum and Dad called next. I was very amused to hear Mum and Dad singing Happy Birthday. I could clearly hear Barney the beagle in the background barking. I presumed that the barking was not in relation to the dulcet tones of my parents. I presumed correctly, as the phone call was cut short as someone was at the door. I promised to call Mum the following day and update her on the party. Lots of kisses from Mum *and* Dad, which made me smile, and we said goodbye.

Knocks on my door, followed by shouts of "out," was my cue to disappear for a few hours. The party was starting at 6 pm, so I was allowed home at four. I was immensely touched by how much effort was being made for my birthday celebration, although I had a sneaking feeling that Eva and Sarah were revelling in the organisation of my "little" party. I was hustled unceremoniously downstairs and literally pushed out the front door straight into the arms of Ben and Daniel. Whoops of laughter erupted behind me as the expletives flew from my mouth in surprise. As I disappeared within hugs and smoochy kisses from my brothers, I laughed as I surfaced, wiping kiss dribble from my face. Tied somewhere on their persons were more balloons in grey and black. I was a little startled to see black, but appreciated the thought, as the inside of the terrace started to resemble a fairground.

Ben and Daniel whisked me away; they had decided on a mini tour of England's capital. I was super keen. Even though I lived in London, I had never played the tourist. We climbed aboard the topless double-decker, a London icon. I was squeezed in between the boys as we were driven around the famous attractions, which were the personification of this very famous city: Buckingham Palace, Big Ben, and London Bridge. The driver, doubling as our tourist guide, bellowed out a commentary of historical facts. It was interesting, if not a little loud, and as we stopped for a closer look at the King's Guard at Buckingham Palace, the boys and I decided to sneak away to the nearest pub for some peace and quiet, accompanied by a drop of alcohol; it was my birthday after all.

We settled at a table tucked away in a corner. I decided to tell Ben and Daniel about my sighting of James. They both became heightened to the threat of my getting hurt again. I assured them that I was fine, just confused. The subject was changed; there was nothing more to say. I did promise that I would be careful in whatever transpired from the possibility of James re-entering my life. We talked about Ben's wedding; the date was set for six months, the wedding would be a small, intimate affair of no more than 30 guests. Ben explained that Lisa wanted a small, rural wedding. The venue, The Barn, sounded perfect, a rustic barn with cascading greenery set in acres of countryside. Ben said that Mum was behaving, not interfering too much; we laughed. I added that the first child to get married was a momentous occasion. The boys both stared at me. Well, it was.

Ben and I turned to Daniel for a little more info on Ivy. Daniel reluctantly described her: tall, just a little shorter than himself; Daniel said he insisted on Ivy wearing flats so as not to be taller than him. Ben and I smirked. She was quite attractive; again, Ben and I smirked. We decided that we would wait to meet Ivy in the flesh, so to speak. Daniel was relieved not to have to find the right descriptives but did say she was quite delightful. "Aaaahh," Ben and I teased. The boys mentioned that Dad had mellowed considerably to a portrayal of an almost human, which was a little harsh; certainly, my recent experiences with Dad showed that he undoubtedly cared.

We shared two Ploughman's Lunches between the three of us, feasting on enormous fresh, crunchy bread rolls filled with cheese and pickles. We chatted some more about my new role as Senior Staff Nurse, and about Ben's promotion at his accountancy firm; he was extremely coy in acknowledging that he had achieved a big step up. Daniel, as usual, provided very little information about his role in the music industry, and even less about Ivy's. Ben and I knew that pushing for any further details was useless. Beers and wine consumed, we decided to head home; a nap was most appealing. Ben messaged Eva and Sarah to warn them we were on our way. I was given strict instructions to go straight to my room for a rest; I was very happy to comply.

Party time; the house was chaos. People everywhere: Eva, Sarah, Dean, Jack, Ben and Daniel. I stood on the stairs witnessing what looked like a frantic response to a global disaster. In amongst the chaos was the most stunning décor that had erupted out of nowhere. Tiny fairy lights were strung up everywhere, intertwined with larger coloured bulbs; the balloons, even the black ones, added to the party theme. An amazing smell radiated from the oven of the usual party fare, and, of course, bottles of alcohol and cocktail ingredients lined the kitchen table. It had been a balmy day; the doors were open into the courtyard, where the small barbecue, thanks to Jesse, stood at the ready for onions and sausages. Milk crates with cushions on served as seating. It looked amazing, and so did Eva, Sarah, Dean, Jack, Ben and Daniel. When they managed to stand still, I could see the effort everyone had gone to: casual but very schmick. The boys in a uniform of chinos and linen shirts; Eva and Sarah in skintight pale blue jeans and beautiful flowing tops, Eva's a rich combination of pink and green florals, Sarah's a subtle mix of grey and white with a pop of orange.

And the birthday girl? I had decided on casual too, but pretty. White jeans, skintight of course, with the palest of pastel green linen tops, a simple ruffle along a low scooped neckline, added a hint of sexiness. This time, the hair straightener was left redundant as I let a few waves do their thing. Footwear for everyone seemed to be optional, a combination of shoes, even slippers, of course, Eva's, were abandoned at various places, to be donned later, perhaps. Not so I; I proudly wore my new knee-high tan leather boots, which accentuated my gold pearl drop earrings and short gold necklace interspersed with tiny pearls, understated with a touch of class.

The music fought to be heard against the excitement of raised voices; we were happy for it to fade into the background whilst the finishing touches were completed. Eva was keen to show me an enormous Happy Birthday banner hanging over the front door, with shiny, colourful streamers hanging down. Fait accompli. Done.

I insisted that we gather round for a group hug. Eva, Sarah, Dean and my brothers were quite used to these occasional open shows of affection; Jack not so. However, he was pulled into the embrace. I thanked them all for being my friends. Eva sniffled a little, and for an amazing birthday, everyone cheered. We were interrupted by the rap of the door knocker, and the party began.

26

The Uninvited Guest

Kate

The builders were the first to arrive, with girls in tow. Maya, Georgia and Belle looked gorgeous in various combinations of denim, topped with a camisole and blouse. I reflected, as they stood next to each other, that they looked like an English candy necklace that we wore as children: a sweet assortment of pale blue, pink and yellow candies. We would bite off the sugar loops, often walking around wearing just the sticky elastic, maybe one or two small candies remaining. The simple pleasures back then.

Next to arrive were the St Barts crew: Lauren and Emma, Adam and Leo, and hanging behind was Charlotte. "Is this ok?" she hesitated. "Yes, this is ok," I smiled as I opened the door wider and welcomed her in. A few nurses and doctors from The Royal London, mostly friends of Sarah, and St Barts joined the merriment. I had hoped to see the Irish girl from the café, but she didn't show.

The festivities were in full swing. The music volume had been increased by several decibels, wine, beer and spirits were flowing, Dean was cooking up a storm on the barbecue, and an impromptu dance floor had been created by pushing every piece of superfluous furniture into the entrance and hallway. Jack turned off the bigger colourful globes so only the fairy lights remained, creating a touch of enchanting charm.

It was perfect, until it was not. I had not heard the rap at the door over the chatter and steady beat of the music. Neil was talking to Eva. I stopped in mid-conversation and looked over to where Neil was standing. Then I looked at Sarah, who had seen Neil and was looking at me. I did not know if this was ok. Ben and Daniel looked at me, sensing a shift in my mood. I had not mentioned Neil to them, as the relationship was never really defined. The remainder of my party revellers continued in oblivion, drinking, eating, dancing, having fun. There seemed to be clouds of worry hanging over Sarah and me, and confusion hanging over Ben and Daniel. Why, in the space of two days, had both James and Neil re-entered my life?

Neil came over, wished me happy birthday, and gave me his trademark kiss on the cheek. We both engaged in general chit-chat. He enquired about the trauma world of The Royal London, and I asked how being a member of the consultant crowd at St Barts was treating him. We both gave gushing responses, overcompensating for not really knowing where the conversation was going. All the time, the music was blaring, and people stopped to wish me happy birthday as they arrived. Ben and Daniel continued to watch, unsure of whether they were needed or not. I slipped them a sly smile, and they visibly relaxed, although they remained vigilant, periodically glancing over to me. Neil then chatted about a planned trip to Europe to present at a conference in Paris. The chat meandered along, and then the line came that changed everything. Neil paused, leaned forward, and whispered, "I can't stop thinking about you." I had no response. I gently shook my head and walked away to rejoin the frivolities of the party, my birthday party. I accepted a sauvignon blanc from Ben and then another from Daniel; both had sensed that whatever had just happened was misplaced, unwarranted and unwanted. I agreed.

Neil left soon after that. Eva and Sarah both checked that I was ok. Now, under a dense cloud of alcohol, I was absolutely fine. I went back to my guests, mingling with everyone, enjoying meeting some of Sarah's friends, catching up with the builders, Scott, Rhys and Chris, and their lovely ladies. The St Barts clan were my favourites. The boys, Adam and Leo, told of hilarious anecdotes and the latest gossip from our previous surgical ward. Lauren and Emma also told some very funny stories of life in the operating theatre. Adam, Leo, and I listened, amused at some of their tales. It seemed that nursing and doctoring were very different within the land of anaesthesia. Needless to say, they were looking for pastures new, where the patients were mostly awake. Charlotte stood on the outskirts of the chat; we made an effort to include her. Adam and Leo, full of beer and spirits, slung their arms around her and dragged her into the circle of frivolity. Charlotte, also full of beer and spirits, was happy to join our little crowd.

As the eloquence of conversation became challenged by the increasing consumption of beverages, dancing took over. Jack flicked a switch, and the fairy lights dimmed, replaced by the flashing brightness of the multicoloured bulbs. A mirror disco ball was hung from the string of coloured lights, and an instant disco was created. A mishmash of 80s, nineties and noughties tunes belted out; arms and legs synchronised to the beat. An impromptu karaoke, minus the microphone, erupted, and piercing singing filled the room. The party atmosphere reached dizzy heights; the terrace was buzzing with the shrill of sing-alongs and shrieks of laughter.

Everyone was dancing: Sarah, Jack, Eva and even Dean, the builders and their ladies, the St Barts crew, Adam, Leo, Lauren, Emma and Charlotte, Sarah's Royal London friends, everyone. The floor was bouncing, the walls shaking as the music, singing and laughter filled the room. It was the best: old friends, new friends, old acquaintances, and new acquaintances, enjoying the night.

Time after time, the playlist was put on repeat until the music slowly became an array of soft love songs, soothing the partygoers to leave or stay, whatever their preference. I warily climbed the stairs to bed. I started to drift off to sleep as my phone signalled a call. I mumbled hello and smiled as I heard Jesse's voice, the best rendition of Happy Birthday ever, all the way from Australia. I stifled a laugh as his voice rose a few octaves. God, I missed him. I asked how Bree was. I sensed him beaming as he assured me she was good, they were good. Jesse asked me how I was. Fighting sleep, I spoke briefly about Neil and then mentioned James. I was perplexed at the reappearance of both, but was especially grumpy with Neil showing up at my party; I was certain that Eva and Sarah had not invited him.

Jesse mentioned that a new registered nurse had started on his old ward at St Barts; apparently, her name was Ellie, and she was the girlfriend of Miles. I sat bolt upright in bed, suddenly very awake. Jesse had heard that she was Irish, with red hair and very lovely. An unsettled feeling swept over me. First, James, now Miles's girlfriend, had crept into my life. I tried to grill Jesse for some more information, but he knew no more. We chatted a little more about his dad and Luke before I finally surrendered to sleep.

I awoke the next morning feeling uneasy, and then I remembered the conversation with Jesse. I was surprised that Miles had a girlfriend. I remembered the warmth of her smile following our brief encounter at the café; she did seem lovely. I decided to catch up with Eva and Sarah later to discuss the latest twist in the Kate and James saga.

I quickly dressed in something a little more presentable than my lacy pink nightie, one of Sarah's beautiful, if not a bit risqué, birthday presents. As seemed to be the tradition with parties at my terrace, when the music stopped, you slept where you stood. Hence, I walked into the living room to many sleeping bodies spread across what was the dance floor and what now looked like a sleepover of epic proportions. I saw Eva and Dean on the floor, intertwined, surrounded by cushions and a very flimsy throw. My mind flicked back to all those years ago, to our welcome-to-Jesse party, and I smiled. So much had changed, but some things had stayed the same.

Grunts and groans were heard as slowly the room came back to life. Wrapped in throws and blankets, the partygoers emerged from various parts of the house, looking very different from the dressy-casual appearance of a few hours ago. The sun shone bright; bleary eyes squinted as they peered into the day, heads steadied by hands as the effects of too much alcohol and too little sleep caused a very subdued crowd to whisper goodbye and thank you before they disappeared home.

Eva and Dean crawled quite literally from the floor to the couch. Sarah, Jack, Ben and Daniel staggered down the stairs, looking very shaky, emitting the odd moan as they tried to navigate the stairs without looking down, gripping the bannister to provide an assurance that they would remain upright. I sat quietly in my grandfather's chair, looking at the landscape around me, and sighed. Party debris was scattered all around. When the others finally reached the living room, they flopped to the floor, being careful to avoid empty beer bottles, plastic cups and plates, and the odd remnant of a sausage. We all agreed we needed coffee; what we couldn't agree on was how we would get it. The café, although not that far away, seemed to be an insurmountable challenge. We decided to start with water and progress from there.

Eventually, Eva and I were able to attempt the journey to the café. Slowly, and exhibiting some very dubious dress sense, we left but soon returned. Sunglasses were a must. We looked quickly around: Sarah and Jack were nowhere to be seen; likewise, Ben and Daniel, presumably, had returned to bed for some more sleep. Dean remained curled up on the couch, sleeping soundly. Eva and I gently closed the door.

We sat in the deserted café, clutching our batch brews. We welcomed the quiet, sitting for a while, embracing the silence. I eased into a conversation with Eva. There was so much that was troubling me, but as I looked at Eva, a little slumped in her chair, looking very pale, I was unsure if I should proceed asking for her opinion or advice. I decided that I would continue, a little selfishly; I just needed Eva to listen, which she was happy to do.

Neil was quickly mentioned; I reflected that his presence at the party had unsettled me. I would welcome Neil as a friend, but he still wanted more. I hoped that he had now finally realised that it was not possible. Next, I told Eva, who seemed a little more engaged with my perplexity, about my conversation with Jesse after the party. This sparked a resurgence of life as Eva listened to the details of Ellie and Miles. Although sparse, Eva was very interested in the fact that Miles had a girlfriend. I added the titbit regarding my brief encounter with Ellie; Eva was excited to realise that she also worked at St Barts.

I paused; Eva seemed to give my obvious confusion some thought. The appearance of James, Neil, and even Ellie. Eva knew me, and she knew that I needed to escape from these perplexities. She gave me a little hug. Taking a deep breath, she quietly suggested I leave.

"Leave?" I queried. She took another breath. "Go… to Australia." Coffee spluttered across the table.

27
The Departure

Kate

Back at my terrace, I called an urgent family meeting. We prised Sarah, Jack, Ben and Daniel from their slumber to join Dean in the living room with the promise of café coffee and various sweet and savoury muffins. They arrived vulture-like, swooping down on much-needed sustenance. Eva and Sarah laughed at my terminology; I became serious for a moment. They were my family. No one disagreed.

The party clean-up fairy had not arrived; therefore, we perched amongst the debris that remained. All eyes were looking expectantly at me. I announced that I was going to Australia. I was met by stunned silence. I quickly explained that I needed to sit on a sunny beach and stare into the ocean; I needed to reflect on my past and plan for the future. I needed to consider where I was at and where I was going. The silence continued. Slowly, one by one, Eva, Sarah, Ben, Daniel, Jack and Dean stepped forward to hug me. I reassured them that I would only be gone for a few weeks, not forever, an audible sigh erupted; relief flooded across their faces. I sensed a barrage of questions was about to erupt, so I continued to clarify that nothing was arranged. I had to organise time off work, money, flights, and talk to Jesse. I suddenly stopped as I realised I didn't have a passport. I had never travelled overseas, never left my homeland.

This became the top priority: how to get a passport. Dean put his hand up. We all laughed. Leave it to me. It seemed that Dean, wine connoisseur, self-proclaimed pizza dough expert, was also an entrepreneur in how to urgently access a passport. I gladly assigned the task to Dean so I could focus on the remainder of my to-do list.

But first, we had to return the terrace to the semblance of a home rather than a post-party disaster area. Still under the lingering aftereffects of beers, sauvignon blanc, tequila and the like, we moved at a snail's pace. A little later, Ben and Daniel had to travel home; both were very excited for me and said they would transfer me some spending money. I absolutely refused, to which they covered their ears and gave me a big kiss. I waved goodbye, watching as they bounded down the front steps, then I watched as Ben bounded back up the front steps to remind me not to forget the wedding. As if I would.

When the terrace had returned to some sort of normal, I showered and called Mum and Dad. I had promised to call them with an update on my birthday and party. I had not planned on telling them that I was going to Australia. They were surprised but very supportive of my plan. Dad offered to contribute a few hundred pounds towards expenses; I graciously accepted. They were keen to know my timeframe for being in Australia. I sensed that they were worried that I might not return. I assured them that it would just be for a few weeks, four at most. I had a wedding to help organise after all.

Jesse could not contain his excitement when, later that night, I called to tell him of my decision to visit the land down under. I had so much to organise, primarily work. Dean was organising my passport. Money was being offered from many quarters, although that truly was not an issue. Jesse did gently probe the reason behind my sudden decision. I explained that seeing James, albeit momentarily, was suggestive of the possibility of James coming back into my life. I wanted to avoid the threat, if that was the right word, of seeing him before I was ready. Going to Australia, in essence, running away, seemed a little extreme, but it also felt right. Just for a little while.

It was a little presumptuous to think I could stay with Jesse and Luke, but Jesse absolutely insisted. I told Jesse that I was not sure when I could be released from work; it depended on what leave was available, but now that Eva had suggested the idea, I wanted to go yesterday, or tomorrow at the very latest. Jesse laughed at my eagerness.

I returned to work the next day. I arranged to have a meeting with my Charge Nurse. Rachael Bently was a manager who led with openness and compassion. Her mantra was fairness and equity, and she was very well-liked. Rachael had the enviable ability to be warm and friendly, yet still commanded respect. It was an exceptional ward in both its care of patients and care of staff. I felt very privileged to work within such a supportive and cohesive team. That said, I was a little apprehensive to ask for leave at such short notice.

I followed Rachael into her office. It was a very busy day; it was always a very busy day. I was appreciative of Rachael seeing me and aimed to be succinct in my request, with my fingers firmly crossed behind my back. Rachael listened to my request, not asking for any specifics, for which I was grateful. Rachael added a twist to her response. She was happy to approve my leave with a small proviso; I was intrigued.

Rachael explained that from a trauma perspective, The Royal London was always keen to benchmark with other trauma centres, and to benchmark globally was very appealing. My visit to Melbourne, knowing that The Alfred Hospital was a major emergency and trauma centre, piqued Rachael's interest in whether I may be able to weave professional development into my leave by researching their processes for the betterment of care at The Royal London. I readily agreed to visit The Alfred and appreciated the opportunity to contribute to positive change. Rachael stated that she would liaise with senior management for further approval and specifics. Confirmation of her proposal came later that day, and it was agreed that my trip would be some work but mostly play. I was very fine with that.

My passport arrived a few days later. I am not sure what strings Dean pulled; I gave him my photograph, and he got me a passport, not quite as simplistic as that, but that was the gist. Packing day was chaotic. Eva and Sarah decided that I needed company and wine. Sarah deemed that I could access her wardrobe of classy attire. They both insisted that I parade different outfits around my bedroom to create piles of to take or not to take. As more wine was drunk, the more questionable the outfits I chose; we conceded I didn't quite suit some of Sarah's luxurious ensembles. Collapsing in giggles and snorts of laughter, I evicted my two beautiful friends from my bedroom. Packing was then soon completed, a little bit of this and a little bit of that. Melbourne was renowned for four seasons in one day, so I packed for every eventuality.

The night before my departure, Eva and Dean came by to wish me Bon Voyage, bearing gifts and the obligatory Indian takeaway. Eva gave me a book, not wrapped, of course: *A Flight to Romance* by John Fishwick. I rolled my eyes in exasperation. Romance was definitely not what I was flying to.

Sarah and Jack joined us. It was a quiet evening, subdued even. A few questions came my way about where I thought I would go and what I thought I would do whilst I was in Australia. Apart from a little Alfred research and beach sitting, I had not planned on anything. I was excited to see Jesse and to meet Bree, Jesse's dad, Tony, and brother Luke, and of course, Bear the Golden Retriever hound. Eva asked if I would go up to the Barrier Reef or to the Harbour Bridge in Sydney, or to the Gold Coast. I smiled at Eva's obvious efforts to investigate where I was going, but I had no idea. I was looking forward to getting my life into some sort of order; anything else would be a bonus.

Indian eaten, wine drunk, time for bed. I was tired; it had been a very busy few days. Good nights were said. Eva and Dean were coming with me to Heathrow Airport in the morning before Eva's late shift. I would see Sarah and Jack briefly in the morning before I left; they both had to be at work.

I snuggled under my duvet, my suitcase at the end of the bed, passport on top. I smiled at the book Eva had bought me, *A Flight to Romance*. No, thank you.

Heathrow Airport was its usual craziness. People everywhere, all shapes and sizes, colours and creeds, big and small, young and old. I was flying with Emirates Airlines, stopping at Dubai before landing at Melbourne's Tullamarine Airport. Eva and Dean were clucking around me like two mother hens, making sure that I had everything I needed. Dean wandered off and came back with a neck pillow, so Dean. They left me a little early as Eva had to be at the hospital for her late shift. Big hugs and kisses, Eva and I bravely fought to hold back tears. I watched them disappear as they got swallowed up by the hordes of travellers. I turned and walked through departures.

28
The Package

Eva

I left Kate at the airport; Dean dropped me home to get changed, ready for my late shift at St Barts. My plan for the next few weeks was to keep busy so I wouldn't miss my best friend too much. Dean readily agreed with this philosophy, as did Sarah. It would be easy, we convinced ourselves; we would be preoccupied with work. Sarah would see Jack, and of course, I would see Dean. So why did I feel a little gap in my heart where Kate usually sat?

I got to my late shift early. Dean had an outpatient clinic and many patients to see, so we travelled in together. I would while away the time in the tearoom; I usually bumped into someone I knew. I took out a book that Kate had lent me in her attempt to introduce me to the pastime of reading and flicked through a few pages.

I was interrupted as the tearoom door opened and in walked a petite registered nurse with red hair. The nurse introduced herself as Ellie, a friend of Miles. I realised I was sitting there staring with my mouth wide open. I quickly blinked and clamped my mouth shut. Ellie handed me a plain white tote bag; I looked inside. There was a package wrapped in brown paper with a yellow bow stuck on one corner. Written on the wrapping paper was simply, *To Kate*. Ellie turned quickly and left. As I watched her go, my phone pinged: *Just Boarding*.

29
The Escape

Kate

The flights were unadventurous, although if only the security and customs officers could smile, I would have felt less like a criminal. I was scanned and rescanned and even searched in a curtained cubicle away from the main security check-in at Dubai Airport. The parade of security personnel carrying firearms in Dubai did nothing to alleviate my feelings of unease. I was thankful to board the next flight to Melbourne. Thirteen hours and 25 minutes, and approximately 19 episodes of *Friends* later, I landed on Australian soil.

I was greeted by Jesse and Bree waving enormous Australian flags. Jesse looked mostly the same; his tan had darkened, and his blonde hair was a little more sun-kissed. He swept me up into a big hug; his whole being radiated happiness, a contentment that had been so obviously missing in London. I guessed the young lady who stood next to him was the reason for that. Bree was beautiful, inside and out, as I was soon to discover; she was warm and welcoming. We instantly connected over our mutual love for Jesse, hers as a lover, mine firmly reset as a friend. I became immensely fond of Bree, for no lesser reason than that she made Jesse so happy. Standing halfway across the world, in a foreign country, I felt an instant calm as first Jesse, then Bree held me close.

Stepping out into the Melbourne air was like stepping into a warm oven. I sighed as the warmth surrounded me. Blue skies, not a cloud to be seen, and a dazzling sun; Australia had well and truly rolled out the welcome mat. My heart missed a beat as, standing next to Jesse's car, were two very handsome figures: one with two legs, Luke I presumed, Jesse's brother, and one with four legs, Bear.

Although five years older than Jesse, Luke was very similar in looks; Luke slightly taller, maybe thicker in stature, but tanned and blonde like his younger brother. But it was Bear that stole my heart. He was adorable, also blonde, long-haired, and a face that would melt many hearts, male or female. He was a little unsure of me at first, sniffed a bit, and then went back to Luke. Jesse made swift introductions before we piled into the car: Jesse and Bree in the front, Luke, Bear, and me in the back, Bear nestled between us, his head now on my lap, friends.

We left the airport and headed to Luke's house in St Kilda. I sat mesmerised, looking out of the window. Melbourne's city skyline coming into view, I swallowed away tears as I realised I had done it, I had left the clutches of Neil and the emotional hold of James, to be me, just me, just for a moment. Luke reached out and squeezed my hand. I returned the squeeze and smiled.

Luke's house was a worker's cottage, which typified many of the homes in Melbourne, situated in a narrow street lined on either side by trees. Luke explained that these trees were London Plane trees, planted years ago as they were known to be hardy and therefore able to survive and thrive in the inner city. Jesse and Bree looked at Luke in wonderment. Luke smirked. Luke showed me around the house; he continued in his adopted pompous tone: the house itself is a mixture of modern whilst preserving the heritage character, boasting extensions to the original footprint which allowed masses of natural light and an outdoor area perfect for the traditional Australian barbecue. Tour completed, and an impromptu applause accepted, Luke showed me to my room, the third bedroom, small but beautifully furnished in pale blues and white. There were two bath towels on the corner of the doona, not a duvet as Luke pointed out with a grin, soap, and an extremely cute plush Koala. Luke showed me a tiny ensuite: a shower, a washbasin, and a toilet with a six-inch shelf for toiletries. Left alone to unpack, I glanced around at my haven for the next few weeks.

I quickly unpacked what I could not fit into the small wardrobe and drawers; I left in my case, which I slid under the bed. Luke and Jesse were adamant that there was no rush; they would put the barbecue on later that evening. I was given options of showering, napping or joining the others, whichever, whatever was fine. I chose showering and napping, but first I would send a few "I have arrived safely" messages.

The first message, of course, would be to Eva, but as I opened my phone, I saw a cryptic message from Eva asking me to call her. She reassured me it was not bad but could be baddish. I sighed and pressed her number.

It was early in the morning, some people would not even call it morning, but knowing Eva, she would be waiting for my call. "Can I tell you a story?" were Eva's opening words. No niceties, how was your flight, how was the food, or even just, how is Jesse and Bree? And so, I listened to the tale about Ellie and the parcel wrapped in brown paper with a yellow bow. Eva said she would put it in my room; we both assumed it was from James. She asked if I wanted her to open it, to which I replied a firm no. I had waited nearly two years for an answer as to why James had left me; I could wait a little while longer.

I sent messages to Mum and Dad, Ben, Daniel, and of course Sarah: *arrived safely, will be in touch soon.* Next was to have a shower.

I squeezed into the ensuite, navigated opening the shower door without being squashed into the side of the washbasin, and was soon standing under a jet of steaming hot water, bliss. And then, nap time. I located a T-shirt and a pair of pyjama shorts, lunged onto the bed, rolled onto my side, and fell into a deep sleep.

I awoke several hours later to a gentle tap on my door. I dragged myself from my slumber to open the door before I realised that I was braless, and my T-shirt left little to the imagination. I crossed my arms over what I sensed to be my protruding nipples. Luke responded by advising me that the barbecue was nearly ready and left me to wallow in my acute embarrassment. Good start, Kate.

My first social engagement in Australia, I looked out my window. I could see Jesse, Bree, and Luke, and I presumed Tony, their dad, and another lady. Bear was sitting next to Luke. What to wear? Backyard barbecue, I surmised, required laid-back and casual. I fished out a pastel pink smock top speckled with tiny white daisies, knee-length white denim shorts, and silver-grey flip-flops, or thongs as the natives would say. My hair did its thing, having left my hair straightener at home. I embraced my obscure kinks and twists. No make-up, just a touch of my pink lipstick. The sun dipped on the horizon, the warmth replaced by a slight chill. I grabbed my pink wrap, or pashmina, as Sarah had corrected me, just in case.

Luke was the first to greet me. "Nice top," he winked. I did not grace him with a response. Jesse sensed an awkwardness; he came over and introduced his dad, Tony, and Tony's friend Allison. I noted a little hesitation on the word friend; they both greeted me warmly and welcomed me to Australia. Tony was very much like Jesse; I was immediately drawn to his easy-going nature. He enjoyed the opportunity to chat to an English nurse, although I had to explain some Yorkshire colloquialisms, much to his amusement. Allison seemed a little less relaxed. I was not sure what their relationship was, but I did not feel it was appropriate to ask.

It was a lovely evening. The food typified the traditional Australian barbecue: steaks, sausages, salads, of course, tomato sauce, not ketchup, onions, and bread rolls. I was used to my beagles begging for food, whereas Bear was impeccably behaved, alternating between lying next to Luke or Jesse; if neither were available, I would do. The conversation was inquisitive rather than probing, and my Yorkshire accent was a talking point, Jesse saying he had not really noticed it over the years we had lived together, to which everyone rolled their eyes in disbelief.

There was so much to talk about: mine and Jesse's new nursing roles, Bree's work as a veterinary nurse, and Luke's wine bar, The Grape, which he owned with his friend Dom. We added a night out at The Grape to my Australia agenda. Tony and Allison left soon after the steaks and sausages had been devoured. I am not sure if it was the Australian air or the accompanying beer, not normally my drink of choice, but the food tasted amazing.

Jesse, Bree, Luke, and I chatted for a little while. Despite my nap, I struggled to stay awake. I said goodnight and thanked them for everything. Luke asked if he could escort me to my room; I assured him that I was fine to find my own way. Conscious of his eyes following me, I walked purposefully, hoping I was going in the right direction.

T-shirt and pyjama pants back on, this time I added a bra just in case, I once again snuggled beneath the doona. I was just able to savour a moment of pure contentment before drifting off to sleep. I was awoken in the early hours by a scraping on my bedroom door. I grabbed my dressing gown, just to be sure. I opened the door to be greeted by my blonde, long-haired, four-legged friend. Bear bounded past me and jumped onto the bed. I was not sure if he was allowed to sleep on beds, but at that hour, I was not about to find out. Bear took up residence at my feet. With a snort, Bear, and a yawn, me, we both fell asleep.

The next morning, I awoke to a furry face and big brown eyes looking longingly at me. It took a few seconds to realise where I was; the sun streaming through the window and the laughter of kookaburras reaffirmed Australia as my location. The house seemed to be asleep, so I indulged Bear with pats, which he shamelessly received, rolling onto his back for belly rubs, legs unceremoniously up in the air. Luke called through the bedroom door, looking for Bear. I opened it to reveal Bear, lying on my bed, on his back, legs in the air. Bear spent many nights on my bed during my stay; it seemed no matter where he was when I went to bed, he would follow.

A couple of days after my arrival, I began to plan my visit to The Alfred. I had reached out to the Executive Director, who welcomed my proposal to visit, having been briefed by the executive team at The Royal London. I was given the names of personnel to meet with to discuss the various aspects of their emergency and trauma centre and the follow-on care to the surgical and trauma ward. Jesse, of course, was able to help too. I was excited to observe how a hospital thousands of miles away from The Royal London worked.

I took my laptop and was allocated a desk space in the emergency department. It was not dissimilar to The Royal London. Sitting there, I felt like I was watching a film clip in fast motion. For 8 a.m., it was super busy. Doctors, nurses, and a myriad of other healthcare workers, together with patients and trolleys, on the backdrop of sirens, pagers, and telephones, culminated into organised chaos with the emergency flow coordinator directing traffic. Everyone had a purpose, a role to play in the care of the patient. I looked at the computer systems, dashboards, data, and databases, making notes, commenting on my perceived negatives and positives. It was fascinating being there as a voyeur, not as a worker, frustrating too; I had to stop myself from jumping up so many times to assist.

I briefly visited the surgical and trauma care ward. The Charge Nurse, or Nurse Unit Manager as they were called, showed me around and introduced me to her nursing team. I was able to talk to some nurses at handover time. Everywhere I went, the friendliness and welcoming were astounding; no matter how busy the staff were, everyone stopped to say hello and were proud to welcome me to The Alfred and to Melbourne. The hospital had an amazing vibe; a culture of togetherness screamed out. I loved it.

At the end of the day, I had so many ideas, so much information, and I felt like I had made a hundred friends. I had a five-minute catch-up with the Executive Director. I felt very humbled at having been given the opportunity to see a part of this hospital at work. I thanked him; he assured me that it was their absolute pleasure, and I was welcome back anytime, a sentiment that was obviously sincerely meant.

Beaming at the camaraderie that I felt, I met Jesse after his shift. Topping off my exhilarating day was a tram ride home. Jesse laughed at my excitement about sitting on a Melbourne tram. I was bewildered at how cars and trams could share the same road without colliding. Jesse explained that the tram lines were on a grid-like system and were renowned for being the world's largest operational tram network. I smiled at Jesse, mimicking Luke in providing some Melbourne trivia.

Back at the house, Luke was at the wine bar, Bree was finishing her day at the veterinary practice, so it was just Jesse and me, and Bear, of course. Jesse suggested beers in the backyard, the Australian term for the garden. It was a beautiful afternoon; so far, I had only experienced one Melbourne season of blue skies and warm sunshine. We chatted broadly about what I wanted to do and see whilst I was in Melbourne. Jesse was keen to play the host; I honestly didn't feel like I was a tourist. Especially after I visited The Alfred, I had an uncanny feeling that I belonged. I felt an affinity to the lifestyle; the culture resonated with what I was desperate to adopt, to live just a little carefree.

We agreed not to plan, but The Grape was a must. I was keen to visit the wine bar situated in one of the city's many famous laneways, and of course, the beach. The St Kilda beach stretched along the foreshore of the St

Kilda suburb, within walking distance of Luke's house, which would be my tentative adventure tomorrow. Before we abandoned Jesse's suggestions, he did mention the wineries; of course, I was very happy to be persuaded to sample the wines of the Yarra Valley.

The evening was a quiet affair. Jesse threw some kebabs on the barbecue. Luke would be home very late. I was happy to spend some quiet time in my room, reviewing my notes from my Alfred visit, so I said goodnight to Jesse and Bree and retired to bed with my faithful shadow following closely behind.

I awoke to the second Melbourne season: pouring rain and very chilly. Bear and I looked out the window, not a beach day, we surmised. I pottered to the kitchen; Jesse was on another early shift, and Bree had already left for the clinic. I presumed Luke was still in bed, as he had worked at the wine bar until the early hours of the morning. I made some toast and coffee for my breakfast and fed Bear biscuits, for his, before having a quick shower. Dress today was jeans and a sweatshirt; the temperature must have plummeted by about ten degrees or so.

A little later, Bear looked at me expectantly. The rain had eased, so I grabbed his leash and a black puffer jacket that was hanging in the hallway, and we headed out for a walk towards the beach.

Many Melbournians were out and about with various breeds of dogs, all wearing a uniform of black and grey Lycra leisure wear and black puffer jackets, accessorised by a takeaway coffee and a mobile phone. I found it amusing to see so many people all looking the same, but I did concede that these clothing essentials were worn with style and class.

Beach visit complete, we headed back. I messaged Luke to see if he wanted a coffee. We had exchanged phone numbers on my first day, just in case I got lost when I was out and about. Jesse obviously remembered my lack of sense of direction. Luke did not answer, but I grabbed one. I marvelled at the taste of Melbourne's coffee, almost worth emigrating for, so good.

Later that morning, I was sitting at the kitchen bench writing up my visit to The Alfred when Luke emerged, looking very sleepy and a little dishevelled. "Coffee?" he asked. "Why not?" Bear was asleep on his bed, so we headed out. The sun had come out. I deliberated over the need for the puffer jacket but decided I wanted to join the in-crowd, so although a little too warm, puffer jacket it was.

Instead of coffee, Luke suggested we take a tram into the city to show me his wine bar; I happily agreed. Hidden in a laneway, The Grape's décor was basic but classy. The minimalistic furnishings were effective. Walking in, a long rustic timber bar was to the left, surrounded by wine-barrel-themed furniture, including heavy wooden chairs and tables. The wooden theme continued to the wooden wine racks lining the walls, the height of which required a ladder to obtain the wine of choice. The wine bar was closed and opened daily at 12 noon, so Luke and I enjoyed the quiet.

Luke took my hand and led me to the back of the room. Stepping through an archway, we entered a stone courtyard with a brick open fireplace, wood and kindling in place. Seating was benches lining the walls; it was a small area that radiated intimacy. Candles on the tables and fairy lights provided soft lighting. Luke invited me to sit, left, and returned with a glass of sauvignon blanc. Although it was only 11:30, I happily accepted the glass and sipped the most delectable crisp white wine. Luke joined me with a full-bodied red; his description, it did look very decadent in a large, bowled wine glass.

Luke was easy to talk to; he explained his transition from chef to owning a wine bar, going on to describe how he had met Dom, by chance, at a food trade show for hospitality professionals. Dom was a few years younger than Luke's mid-thirties; Luke was drawn to Dom's charisma and energy, and they quickly became friends. The joining of Luke's culinary expertise with Dom's knowledge of wines led to the birth of The Grape. From a business acumen perspective, Tony, Luke's dad, lent a hand. It was about to celebrate its second birthday and had quickly become established among Melbourne's socialites.

Luke then twisted the conversation to me. He had heard about my nursing career and was keen to hear about the rest of me. I immediately swivelled the conversation back to him and his personal life on the premise of,

"You tell me, and I will tell you." Interestingly, Luke was a little cagey; he'd had a few lady acquaintances over the years, was engaged to be married once, and was currently on a break. I concurred that I was on a break, too.

The awkward silence was interrupted by the arrival of Dom. Luke had failed to mention that Dom was extremely good-looking, with his Italian heritage featuring prominently in his looks: olive-skinned, darkened even more by the Australian sun, and a mop of thick, dark brown hair.

Dom introduced himself, his Italian accent, and the taking of my hand to place a gentle kiss was charm personified. His manner reminded me a little of Miles and his ability to woo the ladies. It was a pleasure to meet Dom on so many levels, but mostly because he negated a potentially uncomfortable conversation between Luke and me. Dom entertained us with a quick summation of his life: Italy, family, and vineyards. We abandoned any further conversation as we heard voices in the main bar area.

Luke suggested we head home, grabbing some sandwiches from the bakery for lunch. He was working at The Grape later that evening, so he was keen for a little nap. Back on the tram, Luke was a little quiet, pensive. I tried to lighten the mood with tales of Sarah, Eva, and my party tomfoolery, with a little success, but his mood had certainly darkened since Dom had arrived at the wine bar. I asked if he was okay; he shrugged and said he was tired. I did not pursue the subject, and we sat in silence for the rest of the journey home.

Later that evening, when Jesse and Bree were home, I relayed Luke's change in demeanour to Jesse. Jesse explained that Luke had been badly hurt by the ending of a serious relationship; he respected Luke's privacy and did not disclose any details. The consequence was that Luke would put on a bravado of confidence, flirting even, but this act was very tenuous, and the fragility was clear, as it would disappear quickly when the situation changed. I looked confused, so Jesse went on. "When it's just you and Luke, he has a captive audience, but when Dom arrives, the dynamics change, and so does Luke's performance." Wow, I took a moment to process what Jesse had said. I liked Luke. I would be careful. I wanted to be his friend, but I did not want to give the impression that I wanted anything more. I had crossed that line with Jesse without being detrimental to our relationship, but I would not cross that line with Luke. I was grateful for Jesse's explanation.

Dinner was a simple affair: Jesse and Bree both working the next morning, and then they had the weekend off. Homemade pizza, with bought pizza bases, as Dean was not available for his pizza dough prowess and the other chef option was busy feeding Melbourne's nightlife. So, bought pizza base it was, topped with tomato paste, ham, pineapple, and a few grated cheeses sprinkled on top, washed down with a beer or two. Actually, pretty good.

Later, back in my room, I caught up on the motherland communique. I messaged little details of my Alfred visit, the beach trip in the rain, tram escapades, and The Grape, to be revisited.

Eva messaged back, focusing on Luke and Dom, her enquiring mind demanding more specifics. She was particularly drawn to the Italian; I didn't have much to tell but promised more after our wine bar visit the next night. Eva checked that I didn't want her to open the parcel; again, I said a firm no. She did mention that she had seen Ellie a couple of times at St. Barts but had not spoken to her. Sarah messaged me that she and Jack were on a small pause in their relationship and would fill me in when I got home. I wondered if Eva knew; I guessed not.

Mum and Dad had checked in. I felt lucky that my parents respected that I had my own life and, if I was okay, that was all they needed to know. Dad accepted that James was no longer in my life, for now. I asked about Ben and Daniel, and any updates on the wedding plans. Mum said all was fine and that Lisa's parents were fussing over things. I sensed a wariness in Mum's voice and smiled. "There's a big difference between the mother of the bride and the mother of the groom," she begrudgingly pointed out. I humoured her with an agreement, but really, I had no idea. We said goodbye, and I promised to message again soon. I settled down to sleep, Bear at my side.

I awoke the next morning to brilliant sunshine and a very blue sky; no Lycra, puffer jacket ensemble today. Bear and I agreed it would be a beach day, or morning at least. I found some leftover pizza in the fridge and fed Bear his usual biscuits. I tried to be very quiet as I did not want to risk waking Luke. Luke's mood had hovered over me last night, and I woke several times trying to resolve whatever was bothering him. I did not want to intrude on his past; I was only too aware of what that felt like, but I would like to get back to the ease we had when I had first arrived. I decided I would just be me: friendly, sometimes quirky, sometimes together, sometimes not. Put simply, I was nice; that should suffice.

I left Luke a note: *Bear and I have gone in search of sun #beach, you are welcome to join.* With that, I packed water and a couple of snacks, a towel, sunscreen, a hat, a book, and, decked out in floral togs, Australian for swimsuit, under shorts and a T-shirt, both white, and my thongs, we headed out. It was a spectacular day. It was Friday, which seemed to be an approved extension to the weekend, as there were people everywhere. Bear and I located ourselves at the back of the beach against the wall, gaining natural shade from the massive palm trees that lined the boardwalk. I noticed that no one was showing skin but remained covered in shorts, T-shirts, dresses, and the like. I decided to conform and do the same. Towel laid out, a water bowl very thoughtfully located near a drinking fountain for Bear; I sat back to enjoy the sand between my toes and the view of glistening blue water. Absolute bliss.

It wasn't long before I dozed off, only to be awoken by Luke's voice. "Mind if I join?" he asked. "Please do," I replied. Bear was very excited to see Luke, tail wagging frantically, causing a welcome breeze. I was pleased to see Luke looking relaxed in pale khaki shorts and a pale blue T-shirt. When I looked closer, I saw he had a paper bag and two takeaway coffees hiding behind his back. I smiled, my hero had arrived, and we drank and ate, laughing as Bear tried to join in on our impromptu picnic.

We chattered about nothing in particular. Occasionally, I would see a faraway look in Luke's eyes, but I deflected the conversation to some silly anecdote of my life, and he would be back with me. We occasionally touched, a finger or a bare foot in the sand, but it seemed natural, a touch that any friend would do. We left around lunchtime; Bear was getting restless, and I was conscious of my face turning pink.

I wanted to do the final typing up of my Alfred report, so I quickly showered and settled at the kitchen bench. Bear, exhausted from the morning's excursion, headed to his bed. Luke got ready for his shift at The Grape. We were all joining him later; he was keen to show off the wine bar in its active glory; I was keen to. He left a little later and gave me a light kiss on the cheek. "Thank you," he said. I returned the kiss equally as light and smiled.

30

The Grape

Kate

The night was huge, so much fun. It was Friday, and Melbourne was partying. The Grape was overflowing; Luke and Dom looked stylish behind the wooden bar, both wearing black jeans and white button-up shirts, accentuating their tans. Bree and I had decided on dresses: mine a deep wine colour, Bree's a neutral bone colour, both in a very soft linen, fitted at the waist with short billowing skirts. Mine an off-the-shoulder look, Bree a low scooped neckline. I borrowed Bree's hair straightener; no kinks or twists tonight. Bree's blonde bob sat beautifully above her shoulders. Both accessorised with gold jewellery and tan footwear, mine, the knee-length boots that Eva had bought me, and Bree, tan sandals, probably a little more appropriate. Looking around, we were in sync with the rest of the crowd, even my tan knee-highs. Jesse, being Jesse, went a little rogue, wearing shorts and a T-shirt, totally oblivious to Bree's glares. The wine flowed endlessly, so many choices, so many recommendations. The food was delicious: we sampled focaccia and extra virgin olive oils, olives, small plates of deep-fried halloumi, chicken skewers, and, of course, shoestring fries with aioli on the side. Adding a French twist, small charcuterie boards were available to share, groaning with meats and cheeses.

I had been to nightclubs and pubs in England, but this was different: energetic but relaxed and welcoming; unpretentious. It oozed friendliness. Lots of small gatherings, sharing tables, bumping elbows, struggling to be heard, the crescendo of noise punctuated by exclamations of amazement on tasting the food and wine. The Grape exemplified class; the diverse wine selection complemented the food perfectly, with the encouragement to explore, to sip. The food was described on the menu as elevated, and it was spectacular, with unique flavours that were impossible to define, aesthetically presented on glazed stoneware. I asked Jesse what the music was. "Smooth tunes," he replied. Seemed appropriate.

I was bursting to compliment Luke and Dom. I ducked and weaved to the bar, apologised for colliding into numerous bodies and treading on a few toes as I went. I managed to squeeze between two suave-looking twenty-something males and leaned over to Luke, who was meticulously pouring what looked to be a very nice red. Luke paused and smiled. I told him how incredible the bar was and that he and Dom should be very proud. Dom leaned over, obviously hearing my compliment. I tried to think of more adjectives to describe how impressed I was; I settled with a weak, "well done," which sounded a little patronising even to my ears. But the boys smirked, and Dom handed me a glass of red wine. I was not normally a red wine drinker, but I took a sip, and another. I had done a little wine research before tonight, so I attempted to provide the boys with my evaluation of the red: I could only describe it as velvety, silky, and full-bodied. Dom laughed and absolutely agreed; Luke winked, and I grinned as I snaked my way back to Jesse and Bree.

As the night threatened to merge into day, Jesse, Bree, and I decided to head home. We offered to assist with the closing up, but Luke and Dom were adamant that they had it covered. With many thankyous said, we went on our way. Once back at the house, I had a super-quick shower, donned some matching silk pyjamas, thank you, Sarah, thinking that the night called for a continuation of class, and sank into bed, of course, not for long, as Bear scraped at my door.

The weekend started very slowly; no one stirred after The Grape outing until very late morning. I had risen a little earlier to feed and let Bear out. I crept back to bed with a bottle of water and my laptop. I slept a little more, then opened my emails and rechecked my Alfred write-up. I was surprised to see an email from the Executive Director of The Alfred. He again expressed how lovely it was to meet me, but also wondered if I could present my observations, positive and negative, comparisons, and similarities of The Alfred and The Royal London, at the hospital board meeting on Wednesday. I conceded that a proviso of my leave was the work aspect, so of course I agreed. Secretly, I was keen to enjoy the hospitality of The Alfred again. I needed to fine-tune my write-up; I was keen to impress. Thinking back to my student nurse days and Jesse, I grinned. I knew just where to get some help.

The rest of the weekend and into the following week were consumed by my presentation. Jesse was happy to assist. We gathered Luke, Dom, and Bree together on Tuesday night. Luke and Dom catered. The Grape did not open on a Tuesday and provided a couple of bottles of wine, not to be opened until I had given my presentation, much to everyone's annoyance. Jesse set up a screen, which they occasionally used for movie nights or significant sporting events, the rugby league grand final and the like. Luke and Dom did a drum roll on their knees, which caused me to giggle and delayed the start of my presentation and the wine, so the drum roll was quickly aborted. I cleared my throat; the theatrics were noted and began. Cheers and applause erupted as I concluded with the "any questions" slide. Luke and Dom praised the graphics, and Jesse and Bree were impressed with the format. I had posed scenarios in my evaluation, which I think had worked well, and gave the audience stories, which afforded a strong link to reality and a better understanding. We celebrated with wine, of course.

The presentation was very well received; the Executive Director and the members of the board applauded enthusiastically. I was asked many questions, specifically around different aspects of care and processes at The Royal London, which I answered to the best of my ability. They seemed satisfied with my responses, and I was invited to an informal lunch, just your usual hospital catering, sandwiches and small cakes. I smiled at the comparison to The Grape but noted it was very similar to The Royal London.

I had arranged to meet Luke, Dom, Jesse, and Bree at the wine bar later, so I quickly went back to the house to change into something more casual and take Bear for a walk.

Midweek at The Grape was a little quieter. We decided to take over the courtyard. I gave a brief synopsis of my presentation and thanked Jesse for his help. We had just planned on having a couple of wines. Tony had invited us for dinner, so a little later we left Luke and Dom to serve the Melbourne public, whilst Jesse, Bree, and I caught a tram, much to my delight, to Tony's and, it soon became transparent, Allison's. It was a relaxed evening. We feasted on lasagne, my favourite, garlic bread and salads. Warmed bread rolls with lashings of butter and jacket potatoes, also with lashings of butter and sour cream, added a little decadence.

The conversation focused on my last two Australian adventures: to a winery and to the Melbourne Cricket Ground, famously known as the MCG. I had just over a week remaining. I also wanted to revisit the beach and take some time to contemplate my life in London, which I had thus far avoided.

The winery visit was planned for the following Tuesday so that Luke would be free to join us. We were going to a winery in the Yarra Valley. The MCG visit was on my last weekend to an Australian Football League game. I instantly thought of Neil's reference to his newfound interest; I instantly banished the thought from my mind. And in between those two adventures, I was to sort out my life.

31
The Winery

Kate

Luke and I sat in the back of the car on the way to the Yarra Valley. This time there was no Bear in between us. As Luke reached for my hand, I started to pull away. "Please," he said. "Just holding hands, just for the day." "Ok," I replied, "just for today." It was kind of fun to play girlfriend and boyfriend. We snuck in a little kiss and flirtatious innuendoes. We agreed this was a day of fun and would end as we arrived home. That said, it was nice, feeling the warmth of an embrace and the tender touch of a hand. Jesse and Bree pretended not to notice, as Luke and I smothered our laughter; we tried to be discreet.

I had conducted a little research on the Yarra Valley and was eager to sample their famous chardonnay and pinot noir range, and to deviate from my usual sauvignon blanc. The food in all the reviews was described as sensational, with many restaurants overlooking the vineyards providing a sublime experience of one of Australia's premier wine regions. The weather could only be described as dismal, cloudy, rainy, and very chilly, but somehow added to the atmosphere. As the rain lashed against the windows of the bar and restaurant, a fire raged, enticing visitors to sit and sip, which we duly did.

Luke had organised a wine tasting as a prelude to lunch. We were escorted into a dark cellar lit by dozens of tiny tea lights. Finn, who was our designated guide for today, provided a brief introduction to the winery and vineyard, including the winery's history and that of the region's wines. Then the real fun began, as Finn guided us through the wine tasting process, which involved swirling, sniffing, sipping, and spitting. The latter was optional; you could swallow, which, of course, Bree, Luke, and I did. Jesse magnanimously volunteered to be the designated driver for the day, so he graced us with the use of the spittoon. The old oak table had places set for eight, with six wine glasses at each setting, a beautiful fine linen cream napkin placed for "dribbles," and a little plate of vintage cheeses, breads, and wafers. Surrounded by walls of bottles, we explored various wines, which, even to our naïve palates, tasted elegant and refined, or, as Bree commented, very drinkable.

We left the cellar for lunch. The rustic charm flowed through into the restaurant, and seated by the open fire, we sat back to admire the view of the rolling hills of vineyards with a mountainous backdrop, stunning. The lunch was delicious. We sampled the local fresh produce accompanied by more wine, which was carefully matched to our food of choice. We decided not to go on a winery tour; it was pouring rain, and a howling wind blew relentlessly, bending the vines. It was far more conducive to remain fireside with a glass of wine or two. As the afternoon became early evening, the clouds got darker, the rain intensified, and although the fire beckoned us to stay, Jesse, Mr Sensible, Mr Sober, and Sensible, decided it was time to go home. We reluctantly agreed. Full of delicious food and fine wine, we battled the elements to the car, not an umbrella or jacket between us. We sat like soggy messes, ready to be driven home. Luke once again reached for my hand. Head on his shoulder, I napped, encased in a feeling of intoxicated warmth.

Once home, we scrambled out of Jesse's car. The rain had eased. We teetered carefully into the house, full of food and very full of alcohol. I thanked everyone profusely for a lovely day. Swaying just a little, I zigzagged along the hallway for a shower and bed.

I quickly undressed and stepped into the shower; my eyes closed as the water cascaded over me. I opened my eyes as I reached for the soap and saw Luke standing there, naked. My eyes travelled down his nakedness over his tanned, toned body. I stood in a haze of alcohol, desire overcoming rationality, whilst, without a word, Luke stepped under the water, pressing against me, against the wall of the shower. He lifted me, wrapped my legs around his waist. His erection slipped inside. My legs tightened around his hips as I melted into an indescribable euphoria. Slowly, his rhythm increased, thrusting repeatedly, further and further. I could feel his erection pulsating until we came together in a surge of lust. There was no foreplay; this was sex, pure and simple. He lifted me down. The hot water continued to pelt out from the shower jets, washing away the moment. He kissed my forehead, stepped out of the shower, grabbed a towel, and left.

I lay in bed a few moments later, trying to comprehend what had just happened. My wine-induced fog was slowly clearing; that had been the conclusion to our day of pretence, and the dangerous roleplay of girlfriend and boyfriend. That finale was way off script. 'Luke sex' could never happen again. I pulled the doona up under my chin, wrapped my arms around my knees drawn up to my chest, and sighed. It was time to sort my life out.

I had less than a week left in Australia. I planned to immerse myself in the Australian culture for those last few days, to enjoy the company of Jesse, Bree, and Luke, yes, Luke, platonically. My last adventure was to the MCG, then home, but most importantly, my last visit to the beach: just me and Bear, no one to interrupt my thoughts, no one to question my reasoning or argue with my decisions, just 65 pounds of blonde fur that would listen and say nothing.

There was a tap on my door. Luke opened it just enough for Bear to squeeze through and leap onto my bed. "Goodnight," he whispered. "Goodnight," I replied as the door closed gently behind him.

32
The Football

Kate

The MCG on a Saturday afternoon was a phenomenon that I would never forget. AFL, as I soon discovered, was like a religion to the Melbourne fans. We were watching Collingwood versus Essendon. To my left, there was a sea of black and white, and to my right, black and red flags waved ceremoniously in the afternoon sun. The crowd was massive, passionate, and loud. Chanting, cheering, and enticing, an atmosphere of intense emotion. This afternoon, it was just Jesse and me. I was flying home in two days, and Jesse wanted me all to himself for the last time, until the next time.

We were meeting Bree, Tony, and Allison at The Grape later. Luke and Dom would be behind the bar, but for the moment, it was just the two of us.

The game was a little confusing. I stopped asking Jesse questions, much to Jesse's relief, and settled on enjoying the atmosphere. Jesse promised me that the next time I visited, he would take me to a Melbourne Storm game, as he knew my love of rugby league. I assured him that sitting in this famous ground with 105 thousand fans and one of my two best friends was absolutely fine.

I think Collingwood won. Everyone was celebrating, so it was a little difficult to ascertain who the winners were.

The scoreboard was obscured by mascots, flags, and signs of various descriptions. As we started to leave the stadium, Jesse confirmed that Collingwood had won, which was apparently not a popular outcome. It took forever to get a tram, one last ride, to The Grape. There were people everywhere, all desperate to get to the nearest location selling alcohol to celebrate a win or commiserate a loss.

Seated on the tram, I took the opportunity to thank Jesse for the last four weeks. He asked if I was any clearer as to what or who I wanted and what I was going to do. I admitted that my feelings for James, although for the most part were hidden in the back of my mind, had not weakened, changed, or gone, that I did know for sure. What I didn't know was the future of us. Jesse and I both sighed. "So?" he questioned. "So?" I responded. "No idea," he suggested. My exasperation was obvious as I agreed, "No idea."

The Grape was overflowing onto the footpath. As we approached, we saw ad hoc boxes and upturned wine crates masquerading as tables and seating, invading the small pavement space of the laneway. Inside, despite the masses, the relaxed, inviting vibe prevailed. Luke and Dom were the essence of calm, shirt sleeves rolled up behind the bar with a helping hand from their only employee, a casual named Bonnie, an eighteen-something university student; they appeared in complete control.

No one was in a hurry; all were happy to patiently wait a little longer to experience good food and wine. We bumped our way through the archway to find Bree, Tony, and Allison, a little squashed on the seating lining the brick wall, in very close contact with single strangers and obscure couples, all accepting the brief touch of others.

Bree, Tony, and Allison were keen to hear about the football. Jesse obliged with an animated description of the scoring of goals and behinds. I remained a little confused, so I stayed mostly quiet. Jesse explained that I was a Leeds Rhino supporter, to which Tony responded with a long list of the Melbourne Storm's accomplishments over the years. I promised to take him to the hallowed turf of Headingley should he ever visit England. Allison was a little reserved, but I liked her. Tony and Allison had met a couple of years after Lisa's passing. She worked at a law firm; Tony sought some advice related to his various business adventures, and Allison had been allocated to assist. Although I did like Allison, I did not feel comfortable discussing my relationship woes. At the previous dinner, we had chattered about England, London, and nursing; at The Grape, the topics continued the same.

A little later, I accompanied Bree to the bar; we linked arms as we wrestled through the crowd. I had enjoyed our time together, and I wanted a little private moment to say a sincere thank you. Bree replied that she had enjoyed my company during the past weeks; it had been lovely to have a new shopping partner, another lady friend. Bree was easygoing. We discovered we had a lot in common: a love of shopping, fashion, which Bree modelled and I envisaged, and a love of caring for others; Bree through caring for animals, me for caring more for the humankind. Bree would listen when I wanted to talk. She offered advice when I asked for it, but remained silent if I didn't. I would miss her.

The boys were kept busy behind the bar all night, being the epitome of perfect hosts. We chatted fleetingly as they poured me a wine, just small talk, before they were called away in the line of duty. At the end of the night, I shared an embrace with Dom. I had become fond of my new Italian friend.

Fond embraces were also shared with Tony and Allison, with a promise that I would visit again. Jesse, Bree, and I left around midnight, one more full day in Australia, then home.

And so, to the last day before I returned to London, I had received many texts from Eva and Sarah, excited for my homecoming. I sensed a party brewing; I hoped not. Sarah was back with Jack; apparently, they could not live without each other. I quietly wondered who couldn't live without whom, but I was pleased; they were good together. Eva was still madly in love with Dean, of course, came her reply when I jokingly asked. It had only been four weeks, I smiled to myself. Eva and Dean would meet me at the airport. I was to message Mum and Dad, and Ben, and Daniel when I landed. Again, I smiled.

But first, I had a date with my furry friend: beach day, Bear Day. Melbourne turned the weather on, yet again. Bear and I enjoyed a warm and sultry day, maybe a little too warm as Bear panted along, then flopped down in the shade of a palm tree, his head partially submerged in the water bowl, his tail thumping on the ground, happy to be out of the direct sunlight. We were surrounded by umbrellas and sun seekers determined to take advantage of a cloudless, clear blue sky and dazzling sunshine. Occasionally, a little breeze would pop up to bring a little reprieve from the unrelenting heat. I shuffled closer to Bear, both sharing an enormous beach towel that I had found in Luke's laundry cupboard. Sunscreen applied, and Bear snoring gently, his head now out of the water bowl and resting on my legs. Hat on, T-shirt off, in a brazen show of bravery, tog top firmly in place, I stared ahead.

I reflected on the past four weeks, on new friendships and the rekindling of the old. Of the feeling of belonging from that very first day. Being welcomed by Jesse, Bree, Luke, maybe a little too much, I grinned at that thought, and Dom, Tony, Allison, and the staff of The Alfred. I felt privileged to have experienced the Australian hospitality of those who were now my friends.

But I came to Australia to sort my life out, to pause, to reflect on the past, and look forward to the future. To determine if that future would include James. I watched the beachgoers: strangers, singles, acquaintances, friends, couples. Where would James and I fit in? I realised I didn't know, and for the first time in nearly two years, I was okay with that.

Bear was becoming restless; time to go. I took one last long look at the golden sand and the gentle waves, collected the towel and sunscreen, T-shirt back in place, I untied Bear, and headed home.

The house was quiet. I had the afternoon to myself to pack. I wandered down the shops and grabbed some flowers for Bree and a bottle of something special for the boys.

Boarding the flight to London Heathrow, I felt melancholic, sad. The previous evening, Tony and Allison had joined Jesse, Bree, Luke, and me for an impromptu barbecue. The usual Australian fare, except this time a few teardrops fell into the beers as the evening ended and we said goodbye. My flight was early the next morning, up with the sparrows, as Tony had commented.

Bear sensed it was my last night; he had put himself to bed before me and waited patiently for his friends' pats for the last time. The next morning, Jesse drove me to the airport and, despite his vehement protests, dropped me off at departures. We hugged so tight, our tears mingling with each other's. Together we said, "I love you," before I disappeared into Terminal Two, homeward bound.

33
The Transplant

James

All too soon, it was time to leave the gathering in the park, to say goodbye to family and friends, but not before Miles, my spokesman for the day, had informed Mum and Dad, Alex, Dot, Martin, and Ellie that the next few weeks and months would be critical. The stranger, Mr 18-year-old German man, had thrown me a lifeline. Miles went on to explain that I was about to enter the conditioning phase in preparation for the bone marrow transplant. Despite awkward shuffling of feet and mutterings, Miles continued. This would mean high doses of chemotherapy to continue to kill any potentially emerging cancer cells, and to suppress my immune system to prepare my bone marrow to welcome new stem cells. Everyone stood aghast, not even pretending to understand what Miles had just said. I smiled. Put simply, I would go through more of the same, only potentially worse, with once again debilitating side effects. But this was a chance to fight this fucked-up leukaemia journey and to get to live a life, my life.

No one questioned what Miles and I had said. These people would be there for me regardless of knowing the daunting specifics of what this next stage was. It was time to leave. I went home and packed: same sweats and tees, different books, and I was ready.

Miles and I arrived at Ward 5C the next morning with the façade of going into battle, the ammunition being the resolve to win this fight. I was a different man from the man I was several months ago, that first night in a hospital bed, curled up into a ball, sobbing, shocked, confused, and scared.

The day I arrived for the conditioning phase, I was informed, thanks to the clever doctors and my good friend Miles. I knew this was going to be tough; I knew the rigmarole of drug lines, the medications, this time, the anti-rejection drugs, the anti-graft-versus-host drugs to stop the transplanted cells attacking my cells, anti-fungal drugs, and anti-liver-damage something-or-other drugs, and so on. I knew the inhumane side effects of nausea, vomiting, headaches, and fatigue, although I was still sporting the bowling ball look, so hair loss would be one less trauma. Knowing did not make it easier, but the glimpse of survival drove the fight to stay alive.

I was shown to my room, my home once again, for however long it would take. I bid farewell to Miles; we had decided that I would cope with the intensity of the next few days alone. Miles reluctantly agreed. We would message each other, and he would be the conduit, once again, between my family and friends, but this time, this round, I was doing solo.

A new nurse arrived at my door and breezed in. No knock, just entered. I was soon to liken her to Nurse Mildred Ratched, the cold-hearted, passive-aggressive nurse in *One Flew Over the Cuckoo's Nest*. Maybe that was a little harsh; however, her tolerance, as I was soon to find out, for self-pity and self-centred sorrow was nil. Nurse Ratched, I did not know her real name, as she did not feel the need to wear a name badge, would interact rather than care. I was not allowed to be miserable or self-indulgent in sorriness. Her manner was officious and direct. We soon developed an understanding: I would comply with treatment without uttering a moan or groan, and Mildred would deliver my infusions and medications with precision and competence. No fuss, no sympathy, no emotion. I likened Nurse Mildred Ratched's bedside manner to Dr Wilson's no-bullshit philosophy.

Ellie also visited my room. Ellie did knock and wait for a reply before entering. I smiled to myself as I recognised Ellie's very different temperament. Ellie had asked not to care for me as part of her patient allocation. We had developed a close friendship during the past months. Ellie felt an awkwardness and thought it would be improper to nurse a friend. Ellie's charge nurse was happy to comply with this request; Ellie was mindful not to abuse this understanding and visited only very occasionally.

Dr Wilson visited me on my first day back at the Clatterbridge Cancer Centre. He provided a brief itinerary of the next five days before my bone marrow transplant. I listened to the overall goals of the regime, which included further chemotherapy to suppress my immune system so as not to reject the new bone marrow, to make room in the bone marrow for the donor marrow stem cells to grow, and to destroy any residual cancer cells. I was impressed with the similarity of Miles' explanation in the park to Dr Wilson's.

The start time was this afternoon with the insertion of a Hickman's line, a long, flexible tube, like a thin straw, that would be tunnelled under my skin into a large vein near my heart, allowing easier and direct access of powerful medications and infusions, including the new bone marrow cells, to enter my bloodstream. I had escaped this procedure so far along this fucked-up journey, but there was no escape this time.

The next five days were a repeat of the induction and consolidation phases condensed into a brutal barrage of drugs, both similar and different, infusions both similar and different, and side effects both similar and different, night sweats adding to the experience. The oesophagitis returned, and the mucositis paid me a visit. I remained steadfast; I never wavered, and I never lost sight of the end goal.

On day six, I received the news that I had been waiting for: my donor's bone marrow was due to arrive at Manchester airport at 8 am the following morning. Dr Wilson and my other clever doctors described a very large package with lots of cells. Thank you again, Mr German donor man; my family, friends, and I are eternally grateful to you. Mildred, Nurse Ratched, continued to update me. It was like a commentary on the next part of my life: the progression of those cells, the arrival at the airport, the further testing, the final testing, then the planned infusion into me.

Miles informed family and friends. He described the cascade of cautious excitement that invaded his messages. Various messages of love, good luck, and "you've got this" filtered back to me. Ellie visited with birthday balloons, the only ones she could find in the post office nearby. I appreciated the sentiment and reflected that it was like a re-birthday. She agreed. She squeezed my hands, blew me a kiss, and left.

The next morning, Nurse Ratched opened my door with a conglomerate of needles, syringes, dressings, and medication. I had no idea what time it was. Subconsciously, I exposed my Hickman line for the drawing of blood and then sat up to take my 22 tablets, no questions asked, just gulped the ice-cold water and swallowed. Next was to await my blood test results and yesterday's bone marrow biopsy results, or in medical jargon, the pathology, for the green light to go ahead with the bone marrow cell transfusion.

Lastly, Nurse Ratched checked the insertion site of my Hickman's line for any signs of infection, as was the process that she had followed every morning. Nurse Ratched's lack of obvious compassion paled into insignificance as her clinical expertise was exceptional, for which I was so grateful.

The green light came at 11 am. The bone marrow stem cell transfusion at 11:30 am. My chance of a new life literally dripping into my veins one drip at a time. It took approximately two hours to infuse; it did not hurt, nor did it cause nausea, vomiting, or headaches. It just dripped innocuously. I stared and, overcome with emotion, tears trickled silently down my face and dripped onto my hospital gown. Nurse Ratched came in every now and again, took my observations: pulse, temperature, blood pressure, seemed satisfied, and left, as my tears continued to flow. No comment was made. Nurse Ratched had days off after my transplant day. I actually missed her very brief daily exchanges, her attention, and her fastidious care.

I remained in Ward 5C for a further four weeks of monitoring, which entailed multiple blood tests to track the success of the engraftment, the integration of the donor stem cells into my bone marrow, and the production of new healthy blood cells. Dr Wilson had explained that blood tests would also indicate if I needed red blood cell transfusions until the bone marrow had started to produce sufficient quantities of these cells. My mindset continued to be one of trust, but now included a newfound understanding, a logic to this journey, thanks to Dr Wilson and so many others.

I allowed Miles to visit, as the days had turned into weeks. My own company had become very tiresome. Ellie continued to occasionally drop by, and, of course, I had the wonderful company of Mildred, who Ellie informed me was called Jane Morris. To me, she was Mildred, although not to her face, of course.

The day after my bone marrow transplant, I did a lot of research, as on that day, and on the days that followed, it had been like climbing a mountain to shower and get dressed. The conclusion was that everyone had a different experience and recovered at different rates. Miles sat nodding, accepting my newfound wisdom. I continued: ongoing themes were lethargy and fatigue, and my old friend's nausea and vomiting. A common premise in the recovery phase, which I had now entered, was the importance of physical activity; the thought of running again seemed impossible. The key was to move, and progress from there. As Miles astutely reminded me: walk before you can run.

Finally, the day came again to go home. Dr Wilson was happy with my progress and agreed that my monitoring could be continued as an outpatient. Still, lots of pills, lots of clinic and doctor appointments. Still, the usual infection precautions and, more especially, heightened vigilance regarding rejection. Miles and I nodded in understanding. Dr Wilson lapsed into a moment of humanness as he looked between Miles and me. He turned firstly to me: "You've got a good friend there." And then to both of us, "Good luck, boys," and with that said, he left.

Miles helped me pack, collected my medication and outpatient appointments. Before leaving, I was to have my Hickman line removed. I was a bit scared, as I had already googled the procedure. Mildred entered my room, and I relaxed. I had come to trust Mildred implicitly. She ordered Miles to leave while she set up for the procedure. Mildred provided me with a short but explicit description of the process. I nodded mutely and lay down.

I turned my head and closed my eyes. I could feel the methodical movement of Mildred's fingers as she worked, saying little, but just enough to reassure me that I was in capable hands. Mildred administered a little local anaesthetic, and then I felt a slow tug as the line was removed. Mildred barked instructions about the risk of infection to the insertion site, the usual: redness, pain, swelling. I listened carefully; I dared not disobey. Collecting her paraphernalia, she turned to leave. Mildred stopped at the door and turned: "Take care, young man." I lay still as the door reopened slightly. Mildred peered around: "My name is Jane, not Mildred." I stared, speechless, as she closed the door firmly shut.

34
The 100th Day

James

Home this time around was different. This time, it was the prelude to the rest of my life. I had my good days and bad days, lots of clinic and doctors' appointments, lots of sleeping, and still lots of pills. I managed to walk most days, dragging along whoever was available and willing to walk with me. Sometimes Miles, occasionally Dot, and every now and again Martin. Martin, I found, to be great company. He described himself as being quite a lad in his day. He certainly seemed to have had a lot of lady friends. I listened to his romantic adventures with both amusement and envy.

The subject of Kate occasionally entered our neighbourhood strolls. Martin would listen; occasionally he would venture a benign comment in agreement. He never offered his point of view or advice. I never asked, until one day. I remembered that day.

The clever doctors said that the first 100 days are critical after a bone marrow transplant regarding rejection and infection, with the day of transplant being day 0. That day, I was day 74. I was excited to be nearing the magic 100. I was down to once-weekly clinic and doctors' appointments on a Tuesday. It all seemed so surreal that this had happened. I was still in shock at what I had been through since my diagnosis, my fucked-up leukaemia journey, and now I was inching towards the end.

Martin and I walked slowly, both silent with our inner thoughts. A 24-year-old and an 81-year-old. I stopped at a bench and sat down, head in my hands. Martin sat quietly next to me. He had become used to my stops and would always wait quietly until I was ready to continue, happy to be given no reason for the break in our meander. But on this day, I needed to talk about Kate. Martin's eyes twinkled as I mentioned Kate's name; he loved a good tale about a lady, especially, so I had discovered, if it was Kate.

I stumbled through my feelings to find the words. Feeling a little better, my good days were more than my bad, the truck had seemed not to hit me every day. My appetite was at last improving, and I was not collapsing in a heap after my now daily walk. Should I contact Kate? As Martin sat, I stood and hovered, not sure if I should have burdened Martin with this question. Maybe I should have asked Miles. These days Miles was a little preoccupied with Ellie. I was aware that he had devoted so much of his life to me over the past months; he deserved a little of his own time. Miles was soon to return to London. He had already accessed more leave than he had originally requested. He and Ellie were figuring out stuff, as Miles so beautifully put it. So, Martin was it, the person from whom I was awaiting an answer. Martin patted the space next to him. I sat down.

"I have one question for you," he said. I nodded. "Do you love her?" There was no hesitation in my response: yes, yes, I loved her.

And so, to Project Zero, as Martin termed it, or how to rekindle my relationship with Kate. Martin and I both conceded that this was going to be tricky and that sensitivity to a woman's, Kate's, feelings was paramount. We also conceded that this was going to be a gradual project that was going to take patience and time. First, I had to get to day 100; then the rest would follow. Martin did agree that the planning stages could begin almost immediately. We both stood, shook hands, and hugged tentatively to seal our allegiance.

The next 26 days seemed like an eternity. Each clinic visit, each doctor's appointment, the waiting for results, hoping, praying that I would continue to be infection-free and rejection-free on the pathway to full remission. There continued to be no drama dramas. I still got fatigued and nauseated, but slowly my daytime sleeps were no longer needed. I continued to walk every day, and my appetite was improving. I was feeling optimistic, motivated even. The thought of returning to work, whatever that might be, started to filter into my subconscious. I was winning. I kept crossing off the days, nearing that magic number.

Martin and I kept planning. Project Zero was proving a difficult phenomenon to navigate. I presumed Kate was still living in London. I presumed that she was still nursing. I did not, however, presume that she would want to see me. That was one of the stumbling blocks that Martin and I found difficult to navigate: how to see someone that you had left, abandoned, deserted, all that time ago.

I was also a very different kind of man who had walked out of her life, both in looks and mindset. I was mindful that I hadn't survived my fucked-up leukaemia journey unscathed. Martin and I agreed, very reluctantly, that I needed to work out who I was in the aftermath of that journey. I needed a trajectory of my life, a pathway, a roadmap. I needed some hair!! We decided to pause Project Zero.

My family, and Miles, Ellie, and Martin were also focused on day 100 and had planned a small get-together, again in the park. Beth had returned to replenish her funds before embarking on more European adventures.

Day 100 came, the milestone, a very big day in the transplant world. I hoped I would continue to get better and better. I knew life would never be the same again; there would always be pills and check-ups. There would always be the fear of a relapse. But my doctors were ever so hopeful, and therefore so was I. I felt so lucky and in awe of what I had been through, and a little traumatised too. I was deeply grateful to be alive. I looked to my parents. My parents had remained in the background, their way of dealing with a child whose future was unknown. I knew that they were there, their love unquestionable. I hoped that soon they could rejoin my life. And so, as I looked further around, I saw Miles, Ellie, Dot, Martin, Alex, and Beth. I pushed a few wispy strands of hair out of my eyes and smiled.

Miles returned to London soon after my 100-day milestone. Ellie followed soon after. I missed my best friend, but I needed to be cocooned within my family a little while longer. I needed to rebuild my life slowly, methodically, carefully. Walk before I could run needed to flow into my everyday routine, not just running. I was desperate to propel forward to work and Kate, but as Martin sensibly pointed out, I couldn't erase the past twelve months or so of trauma, both physical and emotional, in a moment.

My hair grew back quickly, more in some places than others. It seemed, on my head, to be a little speckled with grey, a detail that Dot was quick to allude to, although she added a positive vibe, declaring it was a very distinguished look. I was not so sure at the tender age of 24. Miles was a little less sensitive with his comments and started using "old man" frequently in our conversations.

The days turned into weeks and months. My body grew stronger. My walks turned into runs, jogging would have been more accurate. It was over a year since the fateful day in London when my world came crashing down. Over a year since I had left, and now I was ready to return. Martin and I were back to Project Zero: plan to get a job, then to get Kate. That was a very simplistic, even crude way of articulating my hopes and dreams, but quite simply, that in my heart of hearts was what I wanted to do.

I allowed myself to think about ELT Finance and Consulting. I revisited the response to the email Miles drafted, explaining that due to emergent health concerns, I was unable to accept their offered position. The response was the usual: We are sorry to hear. Please keep in touch. Maybe it would soon be time to keep in touch.

35
The Glance

James

I looked at myself in the mirror; my hair had grown back mostly, still a little patchy in places, but with careful styling and a little help from Mum, it looked presentable. I was dressed in a grey suit, white shirt and a ridiculously expensive, but very stylish, pale pink and grey tie. Black polished shoes adorned my feet; a tiny sprinkle of cologne completed the effect.

The suit covered my still scrawny physique; I was getting there, slowly. Gymming, a little running, always walking, and most importantly, eating. I had been assigned a dietician, Madeline, who, although a little like Mildred, did have a softer side. I admitted that I needed some degree of bossiness to keep me from wandering off from the often tasteless and healthy to the very tasty but nutritionally bad.

The meeting at ELT was scheduled for 11 a.m. in London. Martin and Dot were driving me to the train station; Dot refused to let Martin drive anywhere by himself since a car had ploughed into the back of him at an intersection. Martin escaped unscathed, a little whiplash that disappeared with the help of a very pretty young physiotherapist, who, according to Martin, could maybe help with my return to running. All agreed Martin was not at fault, but Dot insisted on accompanying Martin on all his driving adventures.

On our walk the previous day, Martin and I were preoccupied with the first stage of Project Zero. We both agreed that the success of the first stage was a little precarious; the plan was to have a brief interaction, just a few words. How this would come to fruition was a little sketchy; in my opinion, a lot had to do with fate, and maybe a little serendipity. The success of the ELT meeting, however, was the priority. I needed to return to London.

So, as I bid goodbye to Martin and Dot, briefcase in hand, I boarded the Warrington to London train. I caught sight of my reflection in the window of the carriage. I looked the part, a little pale and skinny, but the clothing camouflage worked well. I was aiming for the astute businessman look, and I think I nailed it. Now I needed to add an air of intelligence and confidence, and this escapade might just be a success.

I had spent many weeks refamiliarising myself with the original position that I had applied for, cognisant that I had previously passed the challenge; I just needed to repeat the performance and to give the assurance that I could still perform the role. Oh, and that I wasn't going to die, or at the very least get sick. There were no guarantees in that respect. I had decided to be honest and not sugarcoat what I had been through, if asked what the future would look like. In truth, I did not know, but then in truth, did anyone know?

I sat amongst fellow travellers; my mind drifted from ELT to Kate. Where was she? Would she be at work, on an early shift? Where was work, still St Bart's? How was I going to do this? More than a year later, turn up at that pillar-box-red door, rap the gold-plated knocker and brazenly say hi. I shook my head. I wasn't. I couldn't be so insensitive, so foolish in thinking that one word and everything would go back to as it was.

Martin and I needed a better plan. I needed a better plan. I had known and loved Kate for nearly five years. I had adored her, cherished her; I could search the dictionary and come up with a hundred words to describe my feelings for her, but I had left her, just gone. I had broken her trust, our dreams, our future, and now I was trying to get it, us, back. But I was going to have to try harder, because just saying one word was not going to be enough.

Miles stood on the London Euston platform waving like I was his long-lost lover. I grinned; God, I loved my friend. Ellie was standing behind him, waving a placard that said "James Davy". I laughed at these two fools, my fools. It had only been a few weeks, but I had missed them so much.

A quick bathroom stop to spruce up, then on my way to ELT. Ellie was most impressed by my attire. Miles wolf-whistled, causing the London public to stop and stare. I felt good, I could do this. First ELT and then, well, then we would see.

I arrived at ELT's offices in central London. I shuddered as I was reminded that this was where it all began, my fucked-up leukaemia journey. I felt like I had been hit by a bowling ball, winded and breathless, knowing that nearby was the medical centre that had been instrumental in my fate for the past 12 months and more. Miles was still with me; Ellie had a late shift, so with good lucks and goodbyes had left. Miles and I stood there. He gripped my shoulder, as he had done so many times before. He waited. It was 10.45 a.m.; I had fifteen minutes to get it together, to forget, just for a little while, to focus on what life was about to become. I took a deep breath and walked, at first with uncertainty, then with purpose, as I strode into the ELT building in New Street Square.

The meeting went well. The senior executives I met with were genuinely interested in my challenges and how much I had conquered over the past 12 months or so. They did not dwell on the detail. I did not expose all the intricacies; I was succinct in my explanations and welcomed any questions, but surprisingly, they had none. The main focus was on what I could do now and into the future. What I could do and be successful at. Health was obviously important to the company; the rigorous medical screening in the recruitment process was evidence of that. But as Richard Deacon, the senior, senior executive, concluded, "no one is promised tomorrow". And with that said, both executives offered their hands and welcomed me to the team.

I could hardly contain my excitement. I smiled graciously and shook both their hands. I felt humbled that these two men, despite my uncertain future, were willing to provide me with an opportunity to succeed.

Miles was waiting, pacing. He came to an abrupt stop when I emerged from the ELT building. My face spoke a thousand words, my smile stretched from ear to ear and beyond, if that was even possible. For the first time in over 12 months, I truly believed I was getting my life back. We hugged fiercely, this time with excitement and joy, not with fear and trepidation. We both stood in the middle of London, not wanting to move, wanting to savour the moment of my success, as men in suits paraded by, as women in suits paraded by; we stood together, back together.

Miles suggested a celebration, just the two of us, now. My train was not until 6 p.m., so we headed to the nearest bar. No alcohol for me, of course; a lifetime of abstaining began all those months ago with the commencement of all those anti-pills. Miles ordered a beer and a fresh orange juice for me; Madeline would be pleased with that choice. The steak and chips that arrived may not be quite as prescribed, certainly not the thick-cut chips, but I allowed myself a little grace; I took solace in the fact that I would probably only be eating half of the serve.

My commencement date was in two weeks. I had so much to organise. The priority was transferring my care back to London. I would require ongoing follow-up. I planned to link in with Dr Taylor; I had an appointment scheduled with Dr Wilson and so would discuss the specifics then. My second priority was a place to live. Miles became a little belligerent that I would even consider not living with him and Ellie; I retaliated with "one should never assume", for which he kicked me under the table. That sorted, I moved onto my last but not least priority, Kate. Miles had not been privy to Project Zero. As I detailed the plan, Miles was difficult to read. I was unsure whether he was disappointed, or even felt dejected for not being included, or whether he was concerned that I was about to make a big mistake in trying to reconnect with Kate. He listened as I explained the plan and intent. Miles and I had always been honest with each other, even if it meant speaking some not always palatable truths. Miles pushed his plate and beer aside and leaned towards me. "Are you sure?" he asked. Was I sure I loved her? Yes. Was I sure I wanted her back? Yes. Was I sure this plan was going to work? No. We both sighed.

For a little while, we sat in silence; there was so much going through my mind. As Miles struggled through his second beer, daytime drinking had never been our forte, I was conscious of the time. I realised that I was desperate to catch a glimpse of Kate, not to speak, just to see. Was I being unreasonable, even irrational? Miles thought for a few minutes before answering. Miles knew how deeply I loved Kate; he also knew my reasons for leaving her over a year ago. He did not totally agree with my reasons or actions, so should I try to see her, should I try to talk to her, he honestly did not know. He conceded that to see her without being seen would be ok, but nothing more, not now, not today. Maybe in the future, with care, thoughtfulness and humility.

Standing across the road, in a recessed doorway of a 'for sale' terrace, I stared at the familiar pillar-box-red door, the gold-plated knocker shining its opulence in the afternoon sun. The mat at the top of the steps, where I had hidden the key all those months ago, was a little skewed. My heart was pounding, hands clenched, as an edginess made me question for the hundredth time what I was doing. Just as I was about to leave, I saw the prettiest girl I had ever seen. Kate. I stood and stared. Loaded with groceries, as she climbed the steps to the front door, our eyes met, our gaze held for a few seconds before I turned and walked away.

The train journey back to Warrington was filled with chaotic thoughts of the day. After seeing Kate, I had found Miles hiding around the corner in a building alcove, his eyes alight with questions, but he did not ask one. All I knew was that I had seen her, and I loved her. Kate had seen me; I was clueless as to what feelings I would have stirred. I knew that the longing that I had buried had surfaced; the ache that had briefly been forgotten was remembered. What I did next, I had no idea.

Martin and Dot met me at the Warrington Bank Quay train station. The journey home was filled with excitement as I described my meeting at ELT. Martin became a little frustrated at the inability to enquire about Project Zero and Kate, but Dot was scrupulous at unearthing little obscurities; her intuition often wheedled out hidden innuendos, so Martin and I kept away from the subject of Kate. Dot, however, had sensed there was something more to my account of the day; she knew that Kate lived in London, and as Dot was often heard to say, she was no fool. Moreover, she knew her favourite grandson. We arrived at my parents' house, Martin and Dot bid me goodnight. Martin climbed back into the car as Dot gave me an extra-tight squeeze and a wink goodbye. I sensed that Project Zero's membership was about to increase to four.

Once home, the excitement continued. Mum, Dad and Alex, Beth had returned to her European lifestyle, were eagerly awaiting a full recount of my meeting and the day. I was exhausted, and after only a short recap, the need for sleep was overwhelming. I lumbered up the stairs to my room, shoes kicked off, my suit, shirt and tie dispensed to a nearby chair. Dressed in a T-shirt and shorts, I settled into bed. I lay, eyes closed, waiting for sleep.

Martin knocked on my door early the next morning, eager for a walk, eager for an interrogation about my sighting of Kate would be more precise. But I liked Martin, and I had appreciated his conversations and shared understanding over the past few weeks, so I dressed quickly, slurped down my medication and met him outside the front door. He handed me a Warrington cap whilst I braced myself for the inquisition. Martin listened. Martin was pleased that Miles had been recruited to the Project Zero team and that I would be seeking his allegiance in London. Not that Martin would admit it, but I think my quandary was a little tricky for his later years, and he was finding it challenging to hide our plans from Dot. I shared my thoughts that it would only be a matter of time before Dot joined the Project Zero team. Martin acknowledged and agreed with my perception. We continued our walk, arm in arm. I paused, looking at Martin. I told him that his advice would always be appreciated, even from afar. We continued, the older and the younger, companions, friends.

36
The Reprieve

James

The next two weeks were a maze of reviews. I had contacted Dr Wilson before my appointment, and he had insisted that I had a suite of check-ups as I was leaving my allegiance to Clatterbridge, ensuring that due diligence had occurred before handing my care back to Dr Taylor. I was booked into a day at the centre for the "works", followed by results and the planning of the next phase of my life. The works included blood tests and a bone marrow biopsy, but also checking my nutrition, my physical fitness and mental wellbeing.

The blood tests and bone marrow biopsy were crucial in continuing to monitor my progress in recovery, the assessment of my treatment and even the possibility of a cure. I was aware that in all my visits with Dr Wilson, the cure word had never been spoken.

I found it hard without Miles by my side. Martin and, surprisingly, Alex had offered to come with me, but I declined both offers. I needed to start doing things on my own. I felt stronger now, both in my physical and mental health. I honestly believed that nothing else could be thrown at me that I would not be able to cope with, at least not in the first instance. Although I hoped and prayed that I would not need to test my theory.

My parents were amazing, preparing meals and snacks in close collaboration with Madeline, my personal nutritionist. Mum was enjoying experimenting with different foods that were high in nutrients, protein and devoid of sugar, sugar kills, according to Madeline. So do many other things, but I kept that thought to myself.

The week was exhausting and very scary. Waiting to see Dr Wilson, for potentially the last time, I felt like I was waiting for the judge and jury to pronounce if I was guilty or not; if I was going to be sentenced to Clatterbridge or freed to get back to my life. My heart was pounding, deep breaths; I stood up and paced the floor. This was it, this was the cusp of my future. Good or bad.

Dr Wilson came out to greet me and followed me into his room. His face stoic as usual, I sat, he sat next to me. I felt physically sick; I was barely breathing. He leant forward and spoke ever so quietly, "James, you are cured." My world stopped. I stared at Dr Wilson in disbelief; he continued to explain that no cancer cells had been detected, anywhere. I sobbed, tears streamed down my face, the relief was indescribable. Dr Wilson placed his hand on my shoulder, as Miles had done so many times before. For a few minutes, I was silent, my head in my hands, processing the enormity of those few words.

Dr Wilson was very clear that this journey was not over. I would still take pills, but less; I would still be monitored, with regular appointments, blood tests and screening, probably for a few years if not longer, just to be sure. I listened but didn't listen. One word circled, cure. Dr Wilson stood to indicate the appointment was over. He put out his hand to shake mine, but a handshake was not enough. I disregarded all patient-doctor protocols and hugged Dr Wilson, my clever doctor, as I thanked him for the last time.

I left Dr Wilson's room in a daze, this time a good daze, bordering on euphoria. I kept shaking my head in disbelief as people stopped and stared at this human walking along smiling, and occasionally skipping, in the cold afternoon air. I actually didn't know what to do, who to tell first. I wanted to go back to ward 5C at the Clatterbridge Cancer Centre; the person I most wanted to see was Mildred Ratched. I was overcome by feelings of relief, gratitude and happiness. I wanted to thank everyone that I came into contact with; as I left Dr Wilson's rooms, I thanked the receptionist, I thanked the man in the lift who held the door open for me and several others, I thanked a random stranger who had returned my smile. In my own way, I was thanking everyone for my second chance at life.

I entered ward 5C, the familiar faces walked the corridor: nurses, doctors, physiotherapists and domestic staff, and finally at the end of the nurse's station was Nurse Mildred Ratched, her scary stance all too familiar, her face grimaced as she spoke to a young nurse who looked petrified. She looked up to see me standing there, grinning, as I was reminded of that intimidating guise. She paused in the interaction with the nurse, who took the opportunity to escape, quickly fleeing as Mildred's glare followed her. I slowly approached this nursing matriarch, my grin widening as I wrapped my arms around her and whispered, "Thank you." Mildred turned a very deep shade of crimson and became very flustered; the nurses walking by stopped in pure horror at my audacity. "I'm cured," was my unabashed response, to which a massive cheer filled the air, and hugs and even the odd kiss ensued.

I smirked as Mildred shook my hand, maybe a little longer than necessary, turned, and continued with her day.

Delight and relief radiated from my mum as I blurted out my news, her eyes brimming with tears as she drew me close. We stood together; her son now returned to the family fold. No words were needed, as her love permeated through me. I had not felt my mother's arms around me for so long; I had missed that human closeness, that nurturing touch of a parent. Mum insisted on an impromptu dinner at home, inviting Dot and Martin. Dad and Alex would be home soon, and we would FaceTime Bella, now residing in Valence in the south of France. Of course, I agreed.

I delivered my news to the rest of the family, shamelessly tears tumbled in sheer joy at being given a reprieve from my fucked-up journey, to recommence my life. Cure was a big word, but I trusted Dr Wilson, I had to. I would be forever indebted to him and his team, and of course to Mr German donor man.

London was calling, and in three days I would be there.

Once more, Miles and Ellie met me at London's Euston train station. I was easily recognised as I was the only man with what seemed like a thousand cases and a massive smile on my face, bouncing along the platform, still in a bubble of elation. The London commuters stared at our open display of emotion; tight hugs and whoops of delight provided a brazen show of happiness as we embraced.

Ellie insisted on hearing every detail from my last appointment with Dr Wilson. Miles drove as I relayed all the specifics. Ellie seemed content that all was good. Ellie had a very special interest in my wellness, as she, too, had been there since the very beginning.

Miles' terrace was similar to Kate's. I felt a sense of dread as I remembered the last time that I had slept in the spare room, now my room, at Miles's, the night after my appointment with Dr Taylor, the appointment that changed my life. Miles came and stood next to me. I shuddered as the memory of that day reappeared. I stopped and looked around, memories of spaghetti bolognese the first night, scrambled eggs the second, sleepless nights filled with dread. The packing, the leaving, the panic, being frightened, scared. Miles being there, always there. I reached out and squeezed his shoulder, as he had so often squeezed mine. No spoken word could describe the love for this man.

Ellie liked to dabble in cooking, as Miles explained the banging and clatter coming from behind the kitchen door. We were seated around the kitchen table; Ellie presented what I presumed to be a curry of sorts. I quietly thought Ellie should stick to nursing, which seemed to be more her forte. Miles snuck me a tiny wink; we both said nothing.

We talked about their life in London, Miles still at the same accountancy firm, where he was happy to remain for a little while longer. Miles poignantly said that life had got in the way. He paused; he was happy to bide his time until something new came along. Ellie had started nursing at St Barts, continuing her love of cancer care, on the ward where Jesse had worked. I casually asked if she had met an Australian male nurse called Jesse. Ellie gushed about Jesse, enthusing about his reputation that he had on the ward. I learnt that Jesse had gone back to Australia a while ago, but he was still the subject of many a conversation; it seemed he had left quite an impression and was very well-liked. Something made me feel a little uncomfortable hearing about the popularity of Jesse. I had always been a little wary of his friendship with Kate.

Whilst Ellie chattered on about St Barts, my mind became flooded with thoughts of Kate. I had so many questions, but they were for another time. I was too tired. Pills taken, I said goodnight. Back in the spare room, my room, I crawled into bed, and I reflected on how lucky I was. I had done it, I had survived, I had battled unbelievable odds, on a journey marked by resilience, hope, and gratitude. I was humbled by my experience, indebted to so many. But now I was here with Miles and Ellie, in London. ELT on Monday and then maybe Kate.

37

The Plan

James

Miles and I sat at the kitchen table planning our day. Ellie was on an early shift; Miles had taken a few days off to help me get settled and sorted before commencing at ELT. Pills once again swallowed, Miles was astounded by how many I still had to take. A breakfast before a breakfast, he concluded.

On the agenda for today was reviewing my clothing situation and, very importantly, my diet. Madeline had provided me with a dietary guide; Miles and I decided simple was key as it was clear that none of us were chefs in the kitchen. I repeated Madeline's mantra: protein, nutrients, and no sugar. Miles was a little unsure as to how that would be achieved, but if it meant his friend, aka me, would stay healthy, he was willing to try. Miles had given up smoking on the day I got diagnosed, an achievement that made me immensely proud of him; surely a little less sugar was an easy challenge.

An additional item to our day's agenda was, of course, Kate. Miles looked a little apprehensive; I was apprehensive too. I had no idea what was next in the plan or Project Zero, as Martin had called it. We both decided on clothes and food first, then Kate. We did have a thought that maybe we should expand our Project Zero membership to include Ellie. We should tap into a woman's brain to find the answer as to what another female would think. Miles and I high-fived each other for coming up with such a brilliant idea. Now all we had to do was swear Ellie to secrecy and for her to agree to be a part of this elite team.

We had to stall our plan, as Ellie arrived home from her early shift, noticeably a little sad. I left Miles and Ellie alone and disappeared to my room to peruse my new purchases. One more suit, a couple of shirts, a pale blue and a pastel green, two new ties, not as costly as the pink and grey, but still very classy.

Miles and I had decided on grilled steak for dinner, with jacket potatoes and greens. I could hear Miles and Ellie talking in their room, so I quietly went downstairs to prepare dinner. Simple, we had decided; steak, potatoes and greens fulfilled that brief.

Dinner was eaten in near silence. Miles told me later that a very special patient had passed away. Miles and Ellie respected that I did not need or want to hear any details; the threat of my own mortality was still very raw.

We cleared away the dishes; Miles and Ellie conceded that the meal choice was not too bad. I replied that tomorrow night it would be baked chicken. I am sure I detected a slight groan as I sloshed the dishes in the water in my attempt to wash up, Ellie very kindly jumped up to assist.

I didn't sleep as soundly that night; the thought of a cancer patient passing away played on my mind. I was still sleepy when I went downstairs the next morning. Ellie was on a late shift; she and Miles were deep in conversation as I entered the kitchen. It seemed serious; I was about to slip away when Ellie proclaimed, "OK, I can help." Miles gave her a big hug. Help with what I wondered, then I realised, as I saw Miles grin and wink at me, that Ellie would help me in my quest for Kate.

Ellie grabbed a piece of paper and a pen. At the top of the page, she scrawled, "Project Zero, quest to capture Kate." I was not too keen on the word *capture*, so it was duly crossed out; *quest for Kate* would suffice. Ellie took charge; Miles and I smirked as Ellie became invested in my plight. We were both very happy that Ellie was taking this challenge seriously. I made a mental note to call Martin later with an update. Ellie wanted to know what we had done so far. "Not much," muttered Miles. I had to agree. We explained how, on my recent visit to London to meet with ELT, I had stood from afar, across the road from Kate's terrace, and locked eyes with her for a few seconds as she climbed the steps to her front door, and that was it, the only contact in just over 18 months. Ellie looked thoughtful. She needed more. We relocated to the living room and settled on the couch, me in the middle, Miles and Ellie on either side.

Ellie listened, occasionally sighing, likening my story to the love tragedy "Camille", a tale of love and sacrifice, which I conceded resonated strongly with my narrative. Camille's decision to leave Armand, as Ellie explained, was to shield him from the consequences of their relationship, not because she did not love him. Even though Camille was more focused on societal judgement rather than an illness per se, the premise was the same: not to ruin the life of someone that you love.

We decided to make a list of all that we knew and all that we didn't. The list of what we knew was very short: Kate still lived at her terrace, she was still very pretty, and I was still in love with her. Miles and Ellie raised their eyes in exasperation, not very helpful. And so, to what we didn't know. Was Kate still nursing at St Barts? Was Kate still single? This question took me by surprise. I had never considered that she would be seeing someone, but as Ellie gently pointed out, I had fallen in love with her; why shouldn't anyone else? Ellie sensed my despondency and squeezed my hand. I shrugged wearily. To continue. Would she want to see me? We decided before we got to that question, we needed to determine how we were going to give her the opportunity to decide.

We toyed with many options: send her a text, no. Call her, no. Knock on her door, no. We had to be more creative; we had to find a way that would show my feelings for her, my sorriness, my sincerity, my humility, but how? Miles and Ellie left me with that conundrum.

Ellie's mission, in keeping with the Project Zero theme, was to resolve the questions that we could answer. Maybe Eva, Kate's best friend, could help, "brilliant!" shouted Miles. We gave Ellie a brief synopsis of how Eva featured in Kate's life, also a nurse, again not sure where, she was at The Royal London. Would Eva want to help in my pursuit of Kate? I actually wasn't so sure. I had hurt her best friend, and in doing so, I had hurt her. I considered the inclusion of Eva very carefully.

The magnitude of what I caused so many months ago, over 18 months, hit me once more. I had not only lost Kate as a girlfriend and all that encompassed, but I had undoubtedly caused her pain, sorrow, anger, and perhaps the ability to hate someone that she once held so close. I had lost her trust, her friendship, and her love. I was not going to reconcile with a 'sorry'; Kate deserved more than that. Much more. Kate was, is, my world; she deserves everything of me, but how, where did I begin to get back what I had lost?

Ellie was getting ready for her late shift. Miles and I had planned to check my readiness for ELT on Monday. I had mostly everything I needed from when my start date had been delayed by my fucked-up journey. I just needed a couple more stationery items to convey my preparedness for joining a leading consulting firm.

Miles and Ellie had decided to grab some lunch on the way to her late shift, something healthy, they assured me: protein, nutrients and of course no sugar. I laughed. Alone, I scrambled a few eggs and stirred through some grated cheese; my pills had been forgotten amongst the Kate discussion, I silently reminded myself that my pills could never be forgotten. I was meeting Miles after he had lunched with Ellie, so I decided to call Martin and give him an update on Project Zero. I also wanted to ask how he and Dot were. I missed our daily walks and muses.

Martin answered almost immediately; it was obvious that he was happy to hear from me. He listened as I described what seemed to be a worse quandary than the one I had left him with. It was so overwhelming and confusing. Was I overthinking this? Was it really that hard? Could I not just send Kate a text, say I was sorry, explain? But I knew it wasn't, couldn't be that easy; there was too much at stake for that. Martin agreed that it had seemed to have become very complicated. He understood the reasoning for including Ellie, but he was worried that too many people involved would turn into a conspiracy rather than a quest for love. I had to agree. Wise words from my old friend. We agreed that Ellie could ascertain the basic information: was Kate still working at St Barts, had she another love interest, Martin's eloquent words, but I had to orchestrate the ultimate solution. Which was? I asked my wise friend. Martin admitted he had no idea.

I didn't catch up with Ellie for a couple of days. The next day, she was on an early–late shift finishing at nine and then an early shift. I had spent my last free day seeing Dr Taylor at a catch-up appointment before I returned to the ranks of the employed. Ellie had done some very careful investigating. I had told Miles about Martin's conspiracy theory, so to speak, so we were all very mindful of how we progressed. Ellie had discovered that Eva was now nursing at St Barts on the cardiology ward, and Kate was on the trauma and surgical ward at The Royal London, as a new Senior Staff Nurse. I was filled with a range of emotions. I was so impressed by Kate's evolving career, I felt proud. I didn't know whether I deserved to feel proud, as I had become absent in her life. It saddened me as I realised I had missed out on so much of her life. Nearly two years, some would argue, is just a short moment in time. It was crazy to think how much had changed.

It was later that night that I came up with a plan. I was meticulous in the detail; this could not fail, but I was aware that ultimately, that was not my decision. So, to the plan, my strategy to win back the heart of Kate Rose Dixon.

The first part of my plan, and both the most important and difficult to execute, was to compile a letter to Kate. I was anxious to convey to Kate how desperately sorry I was and my need for forgiveness. Unequivocally, I wanted Kate back, but I was very cognisant that small steps were needed. The letter became a note; I was scared that a declaration of my sorrow and wanting her forgiveness would turn into a babbling rampage of emotions that would be discarded into the nearest disposal receptacle. I wrote the following:

Dear Kate,

I was wrong. I am so sorry for the pain I have caused. Please let me explain. Allow me to meet with you, even if it's for the last time. To listen to me, just for a little while, and then if you wish, I will say farewell for the last time, the first and the last time.

I love you, Kate. I have never stopped loving you. I will never stop loving you.

James xx

P.S. This book has no particular reference; I just thought you would enjoy the read.

I read it repeatedly, crossed out words, added words, until at last it was done. I folded it carefully.

Part B of my plan was to go shopping. I included Miles and Ellie in this part. We headed off on Saturday morning to purchase a book, hence the P.S. in my note, a romantic novel, to be specific. This is where we hit problem number one: which book? There were shelves upon shelves of romantic fiction. I tried to think back to the books Kate had back at the terrace. Ellie admitted to liking romantic fantasy, to which Miles and I raised our eyebrows, but was happy to browse in the romantic fiction section, finally deciding on *Watermelon* by Marian Keyes purely based on the striking lime green cover. Miles and I agreed it was a pretty cool cover, bright green featuring two small pieces of watermelon, simple but effective. The sales assistant focused more on the text. She supported our choice, describing the book as humorous and delightful. She did warn that it featured a relationship breakup in the initial pages, but goes on to talk about strength and resilience. At this point, I was a little sceptical, but Miles and Ellie convinced me; the sales assistant agreed, noting that to find a romantic novel without a relationship breakup was near impossible.

Then on to Part C. Once home, I tucked the note into an envelope and placed it behind the front cover of the book. I then wrapped the book in brown paper, placed a sticky-backed yellow bow in a corner. I simply wrote 'To Kate'.

Next to Part D and problem number two: how to get the book and note to Kate. This is where Ellie and Eva came into play. We knew that Eva was now nursing on the cardiology ward at St Barts. Ellie was nursing on the cancer care ward, so all Ellie had to do was find Eva and give her the book to give to Kate. Simple. Except problem number three was that Ellie didn't know what Eva looked like or when she was working. The former was easily solvable. I searched my photos for a clear picture of Eva. I found the perfect one, although it was from a few years ago.

It was a picture of the four of us: Eva, Dean, Kate, and me, taken on one of our many nights out. The one I picked, I remembered well. Kate and I had only just started seeing each other; Eva and Dean had invited us to join them at an Italian restaurant that had received raved reviews despite opening only a few weeks earlier. Kate and I were happy to make up a foursome. Kate was especially keen for me to forge a relationship with Eva. Miles had also been invited with whichever lady friend he chose to bring. Miles declined; there was no female currently in his life, and the prospect of being a fifth wheel did not appeal.

One of the memorable aspects of that night was that we all arrived wearing white tops of some description, shirts and blouses, with jeans. The maître d' commented on the similarity of our attire and insisted on taking a photo. Over the course of the meal, our whites turned into whites with splodges of red, as pastas were spiralled and slurped, splashing specks and drips of sauce. After the meal, the maître d' insisted on taking another photo; not only did we wear the pasta on our white tops, but tomato sauce was smeared across our faces.

The second memorable aspect of that night was that it was the first night I shared a bed with Kate. Despite being somewhat covered with remnants of Italian pasta, we had decided to party on at a bar not too far away. Sauvignon blancs and many beers enabled the four of us to confidently enter, ignoring the stares. We stayed for a little while; more drinks were consumed, the conversation was limited due to the noise of people and music, but the four of us were happy just to sit and absorb the atmosphere. Back at the terrace, Eva and Dean called it a night; Kate and I sat up for a while longer. The 'to stay or not to stay' dilemma remained unspoken. The final nightcap of her grandfather's port was a decision made. We crawled up the stairs and flopped into bed.

I awoke first the following morning to Kate curled up next to me and an exceptionally large erection struggling in my jeans. We had not done the sex thing yet, and I sensed now would not be the time for the inaugural deed. I carefully got out of bed so as not to wake Kate and not to aggravate my extremely uncomfortable situation. I crept to the bathroom, stripped, and took a very, very cold shower whilst Kate slept on in oblivion. The memory brought a wistful smile to my face.

I gave the photo to Ellie, who studied the four of us carefully. She hovered over the face of Kate, explaining that she had seen her in a café a few weeks ago. As she thought some more, she realised it was the day I was in London meeting with ELT Finance and Consulting. Kate had been sitting alone at a table, and as she left, she gave Ellie a warm smile. Even though they had not spoken, Ellie declared she had liked Kate, not knowing it was Kate. I smiled.

Unaware of Eva's shifts at the hospital caused a little issue; however, Ellie suggested she would pop into the communal tearoom at lunchtime over the next few days in the hope of seeing Eva. The book was placed in a nondescript bag so as not to raise any suspicion. It only took three days for Ellie to give Eva the book. Without any pomp or ceremony, just a quick explanation that she was a friend of Miles, Ellie discreetly gave Eva the bag, asking if she would pass on the book to Kate. Ellie disappeared without allowing Eva to ask any questions.

Mission accomplished, thanks, Ellie. I returned to focusing on work, submerged in learning the ELT way, meeting new colleagues, and fitting in. My office, more accurately described as a desk space and a computer, was in an open-plan area on the 14th floor of the ELT building, in the centre of London. I had to pinch myself to make sure I wasn't dreaming. On my desk was a small silver tent card, engraved: James Davy, ELT Finance and Consulting. Since my fucked-up journey, I had a new outlook on life, thankful for all things big or small. That small silver sign was a big deal.

Part E of my plan was the hardest part of all: to wait for a response. It was up to Kate. It was her turn to take the next step into our future, or not.

38

The Wait

James

Two weeks had passed since Ellie had given the book to Eva, and still no contact from Kate. I asked Ellie many times if she was sure it was Eva to whom she gave the book. On about the fiftieth time of asking, Ellie stormed out of the room. I didn't ask again.

I suppose the reality was: how long do I wait? There was no easy answer, but sooner or later, I would have to accept the fact that Kate did not want me back in her life, that she had moved on, that I should move on. The concept hit me like a thunderbolt as I suddenly realised the truth of the situation: I had never considered what would happen if Kate and I did not get back together.

I decided, as hard as it was, that I needed to change my focus or risk jeopardising the other aspects of my life that I valued and was so grateful for: Miles, Ellie, my family, friends, and ELT. I needed to stop constantly looking at my phone, waiting for that elusive ping, so I decided I would go home, just for the weekend, to reconnect with my family and friends. I hadn't seen Tom, Matt, and Lewis since I had been sick. I had received the occasional message, but depending on my circumstances at that time, I often didn't reply. It was time to reclaim my life from before; it didn't lessen my need to see Kate, but it would help close the gap between then and now, to try to dissolve the void that had been created.

Mum and Dad were delighted to have me home for the weekend. Mum began planning for Friday night dinner with Alex and Beth, home again from Europe, this time in pursuit of happiness in Warrington, or at least employment. Beth had deemed Europe to be overrated; none of us questioned this peculiar analysis. We were just pleased to have her home. Dot and Martin would, of course, be there; I was keen to catch up with Martin regarding the progress of Project Zero.

I told Miles and Ellie about my plan to go home; they were keen to join me. Ellie was excited to catch up with the 5C nursing team, and Miles was eager to see the boys. Miles had also lost contact with our friends, as his life had been overshadowed by yours truly. Miles and I decided to make it a boys' night out; Tom, Matt, and Lewis had significant others, but agreed that a boys' night was long overdue. Ellie would be out with the 5C nursing team. Miles was aware that a couple of the nurses were indeed male, but in their late forties, so they did not pose a threat. I smiled at his rationale. I was going to make reference to trust but thought better of it.

We travelled by train to Warrington. I still got tired after a day at work, so propped up against the window, I dozed whilst Miles and Ellie confirmed arrangements for the following night. We were met at the station by various members of our families and went our separate ways to enjoy some family time. Alex and Beth were there to meet me. I couldn't remember the last time we had been together, just the three of us. We decided to detour to the pub on the way home just for one drink, just the siblings. We messaged the parents and Dot and Martin, stating we might be a little late.

Alex got a round of drinks in: two beers and an orange juice for me. Beth entertained us with creative embellishments of her European escapades. She described the sun, sea, and surf lifestyle, but acknowledged the downside of serving holidaymakers who had an air of entitlement and expectation, which became very tedious. Beth described the European males as tedious, too, which made Alex and me laugh. It became obvious that although Europe had been fun, Beth was glad to be home. Alex was a little shady about teaching and confessed that he was looking at different career options and was tempted by medicine. We were sworn to secrecy, not to tell the parents, being teachers themselves, they might be a little saddened by Alex's change of career pathway. Beth and I were surprised, but as we listened to Alex explain why with obvious enthusiasm and excitement, we acknowledged that medicine might indeed be his calling. Both Alex and Beth were still footloose and fancy-free, as Mum would describe her children's single status, often followed by a sigh of disappointment.

Alex and Beth asked how I was; I assured them I was doing well. I tried to eat a healthy diet, with Madeline's ongoing input, from afar. Work was good; I got tired on occasion, but I was conscientious with my pill taking and medical check-ins. Beth asked about Kate; I tried to deflect answering, but Beth was persistent. I loved Kate. Would we get back together? I honestly didn't know.

It was getting late; we reluctantly finished our drinks and headed home. Mum, Dad, Dot, and Martin grappled to give me hugs at the front door. I hadn't realised how much I had missed them, Dot and Martin especially. I always worried that, having not seen them for a while, they would look older and maybe even a little frail, but thankfully, they looked exactly the same. Dot was still a little feisty, trying to boss Martin, and Martin was his usual genteel self.

Mum served up a classic Sunday roast with all the trimmings. Beth pointed out a Sunday roast on a Friday night, but I wasn't complaining. I needed to catch up with Madeline for some further meal advice; the chicken and steak options were becoming a little repetitive. The conversation flowed, with everyone fighting to get a word in. My grilling wasn't too bad, mainly related to work, Miles and Ellie, and no, there was no love interest. Beth opened her mouth to speak, but my look quickly saw her think better of it. The focus turned to Alex, who then quickly deflected to Beth and her travel tales. Beth was very happy to entertain us with a recap of her nomadic living. Mum and Dad, Dot and Martin were content to listen. Dad did add that he had got tickets for the Warrington Wolves versus Leeds Rhinos game on Sunday afternoon; Dad had included Miles and Martin to accompany Dad, Alex, and me. I was excited to watch the Wolves in what was thought to be an epic game, as both teams were playing well this season.

With Mum's apple pie devoured, we said goodnight. I arranged to catch up with Martin the next morning to revisit our walks. Dot asked if she could join; however, she sensed our hesitation and decided to meet us for a cup of tea later. Martin and I were very protective of our walking time. I awoke early the next morning and waited for that familiar knock on the door. I smiled at Martin, decked out in jeans and a sweatshirt, sneakers, and a Warrington Wolves bobble hat. What a sight. Martin grinned at his attempt to be trendy. I did concede that light blue baggy jeans and a very pale pink sweatshirt were in vogue, but maybe not for a now 82-year-old. A candy floss from a fairground suddenly came to mind.

We set off, side by side, again. We were quiet at first, just enjoying each other's company. I asked how he and Dot were. Martin obviously valued the companionship of Dot. In his later years, he acknowledged that he felt privileged to have met someone to share experiences with. He did admit that there weren't too many experiences to share, but he enjoyed a little affection and attention. I stopped him there; that was enough information. Martin laughed as I turned a little shade of pink.

Of course, Martin asked about Kate and the plan. I told him that we were at Part E, aka the waiting game, two weeks down and counting. The question was how long I counted for. Martin expressed that he was impressed with the ingenuity of the plan and commended my intuition, but that said, I was still no nearer to Kate. "Patience, dear boy," was Martin's response. I sighed. "Patience indeed,"

We continued discussing my life: ELT, Miles, and Ellie. Martin was keen to see Ellie again and suggested we invite her to join us for the Warrington game. I had no idea what her interest in rugby league was, if any, but I would ask Miles and then potentially get her a ticket to join us. I told Martin about our boys' night; he was pleased to see that I was catching up with friends who had been abandoned for far too long. I agreed. I did say that I was keen to catch up with Madeline to revisit my dietary options, but that may need to wait until my next visit home.

We turned the corner and headed to the café where Dot was meeting us. It was its usual Saturday morning busyness, but Dot had secured us a table on the fringe of the café, balanced a little precariously between the inside cemented floor and the outside paved area. Dot looked very stylish in a grey trouser suit, with a white, what looked like silk, top poking out at the neckline. I had sat for approximately a minute before Dot quizzed me on Kate. Martin shrugged, acknowledging his failure at keeping Project Zero a secret. We had discussed this eventuality many weeks ago, so I was neither surprised nor concerned.

Over two cups of tea for Dot and Martin, and a batch brew for me, I filled Dot in on the story of Kate. Dot remained quiet, nodded, or shook her head depending on what I was disclosing. I ended with the plan and Part E. Martin and I waited expectantly for Dot's opinion. "Patience," declared Dot. Really! I put my head in my hands. Dot acknowledged my frustration, but this was not a quick-fix situation. Dot believed that I had done everything possible to woo Kate back; anything else would most certainly push her further away. So patience, the three of us said in unison. We were floating in tea and coffee, so we decided to head home. Dot left Martin and me to head back together, solving the problems of the world, which seemed to be a lot easier than solving the Kate conundrum.

The night out was a quiet one. We revisited a pub we frequented in our youth. We felt a little displaced amongst the university crowd: five boys in their mid-twenties revisiting the past and catching up on the now. Tom, Matt, and Lewis had chosen a diversity of careers. Tom, dabbling in journalism, had focused on sports reporting, some would consider an ideal career for someone obsessed with football, rugby, and any sport that involves a ball. Matt had flitted between many careers and was currently studying psychology, the study of the human mind, as Matt felt the need to explain. Miles and I shared a look; this was very different from his previous engineering degree. Lewis was the tradesman and had just started up his own business as a carpenter. Miles and I were impressed to hear that his small business now had a staff of four and was flourishing. Lewis was very humble in his articulation of his achievements; as our friend, we felt very proud. They all had girlfriends and seemed settled in their relationships. We reminisced that the five rogues of the past had settled into respectable citizens.

We touched briefly on my fucked-up journey so I could apologise for my lack of communication over the last couple of years. It was quite refreshing talking to the boys, who accepted that I was sick and was now better, no questions asked.

I hadn't partied, as such, since the night of the Italian restaurant, drowning in orange juice and soda water. I conceded defeat just after ten. Miles and the others absolutely understood as I said goodnight and went to catch a taxi home. Miles decided to find Ellie; Tom, Matt, and Lewis, obviously enjoying a little girlfriend-free time, ordered another round of beers and looked settled in for the night.

Mum and Dad were watching *Mr and Mrs Smith* starring Brad Pitt and Angelina Jolie, a great movie, when I arrived home. They were concerned to see me home a lot earlier than expected. I reassured them that I was fine, just a little tired. They said that Madeline had called and was keen to catch up tomorrow to check in. I was surprised that my nutritionist wanted to see me on a Sunday but was too tired to deliberate. I nodded absently and climbed the stairs to bed. I slept soundly and was awoken abruptly the next morning by a familiar-sounding knock on the front door. "Martin," I groaned. I had forgotten about our planned walk. I scrambled out of bed and slowly went downstairs. I opened the front door, looking rumpled and very dopey. "Big night?" he enquired.

Martin was happy to wait while I tried to assemble some sort of walking attire. I splashed my face with cold water, brushed my teeth, deodorised, and five minutes later we were pounding the footpath. Martin suggested a halfway coffee, which I readily agreed to. Despite needing more shut-eye, Martin and I chattered on with ease. Martin kindly took the lead, delving back into his past with more tales of his youth. Martin's Scottish accent never usually challenged me, but today I had to listen intently to understand certain words. I confirmed with my friend that lack of sleep, rather than alcohol, was contributing to my struggle.

Fuelled by coffee on the return journey, I mentioned meeting with Madeline later that morning. Martin raised his eyebrows, questioning a meeting with a nutritionist on a Sunday morning. I agreed it did seem odd.

Back home, I would see Martin that afternoon at the rugby. He was pleased that Ellie was joining us. Ellie apparently knew very little about the game of rugby league but was happy to watch twenty-six burly men in tiny shorts running around a rugby field. I jokingly noted that Martin seemed to have converted to rugby league rather than football and his beloved Liverpool. He winked and went on his way.

I was running late. I had got back from my walk, showered, swallowed my pills, which now and again proved a little tricky, then started to pack as we were catching the train back to London after the rugby.

39

The Nutritionist

James

Madeline was sitting at a corner table in a bustling café on the main street of Warrington. I opened the door to be greeted by an aroma of coffee. I was surprised to see her. I had not realised how attractive she was; she looked different out of her professional regalia. She reminded me of when I first met Ellie, her hair in a high ponytail, although Madeline's hair was blonde and very straight. Her obvious makeup defied a casual meeting on a Sunday morning. She was wearing a dark green holey blouse, I think known as broderie anglaise, which exuded a femininity, and I presumed jeans, but the table mostly obscured my view. She did look lovely. I was dressed super casually; it was Sunday, after all, in jeans and a navy-blue polo. I caught a glimpse of a mountain of pastries begging to be eaten: croissants, plain and chocolate, muffins, giant chocolate cookies, sliced cheesecake. I remembered Madeline's no-sugar philosophy, so I dragged my eyes back to my nutritionist, who was not looking very nutritionisty, if that was a word.

I sat down and apologised for being a little late. Madeline had a coffee, so I ordered myself one. We went through the pleasantries of asking how each other was. I asked her for any more recipes or food recommendations. I explained that I was living with

Miles and Ellie, who were threatening to divorce me if they ate any more steak or baked chicken. Madeline laughed and gave me a couple of high-protein, high-nutrient cookery books, which were in her work satchel. She noticed me glance at the counter, which appeared to sag under the sheer volume of badness, and smiled.

I felt a small undercurrent of uneasiness. I was confused as to where this catch-up was going. The consultation, as such, was over in minutes. Madeline asked if I had any concerns regarding my dietary intake, boredom sprang to mind, but I just said no. She asked about my weight, which I said was fine. I had maintained a weight that I was happy with and tweaked my intake if I had run, which I admitted had only been a couple of times a week. Madeline seemed satisfied with my answers and then silence.

Madeline tried to fill the uncomfortable void that followed with a little about herself. I found my mind drifting, thinking about the boys and their girlfriends, thinking about Miles and Ellie, Dot and Martin, and then me. I was brought back intermittently as words such as "nearly 30" and "newly single" filtered through. I was unsure how to respond. I was reluctant to define my relationship status. I wasn't yet ready to describe myself as single; I didn't feel that I truly was. I chatted about ELT and living back in London, slowly rebuilding my life. I vaguely described my girlfriend's stance as paused. Madeline looked puzzled; however, I did not explain.

We chatted for a little while longer. I was relieved to find a common interest in reading: Madeline, a lover of non-fiction, especially autobiographies of actors or actresses, admitting that she lived her acting dream precariously through others. I unwittingly let my guard down and said that my interest in reading was due to my girlfriend. Madeline immediately latched onto my faux pas and clarified that I had a girlfriend. I reiterated that I did, but we were briefly separated. I felt bad for lying, for fabricating the truth, but I had not admitted to myself that Kate was no longer in my life; to say the words out loud required a strength that I did not yet have.

Madeline said it was lovely to catch up and was pleased that I was feeling well. I sensed that she was confused and even a little disappointed with our meeting. I did like Madeline. I was conscious not to send her mixed messages, to give her the impression of something that wasn't. I was happy to be friends, but I couldn't promise more. Madeline got up to leave. As she passed me, she leaned in and lightly kissed my cheek. "Call me," she whispered, and was gone. Her perfume lingered, as did the perplexity of what had occurred. Madeline was attractive, smart, gentle, engaging, and apparently somewhat attracted to me, which was flattering, but she would potentially be a band-aid for a bullet hole, and I needed more.

I stayed in the café just a little while longer. I drained my second coffee, third for the morning, went to grab a chocolate croissant, but thought better of it, and headed home. Mum rustled up a cheese omelette while I finished packing. Confused as to whether that was breakfast, brunch, or lunch, I quickly demolished it and polished it off with yoghurt, honey, and a banana. Mum and I acknowledged my healthy choices, which of course brought Mum to the subject of Madeline. I was non-committal, much to Mum's frustration, but there was little to say. We met, Madeline looked lovely, coffee was good, I got two new cookbooks, and we talked. I did voice to Mum that after the commonality of addressing my nutritional needs, it was a bit of a struggle to keep the conversation going. Would I see her again? I wasn't sure.

The rugby was such a good game. The Wolves hammered the Rhinos. We were sitting near some Rhino fans, so it made for some interesting banter, friendly, just. Ellie, surprisingly, was quiet, didn't ask too many questions, although Miles had provided a brief synopsis of the rules before kick-off. She did, however, decide to go for the Rhinos; I think the Rhinos' number 7, or the scrum half, as Miles informed her, had particularly caught her eye. Ellie explained to Miles that his fitted shirt clearly emphasised his defined muscles, which, to be honest, was replicated many times across the field. Miles and I felt a little inadequate by these comments. Ellie gave both of us a big hug and left Miles and me to deliberate on how we could achieve the chiselled look of the twenty-six men parading in front of us.

It was like a meeting of the United Kingdom on the Halliwell Jones Stadium stand, with Martin's Scottish accent, Ellie's Irish accent, and the Lancashire tones of

Dad and Alex. Miles and I added a bit of Cockney just to invigorate the mix. Of course, these idiosyncrasies disappeared when screams and cheers erupted at the scoring of goals and tries, merging into the amplified roar of the crowd.

It was impossible to forgo a visit to the bar to celebrate a great win. Spirits were high, and the noise was higher. After jostling to get served, Miles and Alex finally arrived at our table, which was scrunched within a sea of yellow, blue, and white. We toasted the Wolves' win and a weekend of reunions. Dad raised his beer to family and friends, and we raised our glasses once again.

The train back to London was very subdued. It was early evening, and even though it was full of many commuters, a hush had fallen over the carriage: laptops poised as plans for the week ahead were being scribed, the occasional ping symbolised emails sent and received, sighs heard as many contemplated the week ahead. Ellie slept, her head resting on Miles' shoulder, who in turn leaned against the window. I too dozed, but my mind buzzed chaotically as different thoughts dipped in and out. Strangely, I became preoccupied with my now lifelong abstinence from alcohol; it had never bothered me until now. I realised that that and the pill taking, and continual check-ups, meant that I could never fully move on from AML. It was a sobering thought; I realised that I would never be allowed to forget. I shook my head.

Eyes still closed, I thought of Madeline, and I shook my head once again, then I smiled. I conceded that it was a strange feeling to be wanted after so long, nice even. I liked Madeline, but romantically I was hesitant to take the next step. I soon slipped into a light, dreamless sleep.

A mass of activity symbolised the pulling into London Euston station: the closing of laptops, gathering of bags and cases, the stretching and yawning of sleepiness, in growing anticipation of disembarking into the mayhem of the capital city. After an annoying taxi ride, where we were treated to a commentary of the taxi driver's analysis of the state of rugby, both union and league, we arrived home. Shutting the door to Miles' terrace behind us, bags left strewn in the hallway, we collapsed onto the couch, the three of us, in various states of exhaustion. No one could move. Ellie eventually presented us with three cups of tea and a plate of chicken sandwiches. Miles and I exclaimed declarations of love for her, for which she took a little curtsy. We laughed, ate, and dragged ourselves to bed.

Week three of not hearing anything from Kate saw me burying myself in work. I received a text from Madeline on Thursday, checking that I was okay. I assured her that I was fine; she had added a love heart emoji, I sent back a smiley face. I decided that I would wait one more week for Kate, then I would move on. I divulged my plan to Miles and Ellie, who made some non-committal noises. I sensed scepticism, not believing that I would implement my plan, Part F, as it were. I recognised that I had failed miserably in convincing them otherwise. I had to admit it was hard to convince others when I was not convinced myself.

ELT was a good distraction. Most of my work focused on evaluating business initiatives for clients, looking at the feasibility of success of new ventures by analysing data, examining market trends to determine the viability of ideas, and then providing strategic advice. I had been successful in gaining the trust of ELT to get the job done; my success in the consulting world thus far had been unequivocal, and I was proud to have achieved what I had set out to do. The hours were long, and although ELT were mindful of my health history, they expected results, and if that meant long hours, so be it.

A little twist along life's plan, my life's plan, came at the beginning of week four of the countdown. ELT wanted me to meet a new client, based in Paris. "As in Paris, France?" I qualified, much to Richard Deacon, the senior senior director's, amusement. He confirmed Paris, France. I was to travel on the Eurostar the next day. He checked that I had a passport; by some miracle, I did, I had needed one for a skiing trip in my senior school year. Richard briefed me on the company that I would be linked with. He went on to explain that the ELT Paris office served a broad range of companies from various sectors, including technology and consumer goods. I queried why he specifically wanted me to go; he was a little evasive in his answer, muttering something about my success in the company so far as he signalled me to leave. I closed his office door behind me.

In Paris, I found out that the chief executive had a keen interest in this latest proposal and had specifically asked me to handle the account, to scope out the possibilities and viability of the plan. I was excited, but as Miles helped me to pack later that afternoon, he sensed a little reluctance. I explained I was concerned: what if Kate messaged me to meet up and I was in Paris? I quickly realised that I was being ridiculous. This was work, this was one night, I had to go. Miles was silent, but his face said it all. I was being ridiculous. I had to go.

The next morning, suited up, briefcase bursting, overnight bag packed, passport, pills, I boarded the Eurostar train to Paris, France.

40

The Note

Kate

I landed at London Heathrow after twenty-four or so hours of travel. Security had not morphed into happy, welcoming individuals; their scowls remained fixed as I tried to assume the look of innocence, daring them to further body search me. It failed at Dubai, as once again I was whisked away, much to my frustration, back to the curtained cubicle. In flight, I decided to watch movies; my mind wandered from the friends I had left behind to the friends waiting for me back home. Australia had been surreal, an escapism, with a smattering of work that provided a little bit of reality. It was crazy to think that in a land 10,054 miles away, I blended in so effortlessly. I welcomed the "no worries" attitude, the laid-back and relaxed lifestyle.

I collected my bags from the carousel, deliberately steering them towards the beagle sniffer dogs, and went through passport control. It was a grey, drizzly day; I could feel a blanket of gloom lowering over me. This was England, where the golden sands and blue glistening sea were replaced by grey slippery pavements and muddy grass verges, rivers of rain flowing down the kerbs. The togs and T-shirts were substituted by brown or black duffle coats, boots, and mismatched hats and scarves; it was not quite cold enough for gloves, but hands were firmly in pockets away from the cool air. Welcome home.

Just as I was falling into the depths of bleakness, I saw four sunny smiles coming towards me. I laughed as Eva, Dean, Sarah, and Jack mimicked Heathcliff in Wuthering Heights, all arms outstretched wide, running towards me; the airport arrival lounge was full of people trying not to stare, resisting the joviality. I sank into their open arms, one by one accepting hugs, a little bit of awkwardness from Jack, but I appreciated the sentiment. Dean and Jack took my suitcase and carry-on, as Eva and Sarah whisked me away, quite literally skipping to Dean's car, where we collapsed in fits of giggles. Gosh, I had missed these crazy friends; yes, Australia had sun, sand, and surf, but London had Eva and Sarah.

On the journey home, I sat in the back of Dean's car, on the outer of Sarah and Jack. Dean drove with Eva facing the wrong way as I came under fire by thousands of questions, the focus being mainly on Luke and Dom. Eva wanted to know everything, whereas Sarah was content snuggled up to Jack, to listen; evidently, the path to true love was back on track.

I decided not to divulge my sexual interlude with Luke, even though it was very much a part of my Australian experience; that part would stay firmly in my memory, not for sharing. We chatted about my visit to The Alfred, The Grape, the Yarra Valley, the AFL, the beach, shopping, dinner at Tony and Allison's, Bear, the weather, clothes, from the lycra sportswear and puffer jackets to togs and tees. I had to stop and translate kilometres, doonas, togs, and thongs. I described the Australian population as easy-going, warm, and inviting; they were people who, as you met, immediately became your friend. Put simply, I never felt like I was an outsider; I always belonged. Eva looked a little worried. "We missed you," she said quietly. I immediately replied, "I missed you too."

The terrace looked the same. Eva helped me carry my luggage up to my room. I opened my bedroom door, and my heart stopped; my eyes fixed on a plain white tote bag propped up on my pillow. Peeking out was a brown package, a yellow bow stuck to one corner. I dropped my bag to the floor. Eva walked over to the bed, but I said no. Now was not the time. I had waited nearly two years to hear from James; I could wait a little while longer. We went downstairs to join the others; Dean had made cups of tea and pulled some pastries out of nowhere. I wanted to hear what everyone had been doing whilst I was away.

Eva went first. She told a sad story of how she missed me and spent the four weeks absorbed in work, even doing some overtime. I looked alarmed until Dean interjected and added a little perspective. Yes, Eva had done a little overtime, but had dragged herself out for the occasional beverage and night out. Sarah and Jack supported Dean's version of events, describing the several occasions that the builders, Scott, Rhys, and Chris had joined Eva, Dean, Sarah, and Jack, with their ladies, for a pub night. Eva looked a little sheepish at the exaggeration of her melancholy status. I hugged her, and we moved on to Sarah.

Sarah did not refer to her and Jack's little hiatus; their relationship appeared to be as it was, maybe a little more serious, but I kept that thought to myself. Sarah had also been working long hours and had attended a weekend away in Newcastle on a trauma course, *The Critical Ill Surgical Patient*, which she was keen for Eva and me to attend, as it was for nursing and medical staff. Eva was excited by the idea of a weekend away and promised to look into it.

Dean had started his surgical traineeship program and had been fortunate to be successful with burns as his first-choice speciality. It was a four-year program with many rotations, lots of study, but it would see him rise the surgeon ladder and eventually become a consultant.

The most exciting news was that Jack and the builders had decided to branch out on their own and start up a company focusing on building and design. They were in the inaugural stages of researching the local market and drafting a business plan.

Jack explained that it was a convoluted process of getting permits and licences; it was not without risk, so the background work of assessing the viability of their proposal was crucial, as was funding of the business. There was no rush; they were all happy to tread water where they were.

I was failing in my attempt to stay awake. I conceded defeat and plodded wearily upstairs to bed. The blowing of kisses and welcome homes followed me as I disappeared into my room. I moved the tote to one side, stripped off quickly, grabbed a T-shirt from my drawer, and collapsed into bed.

I woke up sometime later. It was dark. I heard the rain pattering on my window; the house was silent. I sat up, flicked on my bedside light, and grabbed the tote bag. I pulled the brown paper-wrapped parcel out. *To Kate* was written on the front. The yellow bow had come adrift and was now lying at the bottom of the bag. I ripped the paper off: *Watermelon* by Marian Keyes. I loved the vibrant green of the cover and the two tiny pieces of watermelon drawn in the corner.

I read the descriptive blurb on the back cover; the book promised to be uncannily akin to my life. A little chill of uneasiness ran through my mind; maybe I would wait a little while before embarking on the journey of the lead character. I turned it back over and opened the front cover.

A folded piece of paper, a note, escaped and fell onto my bed. I picked it up, held it for a few seconds, and slowly I opened it.

Dear Kate,

I was wrong. I am so sorry for the pain I have caused. Please let me explain. Allow me to meet with you, even if it's for the last time. To listen to me, just for a little while, and then, if you wish, I will say farewell for the last time, the first and the last time.

I love you, Kate. I have never stopped loving you. I will never stop loving you.

James xx

P.S. This book has no particular reference; I just thought you would enjoy the read.

As I read, tears silently spilt down my cheeks. The words blurred; I roughly wiped the tears away, blinked several times, and read it again. Mixed emotions tumbled around in my head. I knew James; I had known James. A nervous anticipation danced inside me. I had been lost in my unknowing; now was a chance to find out the why. Tiredness overshadowed my thoughts. I tucked the note under my pillow, put the book to one side, curled up, mind spinning, and drifted back to sleep.

The next morning, I went downstairs. It was still raining, a very grey day in London town. I wandered into the living room and was greeted by pink and yellow balloons and Welcome Home signs everywhere, with a vase of beautiful pink gerberas sitting a little precariously on my grandfather's chair. An amazing smell of bacon wafted in from the kitchen, and amongst bacon, eggs, toast, and numerous pots and pans were my favourite four, cheesy grins planted firmly on their faces. "Ta-da!" was yelled as I walked in. Eva admitted the decorations were a little delayed due to circumstances but did not elaborate further. We feasted and planned the day. Sarah, Jack, and Dean were working, which just left Eva and me. After breakfast, banned from kitchen duty, I sat back down on my bed and re-read the note.

I decided an urgent meeting with my best friend was needed. Eva had gone home after breakfast, so I arranged to meet her at the café later that morning. I put the note back under my pillow, showered, dressed, started to unpack, and, most importantly, called Mum and messaged Ben and Daniel.

The rain continued. The cold wind howled as tree branches shook, forming a carpet of leaves along the streets of London. I stepped out wearing multiple layers of clothing and an umbrella in hand. I pressed the note deep in my pocket, protected from the rain. Eva had ordered coffee and had secured our favourite corner table. I sat down, pulled out the note, and handed it to her. Her eyes widened as she read, her expression frozen. She put it down on the table, hesitated, then picked it up again and read it once more; this time, a little tear crept down her cheek. She searched my face for an answer.

I took the note from her. I considered the hurt, the pain, the heartbreak, the missing him, the loving him. I could feel Eva's eyes looking, waiting. I sat, not moving, and took a deep breath.

41
The French

James

I took advantage of the couple of hours on the Eurostar to further research my clients. I did break occasionally to enjoy the scenery as we travelled into France, arriving at the Gare du Nord station in Paris at 08:30. Like London, Paris was heaving with commuters, pushing and shoving, everyone apparently in a hurry to get to their destination. Apologies as I was hustled along were scant, and I was relieved to arrive safely at my meeting, mostly unscathed, although a little dishevelled. Straightening my tie, smoothing my hair, and taking a deep breath, I entered the conference room.

Sitting that evening at a restaurant on the edge of a massive roundabout, which I felt should have a name, but I had no idea what it was, I watched the world, or more specifically, Paris, go by. Mopeds, smart cars, whizzing around, so many lanes of traffic, merging, joining, leaving, it was mesmerising. Organised chaos. I reflected that my very brief brush with the French business sector was a little arrogant, although they mellowed, as although I did not speak French, they acknowledged my expertise in analysis and the building of deliverables. A little French hospitality seeped through as they offered to assign me a tour guide to provide an insight into the city's history, attractions, and culture. I politely declined; I was very happy to explore solo.

I decided, in the constraints of time, to visit the Eiffel Tower, the Arc de Triomphe, and the Louvre Museum. The architecture was mind-blowing; I found myself transfixed at these iconic masterpieces that lined the banks of the River Seine. I had been strongly advised to sample some popular French fare: a Nutella crepe. I wavered for a second before sinking my teeth into the most delectable, delicate pancake oozing with a rich, smooth chocolatey spread. I closed my eyes to savour the taste. I had not indulged in such sweetness for nearly two years. It was sensational.

I stayed at a hotel just off the roundabout, a mile or so away from the Eiffel Tower. I could only describe it as purple, small, and quirky. There was no lift, so I lumbered up the winding staircase past purple, red, and gold wallpapered walls, doors, and carpets. The purple theme continued in my tiny room, which barely had space for a double bed. I squeezed into the ensuite, amazed at how a shower and toilet could fit into a triangular-shaped bathroom, a very small triangular-shaped bathroom. I clambered over the bed to open the French windows and was greeted by the most magnificent view of Paris. I could just see a glimpse of the Eiffel Tower. I couldn't stop smiling. It was incredible, so noisy, so busy, so full of life. I stood captivated by a city constantly on the move. The sound of car horns filled the air, police, or gendarmes as they were known, incessantly blowing their whistles to control the pandemonium of traffic and pedestrians.

I showered and dressed quickly. I wasn't sure what to wear in this vibrant city, but I felt a pull towards more smart than casual, so I put my suit pants back on and complemented the look with a crisp white shirt, no tie. Shirt in or out, I was undecided, but went for out. I kept the smart theme somewhat alive by wearing my black shiny shoes. Hair that had all but grown back, combed, the grey speckles could not be ignored, so were embraced; a smidgen of aftershave, Bleu de Chanel, sprinkled. I closed the door to my tiny French retreat and merged into the Paris night.

My clients joined me at the restaurant and assisted with the navigation of the menu, which was written in French. I ordered steak-frites, feeling just a little virtuous to include steak in my choice. I was told this was an iconic French dish. The steak melted in my mouth. I think I actually swooned. The clients were obviously amused at my expression of pure delight, though not surprised. This was apparently a Michelin Star restaurant; good food was a certainty. The wine flowed, but I stuck to soda water, much to the puzzlement of my companions. I did not offer an explanation.

As Paris darkened, it became a sea of tiny lights. I declined the invitation to party on in the 11th arrondissement, a district about thirty minutes from our restaurant. My companions were keen for me to visit, apparently one of the best areas for nightlife in Paris; however, I declined, looking forward to retiring to my room. I did agree to meet for a quick coffee and baguette the next morning, prior to boarding the Eurostar back home.

Back in my room, I stood at the French windows. As I stared at the "City of Love," I heard my phone ping, my heart racing. I glanced at the message on the screen: "Where shall I meet you?" Kate.

42
The Message

James

That night, sleep eluded me as I tossed and turned. Kate had messaged me, I repeated over and over again. I had messaged her back straight away, no stalling, no delays, or gaps in conversation. Kate deserved an immediate response and not to be kept waiting; no more waiting.

I kept it brief. I was in Paris, on business, but would return the next day. Shall we meet at "our" café? You name a time, and I will be there. I did not want to be presumptuous as to put an x, but then a full stop looked bare. So, I put one x and pressed send. A couple of minutes later, she replied that she would meet me at 10 am, no x. I simply said that I would be there.

I bounced out of bed as Paris was charmed by a glorious sunrise, a smile still imprinted on my face as I showered, packed, and dressed for the day. I was bursting to speak to Miles and Ellie, but I would have to wait until tonight after work.

The baguette, butter, cheese breakfast, and the mandatory coffee were perfect. The café was on my roundabout, the circle of chaos, as I now referred to it, much to the amusement of my clients. Between mouthfuls of baguettes, croissants, and crepes, the barrier of nations was forgotten. We parted on good terms, an allegiance secured, with a promise of future discussions and collaborations.

Seated on the Eurostar a little while later, having partaken in handshakes and double kisses with the French in an elaborate farewell, I stared at the message from Kate. I was obsessed, oblivious to the merging of the rolling green fields of France into the industrial landscape of London. As the train pulled into Euston train station, the usual bedlam ensued as every traveller tried to be the first to disembark.

Still smiling, I mixed once again with the suits of London. It was mid-morning; the night of no sleep loomed over me; I was so tired. I had a meeting with Richard, the senior senior executive, and the chief executive at twelve noon. I finished my report and emailed a draft for their review before the meeting. Richard and the Chief Executive, Andrew, stood to greet me as I was shown into the office by Alice, the executive support officer. I noted that everyone seemed to have a grand title. I sank into the chair. Richard and Andrew must have sensed my weariness, as I was given a few congratulatory comments on my successful liaison with the French and then was instructed to take leave for the remainder of the day. I simply thanked them and left. I was deeply grateful. Travelling home, I realised that no sleep was not part of my keeping well plan.

Miles and Ellie arrived home to find my overnight bag abandoned just inside the front door and me sleeping soundly on the couch. I woke up with a start and immediately bumbled through the tale of Kate's message. When I eventually drew breath, Miles sighed, Can you say that again? I grinned and recapped the events, this time slowly. When I had finished, still grinning, Miles and Ellie had joined my obvious excitement with fist pumps and high fives.

Then the realisation that Saturday was just two days away. This was important; I needed to get this right. I had waited nearly two years for this moment, and to put it bluntly, I did not want to fuck it up.

What to wear, easy, jeans and a T-shirt; what to say, problematic, but maybe not. I listened to Miles and Ellie; just be honest and speak from your heart. Sound advice. My heart had been empty for far too long. I needed love. I needed Kate.

43

The Last Chance

James

Miles insisted on escorting me to the café. No words were spoken; we both knew how important this was. He squeezed my shoulder and left me. Kate entered the café, my heart pounded relentlessly. I wiped my hands surreptitiously on my jeans. Did I smile? Did I kiss her? Did I hug her? Did I shake her hand? She looked beautiful in a simple cream dress. I noticed she had a tinge of a suntan. I didn't have time to question why, as she slowly neared my table, her hair tied in a loose ponytail. It suited her; her face showed only a hint of makeup, with, of course, her signature pink lipstick. My heart ached for her touch. I stood and pulled out a chair for her; she sat down.

Her face fixed, impassive, detached. We exchanged a 'Hi'. I said I was sorry; Kate remained still, not a flicker of emotion. I had everything to lose, Kate, forever, but I had to explain. I started abruptly announcing, a little cruelly perhaps, that about 18 months ago, I corrected myself, almost two years ago, I had been diagnosed with AML, Acute Myeloid Leukaemia, but of course, she knew the acronym. I paused. Kate remained poised, but I sensed her façade was faltering just a little. Go on, she said. So I told her my story, my fucked-up journey, all of it, every detail, no more secrets.

Tears brimmed in the corner of her eyes; I shook my head. I didn't want her sadness or her sympathy; I just wanted her to understand. Kate took a deep breath. Why didn't you tell me? This was the question that I had been preparing for, over and over again, from that first day when Miles had asked me why I would not tell Kate, why I was shutting her out of my life. He had listened, but he had struggled to accept my reasons. Now, nearly two years later, Kate was waiting for an answer.

I could have repeated all the reasons that I gave Miles all that time ago, but I looked into her eyes and simply said that I didn't want to hurt her or cause her pain. Kate shook her head, so I tried harder to explain: I was scared, terrified, I couldn't allow her to forsake her career, her future, her life, to watch me succumb to the unknown. I didn't know if I would survive, and I couldn't expose her to that uncertainty. I had missed her; every single day, I had missed her, and I was so sorry.

I saw tears silently rolling down her face, as they were mine. I put out my hands towards her, but she moved away. She stood, pushed her chair back under the table, and ran out.

44

The Journey's End

Kate

I ran straight into Miles, my eyes bleary from tears, my heart thumping, my pulse racing. I fell into his open arms. We just stood there, Miles and I, then I noticed he was crying too. I momentarily stood back. He looked at me; his tiny smile met my tiny smile. Miles spoke softly: He loves you, you know. I know, I replied.

Miles walked with me for a while. Why didn't he tell me? I had listened to what James had said, but I still needed more. Miles stopped. We sat on a bench nearby. He took my hands in his and spoke very gently: He was scared, Kate, we were both scared. I didn't agree with him not telling you, but as the aggressive treatment continued, I understood his reasons. He didn't want you to witness his fight, his struggle, the days when he hit rock bottom, the days curled up in a ball sobbing for a break from the fatigue and nausea, the days when he felt like death, looked like death. I was with him; the missing you, the wanting you, but he could not hurt you and give you his pain. Tears ran down Miles's face. He dropped his voice to a whisper: He loved you, Kate; he still loves you. I nodded slowly. He kissed my cheek; we walked in silence for a while until we said goodbye.

I walked and walked. I understood, but I didn't. Listening to James' story was like listening to a nightmare in real life, James' nightmare, one that I would have wanted to be there for, for James, but I wasn't. For whatever reason, he didn't want me to. So, could I be a part of his future when he didn't want me to be a part of his past? Then the harsh reality hit: James had endured the horrors of leukaemia. I needed to respect what he had gone through, to try and comprehend the enormity of his experience, even though he was cured; his journey of staying well was lifelong. I could, if I chose, be a part of that journey, James' life now and into the future. Did I want that? I stopped walking and stood still. Then I walked a little further and stopped again. I loved James, as he loved me.

I turned around and ran back towards the café, nudging, bumping people, weaving in and out, faster and faster, wiping tears, trying to breathe. I burst through the café doors and stopped. I saw James, his head in his hands, tears dripping into his coffee cup, his shoulders shuddering as muffled sobs racked his body. The barista replaced his coffee, no charge, of course. How could you ask for money from a broken man? I walked around to him, tapped him on his shoulder, he stood, I took him into my arms and held him tight.

Acknowledgments

Wow, I did it, I wrote my first book. Somewhere in my life, there has been a need to write, something, anything. I was never exactly sure what. I always had in my mind the opening line, *"and there he stood, standing, staring"*. I am still smiling in the knowledge that I am sharing my first book with the world's readers.

I have so many people to thank; those who encouraged, advised, and most of all those who were patient with a very novice writer. Of course, immense thanks go to Australian Book Publishers, to Michael Owens and Lilly Reed and her team, to Sebastian, Jessica, and, of course, my editor, Alicia Murphy, for tolerating my naivety with such grace and understanding. The endless questions and "check-ins". We got there. Thank you.

A massive thank you to Bronnie, you know who you are, my beautiful friend who endured Acute Myeloid Leukaemia (AML), who fought through the horrors and unbelievable challenges of both Leukaemia and the life-changing consequences, and survived. Thank you for sharing your story, for your bravery in reliving your nightmare. Thank you to Erin for providing the nitty-gritty details of the AML treatment and for being my first interviewee ever.

And so, to my support crew, my team. Most of all, my mum, Val, 87 years young, sharp as a tack, who provided endless support, advice, and yes, criticism, constructive, of course. My mum was the first to read my book in all its entirety, albeit the "uncut" version. Thanks, Mum.

Thanks to the rest of my family. To my husband, who, one day, Easter Saturday 2025, having listened to another of my entertaining stories as we were driving to the Gold Coast, quite simply said, "You should write a book", and then disappeared into the background. To my children, daughters who listened and made the right noises, and my son, who was my technical support, solving computer challenges with a smile, sort of.

And so, to my numerous friends, especially Fiona, who was the very first person to share my plot and ideas, and to Marina, who was always so positive and ready to listen over countless coffees.

Thank you to my work colleagues who tolerated random questions amongst work conversations, such as "Should I use the word orgasm?" I didn't. Thanks to Sharon, who is on her own writing journey, and to Michael, my sounding board at various times during the workday. Michael managed my emotions extremely well. I do remember his response when I had told him excitedly that I had written two thousand words: "That's not even an assignment", and the look on his face when he saw my despondent expression. Michael was always mindful of his comments from then on.

Thank you to my whole work "corridor", Liz, Melissa, Emma, Emma, Heather, Kate, and Fiona. Fiona read my first thousand words and excitedly told me that she had got "lost" in my book and told me to keep going. My very first critique. Thanks, Fiona. Amanda, Tracey, Rebecca, Beth, Colette, and so many more.

To my boss, thank you for not commenting when pages of my book momentarily appeared on my computer screen. To my boss, boss, I promise I will tell you the "naughty' page numbers, to avoid if you wish.

Thank you to my new readers. That sounds very presumptuous, but hopefully true. I hope you enjoy my first book as much as I enjoyed writing it. My mum's feedback was "Great", "A page turner" and "A perfect ending". I hope you agree.

Finally, they say it takes a village to raise a child; well, it takes a team to raise a writer.

Thank you to the many members of my team.